Journey to Bliss

Also by Ruth Glover

A Place Called Bliss

With Love from Bliss

The Saskatchewan Saga

Journey to Bliss

A NOVEL

RUTH GLOVER

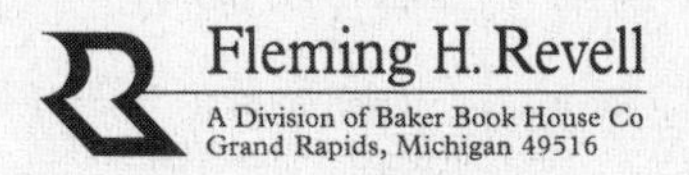

Fleming H. Revell
A Division of Baker Book House Co
Grand Rapids, Michigan 49516

Published by Fleming H. Revell
a division of Baker Book House Company
P.O. Box 6287, Grand Rapids, MI 49516-6287

Printed in the United States of America

Library of Congress Cataloging-in-Publication Data

Glover, Ruth.
Journey to Bliss : a novel / Ruth Glover.
p. cm.—(The Saskatchewan saga ; [3?])
ISBN 0-8007-5758-0
1. Frontier and pioneer life—Fiction. 2. Women immigrants—Fiction. 3. Scots—Canada—Fiction. 4. Saskatchewan—Fiction. I. Title.
PS3557.L678 J68 2001
813′.54—dc21 2001041634

Scripture is from the King James Version of the Bible.

For current information about all releases from Baker Book House, visit our web site:
http://www.bakerbooks.com

To
Ruth McDowell,
a perfect minister's wife
and my dear friend

The harsh winds had ceased their howling down the glens, but not before they had scoured the ancient hills to their bare bones. The scattered growth of bracken, defeated by a lifetime of battling with the elements, rested, spent and torn, under the touch of a tender sun and a rare, blue sky.

High on the hillside above the small village of Binkiebrae, Tierney Caulder sat on a rock wall, sunning herself. Her hand-loomed skirts were spread around her; with a quick brush of one slender foot against another she was rid of her heavy shoes, and her toes, free of winter's cumbersome wool stockings, lifted toward the warmth of the sun, wriggling with pleasure at the unaccustomed freedom. Unknotting her kerchief, she tossed it aside and ran a slim, rough hand through the rich mass of hair that tumbled about her shoulders, glinting auburn in the sun's rays.

Placing her hands on the rocks on which she sat, Tierney leaned back, allowing her hair to fall free, lifted her face toward the warmth of the skies, and closed her eyes. For the moment, she savored the peace that so easily escaped her in the hurly-burly of her days.

Below her the seashore stretched white in the light of the late afternoon, and beyond, the dazzling sea—ever restless, usually turbulent, always bound to the lives and doings of the people of Binkiebrae. On its tempestuous bosom her father had worn out his youth and his manhood and, eventually, his strength. On it her brother James even now prepared to make his weary way home from a day's fishing, the size of his catch the indication of his mood.

Under the shading of her hand, Tierney's eyes searched for and could find no sign of the fishing fleet's approach; the fine day would keep them at their task for hours yet. God grant each man—she prayed automatically, but no less fervently—first safety, then a bountiful catch. The brief request of the Almighty had been the plea of wives and mothers and sisters for as long as mankind had called this hard region home. Too often, anxious eyes searched in vain; too often one boat, watched for above all others, failed to return. That Malcolm Caulder, hard worker that he was, had survived to the age of fifty-nine, was a wonder and a miracle.

Malcolm had survived; it had been his wife, Tierney's mother—weary with watching, exhausted by the weight of life and its unrelenting burdens—who had folded her thin hands in a rest not known for fifty-five years, and gave up work and worry for a better land. How true the old hymn they had sung at her burying—"Land of Rest," they called it.

> O land of rest, for thee I sigh!
> When will the moment come
> When I shall lay my armor by, [they sang "burdens"]
> And dwell in peace at home?

Remembering that occasion of a few months past, for a moment the melody ran through Tierney's mind, and she recalled

the words of the chorus and found them just as fitting, for every Binkiebrae resident, as the verse: *We'll work till Jesus comes.*

Life, for Tierney Caulder, as for everyone on this windswept Scottish shoreline, had never been easy. She was always aware that her "mither" and her "da" loved her; still that had not prevented her from understanding, early on, that life was hard. If it were not the cruel biting of the wind and the wearing anxiety over the safety of their menfolk that pressed down on their spirits, it was the constant need for peat and coal to warm the wee homes, and the ever-pressing need to provide food. Food and warmth—everything else came second to those.

Like all frugal cooks, nothing went to waste in the Caulder household. Even the *faa,* or insides of an animal, were eaten. Tripe was cleaned, stuffed with meat, onions, and dried fruit, if such were available, then boiled and eaten hot, or when cold, sliced and fried. Oats—for the morning's porridge and for oatcakes at all times—were a household staple. And of course they were needed to make that less than glorious but famous dish, haggis. Oats were added to sheep's liver, heart and lungs, onion, and chopped mutton suet; it was all mixed together, stuffed into the stomach bag of a sheep, boiled for about five hours, and served with tatties and neeps (potatoes and turnips). No, nothing went to waste.

Even now, as Tierney basked in the sun, enjoying a stolen moment for herself, the oatcakes were baked and ready, and the kettle was on the boil for tea. Thinking of it and whether indeed the fireplace was burning as it ought, she sought out the one small dwelling that, among two dozen or so, she called home.

"Sma', too sma'," she murmured with a sigh and a shake of her head.

And indeed it was. Though snug and warm, the "hoosie" was small. Her father slept in the one bedchamber, she slept in the loft, and James slept at the fireside, pulling out a pallet at night and folding it away in the daytime. A small scullery at the back of the house was used for washing up and storing dishes and cooking utensils, cleaning vegetables, and similar work. The cooking and baking were done at the fireplace in the main room, the area in which they lived.

Da would be sitting there now, at the fireside, dreaming away his last few days, content just to be warm and fed, free of the need to go out in tempest and storm, snow and sleet, mist and fog, to cast the nets one more time. His once massive frame was pathetically shrunken; the disease eating at his lungs kept his thin body shaken with coughs much of the time. There was no mistaking the touch of death on Malcolm Caulder's pale face and crimson cheeks.

When Malcolm would be laid to his final rest, Tierney and James would find the house adequate for their needs. She could move into their parents' room; James could take the loft.

More than likely, however, it would be the other way round. James, young though he was—at twenty-three just five years his sister's senior—was in love, seriously in love with Phrenia MacDonald. Seriously enough in love to be talking marriage. Tierney approved his choice, even loved Phrenia, whom she had always known. But she shrank from the thought of infringing on the privacy that should be theirs, especially during those first months of marriage. And when the children came, as they surely would, the loft would be needed, and she, with no other choice, would take the pallet by the fire. It was a dreary, even humiliating future, though no different than many a home subscribed to, with a single, unmarried relative to care for.

Never, never would James deny his sister a home, but even that generous gesture on his part pained her by its very necessity.

But she needn't worry—there was Robbie Dunbar . . .

At that moment, as though stepping from dream into reality, Robbie appeared at the foot of the hill, shading his eyes, looking upward. Looking for her.

Tierney saw him with a quickening beat to her heart that she could no more help than she could stop breathing. Raising her arm, she waved her kerchief, signaling him . . . calling him.

Watching him climb, she went over the sweet story of Robbie Dunbar in her thoughts.

How long had she loved him? If not all of his life, then all of hers. First as a friend of James, then as her own friend and confidant, then as . . . she faced the breathtaking thought fully—as *more* than friend, *more* than confidant. Robbie was—her future.

Was anyone more dear than Robbie? Just to follow his rugged form as he leaped from rock to rock, to note his eyes—which she knew to be as deeply blue as the sea and just as familiar—glancing up at her from time to time, to see his lips curl in a smile meant just for her, filled her heart with happiness.

Tierney's love for Robbie had grown in such a natural way—not bent and battling like the bracken, but straight and lovely, healthy and true, like her mother's potted geranium in the window recess. To use Scripture: *First the blade, then the ear, after that the full corn in the ear.* That's how her love for Robbie Dunbar had grown.

It had seemed that there was no need to hurry what would last a lifetime. There were no surprises, no problems. It had always been, it would always be—Tierney Caulder and Robbie Dunbar. Together. Forever.

Tierney and Robbie, sometime, someplace, would settle onto a croft of their own, and life would go on as it had, but filled with the supreme joy of being together.

It was so simple, so right. It flowed along, in her mind and heart, as sweetly as the River Dee, and as steadfast. Love—hers and Robbie's—could be counted on, like the unchanging hills.

That Robbie loved her as she loved him, Tierney never doubted. Unspoken between them, never yet put into words, still that love existed.

And what was the hurry? These were days of sweetness stored up, sweetness to last a lifetime. Tierney and Robbie were young and all of life lay before them, here, where the Dee met the sea. Life for them would be as sure and unchanged as the loves and lives of countless generations before them. From the beginning, life had gone on as it always had. Tierney, content, counted on it, rested in it, bloomed because of it.

At last, breathless, Robbie reached her side, to throw himself down and stretch himself on the grass at her feet.

To lay himself at her feet, and by a few words, tear her world apart. Her world—so dependable, so solid, so unchanging—came crashing down, never to be the same again.

Her first clue that something was amiss, before ever he spoke, was the fact that Robbie's blue eyes, usually as sunny as today's sky, looked hot with something akin to anger. Neither did he give her smile for smile.

"Robbie?" Tierney murmured haltingly, questioningly.

"It's decided, then," he said abruptly, leaning on one elbow, looking blindly at the skyline, plucking at a blade of grass. "It's decided, and there's naething to be done aboot it."

"Decided?" she asked, puzzled. "What's decided, Robbie?"

"That Allan and I," he said in a strange, distant voice, "are awa' to Canada."

Tierney was stunned into silence. Surely she had misunderstood. Had he said he and his brother were away—to Canada, of all places?

Not waiting for a response, perhaps expecting none, Robbie continued, grimly, "Aye. Awa' to Canada. Me father and me mither hae made the plans. The shop . . . it's no' makin' a guid livin' anymair. And Allan and me, neither o' us cares for the thoughts of goin' to sea. Still, we were for it, but me father said na, na. He'll no hae it, lassie. Not the sea; Dunbars hae niver been for the sea, he says. We're for Canada right enow, me and me brother, and sometime, hopefully, the rest o' the family will join us."

"Your da," Tierney said gropingly, "he'd hae you leave Scotlan'? Leave Binkiebrae? And he'd go himsel'? I canna believe it, Robbie! Dinna he askit if ye'll go?"

"Na, he dinna askit. He has spoke, lass, for the good o' the family, and there's no denyin' him his right to do it. I canna tell him nae. And so it's settled, lass. I'm awa' to the new land, the far land, and verra soon."

Then, into the silence that fell between them, a silence of sheer unbelief and shock on Tierney's part, Robbie spoke. With his eyes still on the horizon, Robbie said the words that had never been spoken before; the words that she needed to hear, that he needed to say, and that would make no difference at all. No difference at all.

"There's only one thing that's kep' me here this long, lass. One reason I find it hard to go."

And then Robbie turned those blue eyes on her, and all the things he had left unsaid across the years, he said in that one look.

Da," Tierney said, "I'm goin' to Frasers'. You hear me, Da?"

"I hear ye, lass," Malcolm said, rousing himself from a mid-afternoon doze. "I hear ye."

"Ye'll be a'reet, Da, till I get back?"

"I'll be a'reet, lass. Gang awa' and dinna worry."

"Fenway is coomin,' any moment, an he'll stay wi' ye till I get back."

Malcolm nodded his understanding.

One thing could be said about Malcolm: He was an agreeable patient, seldom causing any problem. The most difficult part of his care was getting him in and out of bed, morning and night. If James were home, he took care of it, but often he was gone, either fishing or courting. At those times, or any time of emergency, old Fenway, their neighbor, was always ready to help. Today he would come and stay with the invalid; they would talk a little, smoke their pipes, perhaps drink tea if Fenway could stir himself to make it.

Once Malcolm was out of bed of a morning, dressed, and seated in his favorite chair by the fire, Tierney took charge of combing his thin hair, giving him his meals, wrapping him against the drafts of the room. No matter her own mood, she spoke cheerfully to her father, sharing any news with him concerning the ongoing life of the home and the community, keeping up his spirits, giving him a little interest in things around him, things that were so silently fleeting away.

Occasionally an old friend would stop by, and Tierney would serve tea, grateful for any small break in her father's long days and, she supposed, longer nights. Malcolm seemed more a part of the next world than this one; it was, surely, just a matter of time until he slipped away, as quietly and simply as he had lived.

But life went on, and Tierney, as homemaker and cook since the passing of her mother, had a routine to keep. Today it was the trudge of two miles to the home of her friend, Anne Fraser, for a replenishment of their egg supply.

In the Fraser household, as in the Caulder, there was no mother and wife. Anne, only fourteen at the time of her mother's death, had, like Tierney, naturally slipped into the role of housekeeper, caring for her father and two brothers.

The Frasers lived on a small croft that was part of the huge MacDermott estate. Paul Fraser, and young Pauly and Sam, his sons, worked at the stables and on the grounds, as had Paul's father and grandfather before him. With such unrest in the land, and with so many families being turned out, willy-nilly, from their crofts, the Frasers were an uneasy lot. Constantly at the beck and call of the MacDermotts, they hardly dared call their name their own, let alone their possessions and their time.

Anne was often called into service in the big house and had the care of the hens and other poultry and the disposing of the eggs. By careful reckoning she was able to come up with a few extras from time to time, and it was worth the sacrifice to share them with Tierney and her family, just to have Tierney come out and visit for a while.

Yesterday, at kirk, as the girls passed each other in the aisle, piously silent, Anne had whispered, "Eggs," in a conspiratorial tone.

There had seemed to be something more pressing than the fact that a few eggs were available. Lovely though they were and filling a real need, especially for a treat for the invalid Malcolm, still Anne had never announced their availability before this.

So, though the day was gray and overcast and the low-hanging clouds were spitting rain, Tierney arranged for Fenway to come over, settled her father with a rare newspaper and a cup of tea, fed the fire, picked up a small basket, and turned her steps out of Binkiebrae in the direction of the Fraser croft.

Rain or no rain, it seemed good to stretch her legs, and she strode out, grateful to have a few moments to herself, if only to think helplessly of her future and the hopelessness of it. Though in the past few days she had moved, worked, talked, as though nothing had changed, still on the inside there was despair over the news of Robbie's leaving and grief that it was so.

Tierney hadn't seen Anne, privately, since that black moment in the sunshine on the hillside when Robbie Dunbar had shattered her dreams, her future, her very life, with his stark announcement. And Annie, her dear and lifelong friend, was the only one Tierney would ever think of telling.

Even if James and Malcolm had heard that the Dunbar boys were to leave for Canada, their inclination would be to keep their thoughts to themselves. Malcolm was close to being past all earthly caring and would burden himself no further with useless and vain problems; James was immersed in his own plans and concerned about how they could come to fruition, what with his father sick and his sister caught up in the womanly round of keeping house for her menfolk.

Hadn't it been that way since time began? The elderly loosing their hold on life and turning responsibilities over to their sons and daughters, girls taking over where mothers left off, tending the home fires and the needs of their men? Sons stepping in and taking over the family business or craft? It all made perfect sense to James; he expected no other lot than the one he had been handed. But just how and when his own future should be worked out, he couldn't yet see. Phrenia, he could sense, was impatient, even as he was, for life to settle down for them in the prescribed pattern.

No, there were no intimacies shared these days in the Caulder household.

So Tierney had made no reference to the devastating news that Robbie Dunbar was leaving Binkiebrae and did her best to carry on in normal fashion. It was surprising and touching, then, that her father, even in his self-preoccupation, appeared to have noticed that something was amiss. Perhaps Tierney had lapsed in her usual cheerful demeanor.

"Is anathing wrong, lass?" he asked gently, watching her prepare to go out. "Ye seem cast doon some wa'."

Da was not to be burdened! His remaining days were to be peaceful! Flinching guiltily at telling a bald-faced lie, greatly touched by her father's insight and concern, Tierney ran a hand lovingly through his skimpy gray hair and said, with as much reassurance as she could muster, "I'm fine, Da! Just fine. Dinna worry about me." Then she added, by way of explanation, "I'm jist takin' the afternoon to go see Annie and pick up some eggs. You'll like one for your tea, I know. And remember—Fenway is coomin' to sit wi' ye."

Quickly past the few dwellings and businesses of Binkiebrae, with her shawl over her head and wrapped closely around her shoulders, Tierney turned her back on any inquisitive eyes, turned her face toward the sky, and wept along with it. Twin tracks of tears—those from a more than generous heaven, and her own—ran down her cheeks, the first tears she had allowed herself. Truth to tell, until now she had been too stunned, too numb, to weep. It had been as though she were caught in a web of thick, agonizing silence, where nothing seemed real, only—Robbie Dunbar, leaving Binkiebrae and Scotland. Forever. It was all too unreal. It was all too real.

Anne saw her friend approaching, had, in fact, been watching for her, certain she would come in response to the reference—the double-meaning reference—to eggs.

"Well, here ye are then," she said, opening the door before Tierney could knock. "Coom on in oot o' the rain."

Urging her friend inside, Anne removed Tierney's damp shawl and spread it out before the fire to dry.

Shivering a little, Tierney held her hands out to the small blaze, which did little to lighten the gloom, but which warmed the small room adequately.

"I guess it were silly o' me to coom today, the weather so bad and all," Tierney remarked, "but I had need to get oot o' the hoose. Besides, Annie, I'm full curious aboot yer signal yesterday. What's it all aboot? Do you really have eggs, then, or is it sum'at else? It is, isn't it? It's sum'at else."

To Tierney's dismay, tears sprang into Annie's eyes. As Annie bent over the fireplace, fumbling with the teakettle, her tears were quickly hidden, but her voice, when she spoke, was unsteady.

"Aye, there's eggs. But there's . . . sum'at mair."

"Tell me, dear Annie. Tell me anythin' ye wish to. I, in my turn, hae something to tell ye."

"It seems to be a day for sharin' confidences," Annie said, trying to smile through her tears. "You go first, Tierney."

"Na, I'll not," Tierney declared, "until I hear tell of wha's troublin' ye."

"Well, then, I'll pour the tea, and butter the scones—"

"A rare treat, Anne." And with appreciation Tierney took the cup and a scone, and in silence the two friends ate and drank, a time-proved healer of many hurts.

At last, looking blindly down into her half-empty cup, Annie could stand it no longer. Once again the tears ran, this time unchecked. With a small exclamation of concern Tierney set her own cup aside and knelt swiftly at her friend's side, her arms going around the shaking shoulders.

"Annie, Annie," she crooned, holding the dark head against her shoulder, and stroking the soft hair. "Is it so bad then? Your da, your brothers—is sum'at wrong wi' them?"

Unlike Tierney, Anne did not have a kind father and sympathetic brothers. The Frasers were angry at life as they knew it.

There was a great restlessness going on in the world, with some people having an opportunity to better themselves as never before. Paul Fraser, finding himself still under the heel of an oppressor—his landlord—and unprepared for any other sort of life, was bitter and short-tempered. With Mrs. Fraser gone, the home was a rough one, with much complaining, some roaring, and plenty of impatience with a young sister who, after all, could do nothing but give her strength and time to keeping house for the three of them. It was a thankless job.

No wonder Tierney suspected something was wrong where Anne's father and brothers were concerned.

"Na, na. Not me da nor me brothers," Anne managed. After a spate of tears, she dried her eyes. "Ah weel, I canna talk aboot it yet, after all," she finally said with an indrawn, quivering breath and a straightening of the shoulders. "I'm not certain sure I should talk aboot it at all."

"But Annie," Tierney said, aghast, "ye must. Ye need to. Who else do ye have to talk with but me?"

"Na, na, I canna, I canna," Annie said, stubborn now. "It's been enough jist to see ye. I'll think on it somemair. It may be that the whole thing is made up of a feeble lie after all. To spread abroad something that issna true—na, na, I canna bring meself to talk aboot it, though I thought I might."

Now Tierney, knowing her friend well, was absolutely certain that something was quite seriously wrong. Nevertheless, she sat down again, shaking her head somberly, and sighing, turning up her damp shoes to the fire. "Ah, Annie," she reproached.

"But Tierney," Anne said, turning the conversation away from herself after a sip or two of the heartening brew, "what's wrong, for ye? I know ye well, and there's sum'at wrong. Yer da jist too much for ye today? 'Twouldn't surprise me; ye've had a long haul there. And not done yet. I'm glad ye came. Let's talk aboot it. . . ."

It was all Tierney needed. The tears, having been loosed on the way, had not dried up, and now they tumbled forth unstopped.

"Dearie! Dearie!" Annie said, greatly troubled, greatly astonished. Her own troubles faded in comparison to what seemed to be a serious problem with Tierney.

Anne waited for her friend to give her the reassuring words, "'Tis naething," but they were not forthcoming.

"Can ye no' tell me, dear friend?" Anne asked, her own heart greatly troubled now, and not for herself but for Tierney. What a day it was for rain and tears!

"'Tis Robbie," Tierney mourned, gazing blindly into the cup in her hand. "Ye'll find it hard to believe, Annie; I do m'sel'. But Robbie . . ." Tierney's voice rose to a broken squeak, "Robbie and Allan are off to Canada any day now—"

"Na, na! It canna be so!"

"Off to Canada to stay. To file for a farm and ne'er coom back to Binkiebrae. Ne'er coom back, Annie!"

"Ne'er coom back?" Anne repeated gropingly, finding it hard, perhaps impossible, to accept the thought. "Ne'er coom back? But Tierney, what aboot ye? I know where ye're heart is. Oh, Tierney, I canna grasp what all this means to ye! And to Robbie—how's he takin' it?"

"Like an innocent sheep harried by a rogue dog," Tierney cried. "He dinna know where to turn; he dinna know anything he can do. His da has spoken, ye see; it's the law laid doon, for him and Allan. An' o' course we know many who're goin'; it's not all that unheard of. There are so many who've gone, had to go, chose to go, niver to coom back. Nae, it's not that surprising, I guess—"

"But Robbie! Did he tell ye, Tierney? Did he tell ye himsel'?"

"Aye, he did that. Bitter, he was, bitter and desperate. An' trapped. But not because of Canada. Hoots, na! He's happy enow to get awa', I think. It's because o'—" Tierney's tears, dried for the moment in the heat of her passion, flowed again. "It's because o'—us!"

Anne set aside her cup and came and knelt at her friend's damp skirt, reaching to console her, comforting Tierney in a pain she could only imagine, herself being heart-free.

"It's the end, then," Anne whispered. "But how much better, lass, that it came before you and he . . . before you and he—"

"I think I canna bear it, Annie," Tierney wept, in her friend's arms. "T' niver see Robbie again! I think I canna bear it."

Staring into the fire over Tierney's damp head, aching for her friend, Anne momentarily forgot her own troubles. Tierney not only had the care of a dying father—that same care dragging out and nibbling away the sweet days of Tierney's youth—but now Robbie, in whom every dream was invested, would be taken from her. It was, indeed, a sad prospect. As a female, Tierney had no choice, no alternative; she was caught as a rabbit in a trap.

"E'en if it weren't for Da," Tierney said finally, "'twould be hopeless. I couldna go with Robbie and Allan. Neither can I hope to go meet them later, when me da . . . I dinna know whaur they'll be, in that vast country. And me without money, or friends, or any idea whaur to go or who to contact—nae, Annie, 'tis no good thinkin' on it. Robbie hasna even mentioned my going; he knows as well as I do that there's nothing in the whole world to be done aboot it." Tierney's last words were a cry of despair.

Anne couldn't argue; there were no sensible alternatives to offer. All that Tierney had said was true. There was no money; there was no way. Robbie would disappear in the vast and stretching prairies of the Canadian territories about which they were constantly hearing, and he would be as lost as a single raindrop in that same landscape.

For love to shrivel and die away before ever it had been allowed to bloom! Anne found no words to comfort her friend. Trying, she started, weakly, "There'll coom along the reet one . . . some day—"

Tierney's flashing eyes, even in the dim light, brought Anne's foolish comfort to a halt.

And so the young women, bound by custom, by poverty, by forces beyond their power to change, mourned together.

Quickly the remainder of the afternoon passed, the rain increasing and the gloom thickening. Recognizing the lateness of the hour and remembering the meal waiting to be fixed when she arrived home, Tierney stirred restlessly at last.

"I maun be off home," she sighed and then recollected Anne's own personal need to talk.

"But first, Annie, tell me, will ye not—what's wrong? Please, dear friend. It canna be too bad to tell me—"

But Annie answered stoutly, "Na na, Tierney. It'll wait. 'Tis nothing that canna wait. I promise I'll tell ye all aboot it . . . some other day."

And no matter what Tierney said, Anne shook her head, insisting it "wasna all that bad," and even managed to smile about it.

Surely, then, the confidence could wait; Tierney had no choice but to accept her friend's decision.

Wending her way back to Binkiebrae through the dusk, she wondered uneasily if she should have persisted. But the afternoon had gotten away all too quickly. What a dear and good friend Anne was . . . had been, across the years. Without a mother or a sister for either of them their relationship had the bonds of a deep necessity—they needed each other! Tierney felt that, in sharing her misery with her friend, she could bear it better. Regretfully, she had not persuaded Anne to divide her burden by sharing it. Another day . . .

Clutching her small basket of eggs and anticipating the boiling of one for her da's supper, Tierney sighed—life's dramatic moments were punctuated with such small concerns—and hurried homeward.

For two weeks Tierney wondered—had she said her good-byes to Robbie Dunbar? Would there be no more opportunity for meeting? And if so, would it be wise?

Wise? Tierney almost laughed aloud at the thought. Wise, where Robbie Dunbar and her future were concerned? Given half a chance, Tierney would have forsaken all—home, kirk, friends—and sailed away, in a heart's beat, with Robbie Dunbar.

But Robbie knew, as did she, there was no future in such a scheme: He was destined to go with his brother; she was destined to stay. He couldn't ask her to do otherwise; she couldn't offer. But her wild Scottish heart may yet have broken all bounds, forsaken all sense, except for one thing: Da.

Desperately as Tierney's thoughts sought a way out, passionately as she, at times, threw reason to the winds, all roads led her back to Da and his need of her. Not in her wildest dreams could she imagine herself saying good-bye to Da, shutting the door, turning away, and leaving her father in his final illness. And, as the days slipped away, it was increasingly difficult to leave him at all, even for the buying of food and the collecting of fuel. Rarely was she outside, for any purpose.

The little house, kept especially warm for the invalid, grew heavy with the odors of illness, and Tierney, at discreet moments when her father was abed in his room, flung open the windows and door, and in spite of the chill, gave the home a good airing.

Always, the hilltop called to her, and her silent, secret place beckoned. Only up there would it be possible to breathe deeply, to clear her head, to begin to understand the dreadful import of what was happening to her. Down below, acceptance eluded her; she found herself bitterly resisting the fact that Robbie, any day now, would be gone.

Phrenia proved to be a blessing; she came often and took her place at Da's side, sometimes reading to him, sometimes watching him drift in and out of a doze, and dreaming, Tierney supposed, of when the small house would be her own, hers and James's. Her eyes would roam over the rough walls, mentally cleaning, fixing, changing. As she has every right to, Tierney reminded herself constantly, and felt no better for it.

And so the days slipped away, lost in the routine of nursing, meals, washing, baking. The normality tended to help Tierney become numb to the reality.

And then there came the day and the knock at the door. Opening it, Tierney saw Robbie's younger sister.

"Please, Tierney," the girl said brightly, "Robbie wants ye to meet him at four o' the hzour, atop the hill."

"Thank you, Willa. Thank you, I will." With never a hesitation, Tierney responded. If Robbie Dunbar had asked her to sail for Timbuktu at the cock's rising, she would have gone, at a moment's notice. Except—for Da.

Even now, agreeing to meet Robbie, the thought of Da caught her up short. Quickly she turned back to the door, stepped out, and called, "Willa—come back a moment, please!"

"Aye?"

"Willa—if I'm to meet Robbie, I'll need someone to stay a few moments with me da. Would ye be able to do that for Robbie and me?"

"I'll coom back in plenty o' time," Willa replied agreeably.

As good as her word, Willa showed up at the door at the proper hour, and Tierney, snatching up a shawl, stepped outside, paused on the flat rock that formed a stoop before the low door, and looked up. Looked at the high hills, brooding today under a cloudy sky. Spontaneously, without conscious thought, a verse from the Psalms sprang into her mind—suggesting, offering solace: *I will lift up mine eyes unto the hills, from whence cometh my help.*

Ah, if only it were so! If only the everlasting hills, having seen so much of life and pain and parting, would speak benignly, promising that in their time and way they would make everything right. Tierney couldn't believe it to be so simple, and the tentative offer of divine help slipped away and the hills remained, silent and voiceless, as they always had, as they always would.

Resolutely closing her mind to foolish fancies of divine help, Tierney fixed her eyes on the hilltop and the one spot that was her own special hideaway and retreat, and began to climb.

Though the sun hid itself most of the way, the day was warmer than she had known, and she soon pulled off her shawl and carried it over her arm. Next, the kerchief came off, and the slight breeze blew the auburn tresses into vibrant disarray; the coolness felt magnificent as it pushed against her slim, young body, challenging her progress, teasing her steps.

Robbie was not yet there. Looking out over the sullen sea, imagining the far distant place to which its restless movements would take him, Tierney felt its cold unconcern seep into her very heart, and she shivered and drew her shawl around her once again. Why had she imagined there would be consolation up here? Surely, from now on, the stretching sea and the wide sky would only serve to remind her of the vast distances that served to separate her from Robbie Dunbar.

Some movement down the glen caught her eye, and she left off searching the sea. Once again—for the final time—she watched Robbie Dunbar climb to meet her. He was, she understood poignantly, no more able to go without seeing her than she was to refuse him.

To see him, and ache; to not see him, and grieve—those were her options. She had grieved for two weeks; now, seeing him, she ached. Truly their love and the uselessness of it were as sheep's gall mixed with honey.

But it would be a strange meeting, this one, like none other. Unless, of course, he were coming to say he would not be going after all. Otherwise, what was there to be said, what done? Not only were their hands tied but their tongues also—nothing that was of import had been said between them, could be said, would be said.

But nothing could stop the language of the eye, and Robbie—two weeks ago—had spoken all things to her whatsoever she desired to hear and said it passionately.

Remembering again that moment when he had looked at her, his heart in his eyes, brought an exquisite thrill to Tierney again today, as it had a thousand times in the past two weeks. But it was a thrill threaded with a pang, a pang that was becoming as familiar as the thrill that brought it. Again—the bitter and the sweet.

He was at her side almost before she knew it, so engrossed in her thoughts had she been. Rather than throw himself at her feet as he had done so often in the past, Robbie leaned, as she did, against the ancient rock wall, breathing deeply—from the exertion of the climb, one would suppose. The effort had tinged his lean brown cheeks with color; his blue eyes, under deep brows, burned darker than she remembered.

He was, Tierney thought, beautiful, all things a man should be.

Robbie Dunbar. He was indeed all Tierney's heart had dreamed of, all her body needed, all her mind could imagine. And he was not to be hers. Not ever.

Tierney had not known that love, being an intangible thing, could be felt so keenly. Was it possible, given time, for the anguish and grief to ease? Perhaps. But love would endure, unchanged, for all of life, and this Tierney never questioned.

Whatever life brought her from this day forward, wherever she was and however far from him, she would go on loving Robbie Dunbar.

And he had declared his love for her. Not in words but in that one deep, speaking look. One long look, saying everything. After that passionate, heart-to-heart message of undying love, filling her with its exhilaration and joy, had come the pain. Such pain! For something so tender, such desperate misery! For something so precious, such loss!

Remembering, they gazed broodingly over the pulsing sea, the bending sky. And, seeing, comprehended neither.

Did his eyes mist, as did hers?

Was her throat aching, as was his?

So passed a few moments in time, a broken bridge that could never be recrossed to the way things had been.

"Robbie . . ." It was a whisper.

"I couldna go, lass," he answered abruptly, "withoot sayin' guid-bye."

"Aye."

"I'm awa' tomorrow, Tierney. The *Solway,* berthed in Aberdeen, will lift anchor at noon, and I—"

"Aye."

"I go, but I willna go heart-free."

"I know." How well she knew! With every word, every glance, the bonds tightened.

"I canna. There's nae mair to be said for it. And still—I maun go."

It was as simple as that: He would not go heart-free. But he would go.

He swung around to face her, his hand reaching to touch her, and drawing back.

"Time to go," he said roughly. Back down the hill, back to reality. Time to leave all dreaming, all supposing, all hoping.

"It's guid-bye, lass," Robbie continued doggedly, meeting Tierney's eyes with a sick determination. "I'll nae be seein' ye again."

And then Robbie touched her. For the first and last time, Robbie touched her. It would be a touch to remember the remainder of her days.

Tenderly Robbie reached for her and took her chin in his hand. Tenderly he turned her face toward him. Tenderly he placed a hand on each side of her face, her tear-streaked face, and looked deeply into her eyes. Slowly her eyes closed and her face lifted.

With a low sound which, on a less fine man would have been something between a curse and a groan, Robbie dropped his hands, stepped back, clenched his jaw, and rasped, "I canna, lass. *I canna!* I canna kiss ye, else I'd never leave ye."

And so saying he took one stumbling step backwards, turned on his heel, and was off, leaping and bounding like a madman down the steep hillside.

And so Robbie Dunbar took his departure from Tierney Caulder. And so, through a shimmer of tears, Tierney Caulder watched her true love grow smaller and smaller until, as she had known it would be, he disappeared altogether.

Never, as long as Tierney Caulder had known Anne Fraser, had Anne avoided meeting her; it was unthinkable.

Anne Fraser was one of those fortunate individuals whom nature had touched—body and soul—with perfection. She had a face like an angel, cream-colored, daintily pink as to cheeks, dewily red as to mouth. Surrounded by a cloud of soft dark hair, her features combined to give her an expression of unusual sweetness. With a softly rounded figure, which might well develop into that of a full-bodied woman by middle age, still nothing would erase the basic simple beauty of her face and form. By temperament she was good-hearted, good-natured, good-tempered. Anne was too kind to hurt a flea, everyone agreed. Neither did deception have any part in her makeup; she was naturally honest, without pretense. In light of these things, what happened was curiously puzzling.

Having left Fenway sitting with her father, Tierney used the free time one afternoon to do some necessary shopping. Making her way to the Dunbar shop, it was to see, ahead of her and coming out of the town's only place to buy provisions, the familiar form of Anne Fraser. Her shawl was quickly pulled over her head; though her face was partially obscured, there was no mistaking the figure for that of Anne Fraser. And there was no mistaking her gown, which was as well known to Tierney, who had helped stitch it, as her own.

And yet it could have been a stranger, a stranger hurrying on her way. Or was it possible that Anne didn't see her, Tierney wondered, perplexed.

"Annie! Wait! Annie!" Tierney called. At the second summons Anne slackened her pace, hesitated, then quickened her steps and once again pursued her hasty course in the opposite direction.

It was so unlike Anne that Tierney was almost deceived into thinking she was mistaken and it was someone else, after all. But that was ridiculous! Annie it surely was.

Tierney watched Anne disappear around a corner. What could have been so pressing that she had no time to spare for a few words with her friend? Only slowly did the realization come that Anne's face, mostly obscured by her shawl—briefly seen, quickly concealed—was not quite as usual.

A mark . . . a bruise, perhaps? Surely if it were innocent, meaningless, an explanation would have been ruefully offered, perhaps even laughingly.

There was no time to follow; perhaps Anne had counted on that. At any rate, Tierney, troubled at heart, uneasy and not knowing why, watched her friend out of sight before she entered the shop and began assembling the items she needed.

"Was that Anne?" she asked Willa, who was presiding behind the counter.

"Aye—poor thing."

"Poor thing?"

"Dinna ye see her bruise? I askit what was wrong, and she jist pretended like she didn't hear me."

"Ye askit, and she dinna say?"

"Reet. She was, well, flustered, rather. Kep' her head doon and did her buyin' and jist hurried oot o' here. Poor thing."

"Why do ye keep sayin' poor thing?" Tierney asked, her concern for Anne making her peevish.

Willa shrugged. "It looked sore," she said defensively. "All black an' blue."

"Well, there's a perfectly guid explanation, I'm sure," Tierney offered doggedly and wondered why she bothered defending a bruised cheek to this child.

Only afterwards did she make a connection with what was really troubling her. Hidden away but not forgotten was the incident of several weeks ago when Anne had been in tears over something and had refused to talk about it. Now Tierney recalled the occasion and found herself becoming more and more alarmed. Was something, after all, seriously amiss at the Fraser croft? Something that Anne did not want to talk about, did not want known?

The days were too full and Da was too ill to pursue the conjecture. Anne might as well have been on the moon for all the opportunity Tierney had to see her.

When next at kirk—Fenway again doing duty in Malcolm's sickroom—Anne's pleasant face showed only the smallest stain, and it might have been overlooked except for Tierney's keen study of it. Though Anne flushed under Tierney's scrutiny, the smile on her lips remained fixed, and she returned her gaze steadily.

Once again there was no opportunity to speak privately; Anne seemed to see to that. She remained surrounded by others, and though Tierney darted meaningful looks at her, with signals that her friend should have caught, Anne either misunderstood or deliberately ignored the questions that flashed from Tierney's eyes.

Walking home no wiser than when she went, Tierney was as annoyed as she was anxious; it was a troubling combination. What was wrong with Annie, anyway! Whatever it was, it seemed clear Anne intended to ignore it, even act as if it didn't exist. And did it? Tierney found herself questioning her own judgment. Everyone sustained bruises from time to time; everyone found themselves hurried and unable to stop and talk, even for a good friend.

Once home, Tierney dismissed her concerns for Anne the second she stepped inside: Malcolm was slumped half out of his chair, pale as death itself, and breathing shallowly.

Fenway had apparently just leaped to his feet, overturning his chair, and could think of nothing to do but wring his hands and cry, over and over, "Wha's wrong wi' ye, auld gowk! Wha's wrong . . . wha's wrong?"

"Help me, Fenway!"

Tierney ran across the room to her father's side, and with Fenway's meager assistance raised Malcolm, tipping his head back and clearing his air passages. Leaving Fenway to hold the flaccid body in place, Tierney flew to bring a wet cloth and began bathing her father's brow, alternating with rubbing his hands. It seemed ages before Malcolm stirred, his head bobbing on his thin neck like a bruised flower on a broken stem, his eyes half open and apparently unseeing, his mouth slack.

Stepping to the doorway Tierney called a neighbor who was walking past, and between them they got Malcolm into bed. Though Fenway stood around helplessly for a while, there was nothing he could do, and eventually he returned to his own fireside. Tierney couldn't blame the old man; he had simply been doing her a favor by sitting with the invalid, probably dozing in his chair when Malcolm collapsed. Hard of hearing, poor of vision, Fenway never knew when his charge slipped into unconsciousness. Upon waking and seeing that something was amiss, he had struggled to his shaky feet, and was in the midst of an anxious outcry when Tierney returned home.

The village of Binkiebrae, with its two dozen or so poor, low dwellings, could not boast a doctor of its own. There was nothing a man of medicine could have done that had not already been done; everyone knew old Malcolm was worn out and fading away, and nothing could change that. Maggie Gaul, the next best help, was soon present. Malcolm was made comfortable and warm, propped to ease his breathing, which was labored and slow, and watched tenderly—by Maggie who had known him since his boyhood, Tierney who loved him and grieved over his final, difficult misery, and others who came in the next few days to do what they could.

Among them, bringing eggs and milk, was Anne. Even in the dim room and in the midst of her distraction, Tierney's keen eyes caught the half-hunted look on Anne's face—once again something had happened.

"Annie," she said, shaking her friend's arm gently, "sum'at's wrong. I know it."

Anne didn't attempt to deny it. How could she, with her miserable expression speaking for her?

"Aye, Tierney," she admitted. "You know it; you know it verra well. I willna hide it from you any longer. I hoped 'twould come to naught. . . . But it'll wait; I canna stay and talk aboot it, with your da so sick an' all. Anyway, it's goin' to take mair time than we have jist now."

With Malcolm's every breath threatening to be his last, Tierney knew there was no alternative, and though she longed to insist, she sighed, lifting her shoulders in helpless resignation.

"Promise you'll coom as soon as you can when . . . when it's all o'er, Annie. I canna bear to think of you goin' through sum'at and me not standin' by you. What it is I canna imagine."

"Dinna fret. I'll be a'reet . . . I think . . ." Anne's voice faltered.

The end, when it came, was peaceful for Malcolm Caulder. He died as he had lived, quietly, to himself. That it happened in the wee hours of the morning was not unexpected; it seemed to be when people gave up, gave in, and, unresisting, left one abode for Another.

A God-fearing man all his life, Malcolm had no need to fear now.

Sitting at his bedside, as she had for so many long hours of so many long days and nights, Tierney had fallen asleep. Perhaps it was the absence of sound that woke her; the long, slow rale was silenced at last. As she opened her eyes, she was immediately intensely awake and aware, and the stillness brought her heart into her throat. There was no need to check pulse or breath—Malcolm was no longer there.

It was her first coherent thought—Da's gone. The shell of a man, all that had lingered of her once-powerful and vital father, rested, quiet and empty, at her elbow, but Da was gone.

Dawn was so close, and James was so needful of his sleep, that Tierney sat at the side of her father's earthly remains until a weak sun streaked the sky and light began to filter in with its assurance that life went on. It always had, and it always would. But without Malcolm Caulder.

Now Tierney roused herself, slipped quietly out to the pallet at the side of the fireplace, and touched her brother. James's eyes flew open; even in the gloom she could see the question in them. *Is he gone, then?*

"Da's gone, James," she said quietly. "I dinna know in time to wake ye . . . I'm sorry—"

In spite of the long months of expectation, an involuntary sound of grief escaped James's throat, and he covered his face with his hands. Tierney ran her hand gently over his dark tousled head, as together they did their mourning for the good man who had brought them thus far and would never guide or direct them or provide for them again. It was, perhaps, the threshold of maturity for both of them—James to carry on without the wisdom and strength that had always been there for him, and Tierney to face total responsibility for herself in a way that had never been necessary before. For James—along with marriage to Phrenia—there awaited the new step into becoming fully and completely the head of a home; for Tierney—what?

Thankfully there was no time to pursue the strange and new thoughts that surfaced at that moment. Time would bring answers; time would bring solutions.

"Get dressed, James," Tierney said eventually, "and get Maggie."

The slow cortege, as it wound out of Binkiebrae the next day, over the hill to the burial ground, had a simple dignity that relieved the occasion of being just another pathetic moment—

there was so little to show for a lifetime of living and loving, working and striving. But the friends walking behind the coffin spoke of the goodness of the man whose mortal remains rested so lightly on the strong shoulders of Binkiebrae's stalwart males. "A guid mon," they said, and the words were a fitting eulogy.

With Malcolm laid to rest beside his wife, the mourners returned briefly to the Caulder home. Maggie and others had cleared the place of any signs of death and sickness and provided food. Soon everyone said their farewells, and life, for the good people of Binkiebrae, went on in its familiar, unchanging fashion.

Closing the door behind the last departing guest, Tierney turned to the room where she had been born and lived all of her eighteen years, and knew it to be a different place. It was James's. And Phrenia's. James, whatever his thoughts, moved restlessly about the room.

Watching him and understanding, Tierney released him. "Go on, James, to Phrenia. I don't mind. It's something I'll hae to get used to . . . the empty hoose."

Though he gave his sister an apologetic look, James was obviously relieved and took her up on her suggestion. He was not accustomed to lingering around the house in the daytime, and it was not fitting to go about work or business of any kind on this day. But time spent with Phrenia—that was allowable. James made his way gladly to the home of her parents, where the young couple—guardedly, lest they seem too precipitate—planned for the happy day, now in sight, when they would marry and set up housekeeping, and life would go on as it should.

With evening coming on, the house almost unbearably empty around her, Tierney lit a lamp and pulled the kettle into position to begin its boil for another cup of tea. The room seemed to echo silence. . . .

The stillness was broken by an outside sound, something Tierney couldn't identify, something, someone, touching, scraping the door. Tilting her head, listening, she heard it again.

"What—" she murmured, finding the sound foreign, strange.

Once again the peculiar scrabbling came from the threshold. Tierney set aside the teapot, stepped to the door, reached for the latch, turned it—

With a crash the door slammed inward. Startled, Tierney stepped back, and just in time to avoid being struck by the figure that had been crouched there and that now tumbled into the room.

Out of the bundle of clothes, torn and askew, came a sound like the mew of an injured animal. Horrified, Tierney watched as the figure slowly stirred, raised itself slightly, and fell back to the floor.

"Annie? *Annie!*"

Annie!

It was indeed Annie. Battered and soiled, with her dark hair escaped from its confines, spreading like an ominous cloud about her head and shoulders, she crouched at the doorway. No sound escaped the prostrate figure, but when Tierney knelt and attempted to lift her, the face that was raised to hers was runneled with tears.

Tierney wasted no more time on speech. Getting her arm around Annie, she lifted her until she could slip her arm firmly around her waist. Then, Annie doing a sort of hop on one foot, they progressed enough so that Tierney could shut the door.

The room closed around them, quiet and shadowed; the fire flickered invitingly against the evening's chill, and the lamp shed its steady, cheering glow over all. Annie, as though come into a haven, gave a long, shuddering sigh, and sank onto the settle before the fireplace. Not knowing whether to tend to whatever injury there might be or simply to offer comfort, Tierney knelt at her friend's knee.

"Annie. Can ye talk, lass?"

Anne's head drooped. "Aye," she whispered. "Though I dinna wish to."

"Even now!"

"I canna imagine where 'twill end, once 'tis said."

"'Twill end here, Annie, if that's what ye wish."

"It must, Tierney." Fresh tears ran, silent and unchecked, from Anne's puffed eyes.

"Lean back, Annie. Get yer breath. I'll be back in a second."

Annie obeyed, as one deathly weary, deathly ill. Tierney searched out the cloths used during her father's illness that were washed and carefully stored away for any future need (nothing went to waste in the crofts and shanties of Binkiebrae). A little hot water from the kettle, a little cold water from the pail, and Tierney applied the warm and comforting application to Anne's face, dabbing away the soil and tears, exposing bruises and a cut not noticed before.

Anne was shivering, and Tierney put a shawl around her shoulders. While Anne's breathing slowed and her tears dried, Tierney tended the fire, emptied the basin and put away the wet cloth, filled the teapot that was ready and waiting, and, finally, filled two cups with the fragrant brew.

Anne came up out of the settle's corner to an upright position, to take the cup and eventually try a cautious sip. Soon a bit of pink was returning to her white cheeks, the result being that the bruises rising there stood out, stark and ugly.

Tierney, watching over the rim of her own cup, was horrified at the marks of abuse. Someone—Annie's father? one of her brothers?—had wielded a cruel hand against her. How could they! Annie, gentle and easygoing, spending her young womanhood taking care of those same males . . . had they, in careless disregard and with cruel intent, turned on her? If so, it wasn't the first time. Tierney recalled, darkly, the other time Annie had hidden a face that had been, to a lesser extent, similarly battered.

Paul Fraser was known to be a rough man; his sons, cheerful, laughing young men, were quick-tempered and undisciplined.

Anne's mother, a woman of virtue and grace, had been the gentling influence in that home. With her gone, was Annie at risk? Tierney grew cold thinking about it and again stirred the fire to greater efficiency.

When Anne handed Tierney her cup, straightened her clothes, put a hand to her hair and drew a steadying breath, Tierney could wait no longer.

"Was it your da?" she asked quietly but pointedly.

"Na, na."

"Pauly? Sam?"

"Nae, not me brothers."

Tierney was confused. No other possibility came to mind. Was Anne physically impaired so that she stumbled, fell, went unconscious perhaps? It was a wild solution but one Tierney grasped at; it would be preferable to a revelation that pinpointed another human being as the reason for such barbarism. But it was a vain and futile hope.

"Then who . . . or what, Annie? For heaven's sake—what has happened to ye?"

Annie seemed to be gazing blindly into the fire. After a long moment, she said quietly, "Lucian."

"Lucian MacDermott," Tierney whispered. And suddenly it made great sense.

Lucian, the scion of the MacDermott clan, spoiled, known for his cruelty to man and beast even as a child, was home again. Sent off to Edinburgh to receive his education and home only occasionally over the past half-dozen years, Lucian, as a young man, had already earned an unsavory reputation, and tales of his arrogance and thoughtless unconcern abounded. If he were cruel abroad, how much more so on MacDermott land where he felt himself to be a young king.

Tierney well knew the power and authority held by landowners; for centuries her people had known the harsh treatment of the titled and wealthy, and the subservience expected of them as servant to master, lackey to overlord, subject to ruler.

What had Anne done to bring on herself such dire retribution? Or—and Tierney went still momentarily, thinking of the possibility—what had she *not done?*

"Aye," Anne was repeating, starting off another round of trembling so that she pulled the shawl closer about her. "Lucian."

With Lucian home and several guests with him, the MacDermott house was understaffed; Anne, as usual, was called into service. It had not been in the great house, however, that she had again encountered Lucian, the first time in several years; always before she had been busy elsewhere when he came home, briefly, at holidays.

She had been crossing the yard, a basket on her arm, her bonnet flung back and her dark hair smoky in the late-day sun, when Lucian and two other young men had come from the house, intent on reaching the stables, and dressed for riding.

"Well, would you look at that!" Coming face-to-face with the lovely young woman, Lucian had stopped, thumbs in vest pockets, with his young companions alongside of him, uncertain.

The three quite successfully blocked her path. Anne found herself flushing; Lucian's stare was bold. The eyes of the two strangers were fixed on her rather blankly.

"Don't tell me. Let me guess—it's Fanny." Lucian put a finger below Anne's chin and tipped her face up.

Anne stood quietly under the scrutiny, waiting for the awkward moment to pass so that she could move on.

"Fanny—all grown up. And everything." With the "everything," Lucian's eyes swept brazenly over Anne's sweet figure. "Fanny. Am I right? Eh? Eh?"

He was demanding an answer. Feeling that to do so might settle the embarrassing confrontation, Anne said, with dignity, "I'm Anne."

"Annie Fanny! But not a mannie. Agreed, men?" Again Lucian's eyes swept Anne's body, and his laugh was rude and loud, spraying spittle into the face that had first flushed pink and was now paling before their very eyes.

One young man joined the laughter, braying rather like an ass in the process; the other put a hand on Lucian's arm and said quietly, "Let's go. Leave her be, and let's go."

"You yearn for horse flesh when there's female flesh around? And such flesh!"

Unused to rudeness, a stranger to lasciviousness, totally unaccustomed to such a blatantly disgraceful reference to the human form, her own in particular, was Anne's undoing. Eyes glittering with suppressed fury, "I thought ye might have grown up, Lucian," she said bitingly. "It seems ye're nothin' but a bairn still."

It was then Lucian MacDermott, unprincipled youth as he had been an unprincipled child, belittled in front of his friends and furious because of it, drew back his arm and backhanded Anne across her face.

The basket flew from Anne's arm; as she staggered momentarily, her hand went to her cheek, already scarlet and hinting at the bruise that would swell there and the discoloration that would result.

"Enough!" The two young men, shocked, drew Lucian back. Shrugging them off he would have returned to the attack except that someone, calling from the stables, demanded to know what was keeping them.

Turning reluctantly away, Lucian, his eyes hard, flung back over his shoulder, "Just who you think you are, I can't imagine! Frasers have ever been available to the MacDermotts, no matter what the need. And my needs are not met—yet!

"And clean up that mess, wench," he shrieked, his tossed head indicating the dozen or so eggs that had flown from the basket and were lying smashed on the ground.

Anne, deaf to everything but the roaring in her ears, was fumbling for the basket. Ignoring its broken contents, she stumbled homeward. Here, she bathed her cheek and eye and groaned at the sight, knowing it could not be disguised. As in most emergencies, her thoughts went automatically to a soothing cup of tea. Waiting for its medicinal purposes to bring a degree of calm to her spirit, which was as bruised as her countenance, she shrank from the thought of explaining to her father and brothers.

There was no hiding the injury. Her father, a most careless parent, noticed as soon as he came in the door. It seemed that he inquired about its cause almost reluctantly.

"It was Lucian," Anne, ever truthful, admitted, and recounted briefly the meeting with the young men and its outcome.

"What in heaven's name did ye do to cause him to act so?"

"Nothin', Da, nothin' at all!"

Paul Fraser's face grew red. "You got in the lad's way. Don't be a fool, girl. Stay out of that'n's way—"

"He's no lad, Da. He's older'n I am . . . old enough to have some sense and to know better, I'd think."

"It makes perfect sense to him," Paul said bitterly. "Dinna ye know, lass, that the laird has full say o' all of his tenants? All o' us is at his beck and call, and that goes for the young laird too."

"Even wives and sons and dauties, is that what ye're sayin'?"

"That's the way it is. It's always been that way, and it always will. Ye have nae right tae think things'll be any different."

"Are you tellin' me, Da, that he can get away wi' . . . wi' whatever it is he's threatenin', and naebody can say him nay—not e'en me own father?"

"Not me, nor yer brothers. So leave them oot o' it, ye hear? I dinna want them in any mair trouble than they have a'ready. Ye hear me, Anne?"

Anne, more blinded by tears than when Lucian had so summarily struck her and more injured in ways that matter, put supper on the table and escaped to the loft. Here she stayed throughout the evening and night, never coming down to subject herself to her brothers and a further confession, from them, of helplessness in the face of Lucian's abuse.

Cook, the next day, gave Anne's face a keen look and shook her head, muttering darkly, but apparently not surprised. Mrs. Case, the housekeeper, studied Anne's face grimly and set her to cleaning silverware rather than servicing the rooms above stairs.

"I can't keep you downstairs forever," she said almost crossly, as though angry at the need to face the problem. "You aren't the first in the world, by any means, to have such a problem. It's the price you pay for having a pretty face." She spoke as if it were Anne's problem, not Lucian's. "If you're lucky it'll be a passing phase. These things never last; no young laird can think seriously of a serving girl or maid. Lucian knows that; he knows his place, all right. Just keep out of his way. And if you can't—" Mrs. Case shrugged and left her sentence unfinished.

Later in the day Anne was sent to Binkiebrae by Mrs. Case, almost coming face-to-face with Tierney. Having been adjured to say only that she had tripped and fallen and hurt herself, and knowing she could not lie to Tierney, Anne had hastened on her way, heart beating hard and sobs near the surface. Even so, Tierney suspected, Anne knew that.

The second confrontation with Lucian took place in one of the upstairs bedrooms, not Lucian's. Anne had been careful not to enter his room whenever he was in it. Laying a fire in one of the guest rooms, she heard the door open and close behind her. Turning her head she saw Lucian leaning against the door, a triumphant smile on his face.

"Think you're smart, don't you, slipping around, avoiding me. Well, I knew you couldn't do it forever. And here you are! And on your knees! Perfect, just perfect. Before you get up, *Fanny,* apologize for your rudeness the other day and I might, I just might, let you get away with it. In fact, I promise I will—if you ask me properly. Now what do you say, *Fanny?*"

Anne never knew what prompted her; she would never understand where she got her courage. But her brain, icily calm, seemed to put words into her mouth, deliberate words, coldly spoken.

"I told you me name is Anne."

The words seemed innocent enough, but they both knew she was insisting on her independence. No matter his anger, she stubbornly insisted on her right to be her own person.

About to rise from her knees, she was startled when Lucian leaped across the room, bent, and savagely took her by the throat, pressing cruelly, while his face was thrust into hers.

"Who cares what your name is, you stupid jade! It's your position that counts, and you've got the proper one—on your knees! Don't you know I have the right to treat you like the baggage you are?"

Lucian's hands, slim as a woman's, had remarkable strength. In the awkward position of kneeling, Anne had no leverage, nothing in her favor for breaking free. Choking, pulling at his hands, the best she could do was scratch, which she did, raking great gouges into Lucian's flesh. Finally, with a curse, he let go, throwing her sideways and down, so that she lay, gulping great gasps of air into her lungs, unable for the moment to so much as get to her feet.

Where it all might have ended is a question, but there came a tap on the door that the young man had cannily locked behind him. Lucian's mother, Mrs. MacDermott herself, called out in low but carrying tones, "Lucian, are you in there? Come out, dear. Your guests are waiting, and the carriage is ready. Lucian?"

"Coming, Mother." Lucian's voice was sweetly obedient, and the smile had returned to his face. Just that sweetly, just that smilingly, he kicked the recumbent figure lying prone on the rug at his feet, stepped to the door, turned, looked down, and said gravely, "Good little girls have nice things happen to them. Keep that in mind, Fanny. Don't forget it again; be a good girl, and you still may have nice things happen to you."

That Sunday, at kirk, Anne had spoken the enigmatic word that she knew would bring Tierney to see her: "Eggs," she had whispered. She knew her friend would see through the small subterfuge and respond.

But before that moment arrived, Pauly came into the house with a battered face.

"Pauly!" Anne cried, appalled, reaching a hand toward her brother.

"Leave me be!" Pauly half sobbed. "Ye've done enough a'ready!"

"Me? What've I done?"

"Don't ye know that that scum, Lucian, can do whatever he wants, and we've no rights of our own? Jist know this—me and Da and Sam, we're payin' for yer almighty independence! Ye might as well give in and git it over and put behind ye, jist like generations of lasses have had to do. What makes ye think it'll be any different for ye?"

And Pauly, hurting and bitter, refused to allow his sister to minister to his bloody face, and lay down on a pallet near the fireplace, put his head in his arms, and would say no more.

When Tierney came, any notion of sharing her problems was silenced. Though she needed desperately to talk, it occurred to Anne that the long arm of the MacDermotts reached into the heart of Binkiebrae. Would the Caulders inexplicably lose their house? Would James find his boat confiscated for some vague reason? Would Tierney herself come under the scrutiny and attention of the loose-living, free-thinking Lucian?

"I canna talk aboot it," she had said to Tierney, and she would not be persuaded.

Perhaps, with discretion and care, she could avoid any further contact with Lucian. Perhaps, before long, he would return to Edinburgh and society life, and all of them on the crofts and in Binkiebrae could breathe easily again.

It was not to be.

Evening was coming on, tea over and chores done, when Anne left home to make her way toward a small house on the edge of Binkiebrae, this time with several newly hatched baby chicks in her basket, a gift for old Maggie.

She was absorbed in checking on the chicks, running a finger lightly over their downy heads as she went, and so heard the approaching horse's hooves too late. Caution, ordinarily, would have sent her scuttling for the brush at the side of the road in time to avoid a confrontation with Lucian, if it were indeed he.

By the time she recognized him, pride kept her in the middle of the road, kept her moving, chin up, eyes straight ahead, mouth suddenly dry, heart beating hard.

Lucian drew his horse to a halt. When he saw that Anne continued on her way, he flushed an angry red, yanked his horse around so that he came abreast of her, and pulled in front of her.

"Hold on, Fanny. Haven't we got some business to take care of?"

Still Anne did not pause but routed herself around Lucian and his mount, walking steadily, silently, though the hand on the basket shook and the chicks set up a twitter.

Once again, now cursing angrily, Lucian yanked the animal around and came alongside the doggedly proceeding Anne. Again he pulled in front of her; again she attempted to sidestep rider and horse. She never made it.

Curses exploding from his twisted mouth, Lucian removed his foot from the stirrup, pulled it back, and with a powerful kick from his heavily booted foot sent Anne staggering, stumbling back, turning an ankle badly in the process. Before she could right herself Lucian sprang from the saddle and, for no reason at all except meanness, kicked the fallen basket so that it bounced and rolled, the chicks escaping to run peeping into the grass. With surprising strength for one with his girlish build, he gathered a handful of Anne's clothing into his fist and pulled her startled, wide-eyed face to within inches of his own.

"This is as far as you go, Miss Hoity-toity!"

Anne was small, Anne was womanly, but Anne was a fighter. The pain of the ankle was forgotten as she battled the raging, cursing youth. Lucian's purposes seemed clear; he kept his grip on Anne's clothes and began dragging her toward the weeds and brush at the road's edge. With one booted foot he tripped her feet, already unsteady, and toppled Anne to the dusty road. From there it was simpler to drag her, with her torn hands grasping at the roadside growth and her feet scrabbling to gain leverage. Lucian's punches, Lucian's kicks, Lucian's questing hands—all found more than they could deal with in the raging, spitting, fighting scrap of humanity that was Anne Fraser. When Lucian's feet became entangled in the undergrowth and he lost his balance, falling heavily on the thrashing, heaving body, he lost his advantage.

With a strength she didn't know she had, Anne pushed with both hands, drawing up her knees and shoving with them at Lucian until the tender anatomy was excruciatingly gouged. Lucian rolled, screaming, from her, to huddle in the fetal position, cradling himself in his own arms and sobbing.

Anne made her escape, crawling into the brush and hiding until Lucian gained some measure of control, got to his feet, limped to the road, and headed down it in pursuit of the missing horse, still moaning, still cursing, threatening.

Already near Binkiebrae, and not wanting to go in the same direction as Lucian, Anne determined to reach the Caulder home, and Tierney. Greatly hampered by the sprained ankle, her progress had been slow—a crawl much of the way, a limping walk at times. Soiled, clothing torn, battered and degraded—but intact, Anne reached the Caulder doorstep the victor.

"But I can never go through it again," she concluded, her eyes reflecting, in the firelight, the horror of her experience. "Whatever am I going to do, Tierney? Whaur can I go that I can escape the MacDermotts? How can I ever be safe again?"

It was Tierney herself who took the word the following morning to the Frasers that Anne was in Binkiebrae and would be staying, for the time being, with the Caulders.

Paul Fraser laid aside his pitchfork and walked with Tierney from the great stables to the yard. Though his face took on a red, congested appearance, his voice, when he spoke, was controlled.

But it was grim. "Perhaps that's best," he said. "Lord knows I canna do muckle for her. And her brothers—weel, Pauly learned the hard way; he'll no' be protectin' his sister any mair, the young master seen to that. Oh, Pauly's bigger and stronger, a'reet, but one raises his hand to his master—and his master's son—verra carefully indaid. I mysel' barely stoppit the brawl that was a'risin', and thereby saved our Pauly from heaven alone knows wha' terrible consequences."

Paul Fraser shook his head, while his defeated eyes gazed into space, refusing to look at Tierney as he confessed his inability to stand up for his daughter against his employer and master. And that master's son, bully that he was.

"I dinna know," he continued, "how long Anne can get away wi' stayin' wi' ye. I'll tell them, up at the big hoose, that she's sick, but I dinna know how long 'twill work. I seen the young master come limpin' in last night; in a foul mood, he was, and his clo'es torn and dairty. I kep' me'sel' oot o' his way. And then when me dautie didn't coom home, I was half sick wi' worry and shame—"

Paul Fraser bowed his head and scuffed his boot in the dirt of the yard. "Ye tell her it's a'reet wi' me if she stays wi' ye fer a time. Best to be careful, though, and stay oot o' the way—"

"Oh, she'll stay oot o' the way, never fear. She's a sight to behold, Mr. Fraser—scratched and bruised, not to mention her ruined clothes. . . . Now, if ye dinna mind, I'd like to go into the hoose and pick up some of her things, if that's a'reet wi' ye."

"Go ahead," Paul Fraser said, adding hesitantly as Tierney turned away, "Anne . . . she's a'reet? He dinna . . . that is, she's a'reet, is she?"

"Depends on what ye mean by a'reet," Tierney said with heat. "Ye should see her face, Mr. Fraser, and her torn garments. But yes, she's a'reet."

Paul Fraser drew a deep breath and said gruffly, "Tell her to take care. And then," he added doggedly, "if we're not tae be in serious trouble, she'll hae tae coom back. I can only make excuses so long, ye know."

Tierney swung away, as angry as it was possible for her to be. The helplessness of her friend's situation, the uselessness of speaking out, the impotence experienced in the face of terrible unfairness, infuriated and frustrated her almost past enduring. A female's lot was a hard one! Was there no equality anywhere?

Though she herself suffered no such physical abuse, though she herself experienced no deprivation of home or food, she paid the price for her femininity in many ways. While James worked and made the living, she was reduced to sitting home, waiting, as it were, for some other male to come along and offer his provision, his protection, his name. In Binkiebrae, as in most of the world, this was her option.

As she made a parcel of Anne's things, Tierney's thoughts turned from the limitations of Binkiebrae to the nearby city of Aberdeen. Women worked there. Oh, not the respected and the cultured—she had seen the ragged, sometimes scurvy lot that could be found around the streets of the city, doing all manner of things—selling flowers, peddling odds and ends of cooking pots, offering secondhand clothing for a few pennies. Tierney shivered at the prospect, considering her present lot much preferable, though it wasn't productive.

There was work on the wharves, in the fish markets—Aberdeen was an important fish-trawling center—and many women could be seen on the docks. Too, Aberdeen had a flourishing trade, with many mills manufacturing woolens, linens, paper, even combs. Tierney had seen women coming out of these vast buildings in long, weary lines. Women did char work in the granite buildings of the city, perhaps in the granite works themselves. Called "Granite City," Aberdeen was known for its granite, and many people were engaged in its hewing and polishing. There were fine docks and a good harbor, and Aberdeen did a large import and export trade, being the leading port for the White Sea and Baltic trades. Surely, somewhere in this thriving city there would be something a healthy, strong, willing girl could do.

Tierney sighed, close to feeling defeated before she ever began; it was an unexplored frontier for women she contemplated entering. And did she have enough gumption to get out of Binkiebrae, with its familiar environment, and try to fit into the enterprising competition of the masses of people on the streets of Aberdeen?

By any chance, would Anne throw in her lot with her? With the possibility of Anne's agreeing, what was just a vague dream with shadowy dimensions in Tierney's thinking took on possibilities, if not probabilities. Nothing ventured, nothing gained! Perhaps she was more of a modern woman than she had known!

Women everywhere were becoming restless, aware of opportunities for their gender where doors had been shut before. True, it would be hard to be a pathfinder, but someone had to break ground! Someone had to dare to break free! In an impossible situation, almost literally thrust out of home and croft, Anne might indeed be amenable to . . . at least . . . listening.

And listen she did. With her poor eyes half shut and the skin around them turning greenish blue, with her arms scratched and one ankle painfully swollen, Anne listened.

Tierney had returned home to report to Anne her father's reaction and message. Anne's puffy face crumpled, her slitted eyes leaked tears, and her broken lips twisted to think she would be expected to return, and to the same impossible situation.

But what else was there for her? She couldn't go on sharing Tierney's small loft, sleeping in her narrow cot while Tierney slept in a pallet on the floor beside her. She couldn't expect James to provide for her, though he had been kind, expressing shock at the sight of her injuries, and assuring her that she was welcome at his fire and table.

But Anne had seen Phrenia's expression when she stopped by—first blank and questioning, then coolly accepting. But it was clear it troubled her to have another female under the same roof with her intended, and Anne and Tierney both caught numerous pointed references to the marriage that would take place "as soon as it seemed a'reet."

Sitting together at the fireside with the inevitable "cup o' tae," Tierney talked about what had occurred to her—a solution not only for Anne but for herself.

"Ye know, Annie," she said, "that I dinna relish livin' here with me brother and his new wife. But what is there for the likes o' me to do? I'll never marry . . . na, never. Dinna expect it o' me, Anne! It's an auld maid I'll be, and that for all o' me days. I canna imagine wha' 'twoud be like to live here wi' a growin' family, and the bairns not mine. I'd be in the way—for there's no' enow room—helpin' raise another woman's lads and lassies. Nae, thank ye, I'll not! So, ye see, Annie, I'm fightin' to have some kind o' a life o' me own. I'll live in a tenement or wheree'er I can, if 'tis clean, and do what I hae tae do to make a livin', so long as it's honest."

"I know how ye feel," Anne said softly, as though her injured mouth hurt to make the sounds. "I hae no' place o' me own, either. It's a harsh life, Tierney, and a pitiful one for many in our shoes." Glancing down at Tierney's castoffs on her feet, she added ruefully, "E'en our shoes are apt tae no' be our ain."

Many hours were taken up with restoring Anne's despoiled clothes. They were laundered and ironed and mended and patched. Though they resembled nothing better than rags, there was no way they could be consigned to the rag bag while there was a day's wear in them.

"We better take the opportunity to let oot the seams," Anne said practically. "I've been wearin' this gown for three years, and have done a bit of . . . growin' in that time."

Even with Tierney, her natural reserve brought a flush to Anne's cheeks as she referred to the natural development of her body from age fifteen to eighteen.

Tierney, not quite so self-conscious, or perhaps with a more teasing nature, said, "Aye, and very nicely, too." Growing serious, she added, "An' it's one reason that Lucian canna stay awa' from ye."

Now Anne's face flared crimson. "Beast that he is! At any rate, we best let these seams oot . . . maybe put a wee bit o' lace here in the bodice."

No matter what they did, nothing would disguise Anne's lovely womanhood, Tierney knew, and she worried for her friend. Tierney's own build was slender where Anne's was rounded. Not the beauty Anne was, Tierney's chief attraction was her wide and ready smile, her golden-brown eyes usually lit by a sparkle of life, and the abundant auburn hair that glinted fire so readily.

Again and again, no matter what they were doing—mending, making bannock, cleaning neeps or tatties, washing each other's hair, eventually venturing out in the evening's gloaming to walk a bit—they came back to thoughts of moving away, obtaining work . . . finding a life somewhere other than in Binkiebrae.

There came a day when Sam, Anne's brother, stopped by "to see how ye be." Before his short visit was over he made it clear that Da was making noises about Anne getting home again. "He's gettin' verra restless aboot it. Think ye that ye'll coom back anytime soon?" he asked her.

"Not yet, Sammie," Anne pleaded. "Tell him not yet. Soon . . . perhaps soon. See—there's still signs of bruisin'—"

Sam looked gravely at the cheek that was blossoming pink and fair and said sturdily, "Aye, I see it. I'll tell 'im, Annie. But look fer him to coom hisself one o' these days."

With these words of warning Sam took his departure; Anne sank onto the settle, with some difficulty controlling tears and a fit of the shakes.

"How can I go back? Oh, 'tis dreadful, dreadful to think on! 'Tis time, Tierney, to do more than talk aboot leavin' Binkiebrae! It'll ne'er happen if we don't do somethin'!"

And so it was decided to go to Aberdeen as soon as a ride could be obtained, though "we could walk it," Anne persisted.

"Na, na, Annie. Ye're still shaky and summ'at weak. I'll see if there's a cart goin', and we'll ride along."

It was the custom; within a day such a ride was available. Tierney said nothing beforehand to James, hoping they would be home before he was—the weather being advantageous for fishing, the boats out long hours—and have tea ready at the usual time. Nevertheless, she left a brief note: *Anne and I are out for a change. Home soon.*

They reached Aberdeen in less than two hours, travelling deep into the heart of the city. Thanking the old huckster, a neighbor who was trundling sacks of new onions to sell at a market where stands of such merchandise were displayed, the girls struck out on their own.

"If ye're here aboot four o'clock," they were advised, "ye can ride back tae Binkiebrae wi' me. Else, ye'll hae tae walk it."

"We'll be here, and thank ye, thank ye verra much," Tierney said warmly.

"I hardly know where to begin," Tierney said, more independent than Anne and therefore the expected leader. "Let's ask around."

Inquiries at the stalls brought no results. Even the red-faced, plump-bodied women who surely understood the need, seemed too busy to give the girls more than a brief hearing, responding with a discouraging shake of the head, and a quick return to their tasks.

"Try the docks," one said.

Tierney sighed; it was a long walk. "We'll head that direction," she said, "and see what might turn up as we go."

Walking and asking, the distance went by slowly and the time rapidly. Finally, tired and footsore, the girls found an upturned box, rested their feet, and ate the bannock and cheese they had brought with them.

One woman, not much older than they, turned from the cart she was pushing along the street, to offer them a drink. Unscrewing the glass jar, she listened patiently as Tierney explained their purpose.

"Losh now," she said, wiping the sweat from her brow, "if 'twas me, I'd go see that woman around the corner . . . over there. But I have a hooseful of bairns," and sighing, "so I'm fer Aberdeen and the streets all me days, it seems."

"What woman is that?" Anne asked, as she and Tierney studied the corner and could see nothing out of the ordinary.

"There's a sign hangin' there, around the corner; it'll tell ye all aboot it."

Their benefactress, having said her bit, screwed the cap on the jar, tucked it back among the apples on her cart and, without another word, went her way.

"I suppose we might as well look into it," Tierney said, weary of walking, hot and dusty and discouraged, but determined to make the most of their day in the city, the only place there was any hope at all of a change for them.

The sign was easy to spot. Fastened to the front of a shop that offered books and other reading material, it was set over a table on which rested a stack of pamphlets. At its side, disregarding the straight-backed chair available at the side of the table, stood a tall, abundantly endowed woman. Her hair was piled tidily atop her head and supported a serviceable hat. Her dress was neat, her shoes sturdy. Her voice was resolute; no one, surely not the seedy collection of females before her now, would doubt her authority.

BRITISH WOMEN'S EMIGRATION SOCIETY, the sign read. Beneath it was tacked a large poster. It was like nothing the girls had ever seen. The first line caught their attention, and the further they read, the more intrigued they were.

ATTENTION!

Nice girls are needed in the Canadian West!

Not ten, not a hundred, but THOUSANDS!

More than 20,000 men are waiting for WIVES

and none are available. SHAME!

Anything in skirts has a chance. No tomfoolery! This is serious!

DON'T MISS THIS OPPORTUNITY, GIRLS;

you may never get another!

If you can't come yourself, send your sister!

Application forms available

Four or five women, having read the catchy advertisement and obviously interested, had sidled up to the woman in charge of this display, and a conversation was in progress. Tierney and Anne edged near. When pamphlets were offered, their hands went out for them. It seemed to be promotional material explaining all about employment possibilities for women in—of all places—Canada.

"Domestic Servants Wanted," the pamphlet announced, and went on to urge the migration of young women of marriageable age. Canada's federal government, it seemed, was actually recruiting young females.

The woman, who introduced herself as Ishbel Mountjoy, was saying in beguiling but businesslike tones, "Canada promises greater economic mobility, by far, than you may expect in your homeland. The opportunities are boundless—you see what the poster says. If you are not interested in becoming a wife, take the opportunity to get moved to a new and vital part of our world, where your skills are needed and wanted. And *will be paid for!* You may," she went on in thrilling tones, "by your choice, elect to have a domestic role in the settling of the far West! Think of it!" More mildly now, but with the power of the government behind her, she continued, "The Canadian government considers women the 'gentle tamers' who help to equalize the ratio of women to men on the frontier."

What a complimentary phrase: gentle tamers. It spoke of the power and strength of a woman, yet the tenderness that accompanied all that she undertook. The two words and the pride they conjured up, it was plain to see, made an impact on the hearers. But it seemed clear, in all she said and did, Mrs. Mountjoy was absolutely serious, a paragon to be trusted, an advisor to be heard.

Not said, but intimated, was the idea that marriage was more than a possibility. But when Tierney boldly asked if that's what she meant, Mrs. Mountjoy assured her, "No, indeed! Though for those who wish it there is every possibility of it happening. That's the excellent part of it—a woman is free to make up her own mind. She may work and support herself, helping build the great Canadian North West at the same time, or she may marry, if she so wishes, having her choice of many sturdy, hardworking but lonely bachelors, and becoming mother to the next generation of Canadians."

Tierney heard only the part "a woman is free to make up her own mind."

Ishbel Mountjoy was continuing. "At this time, Europe and Britain—including your corner of the world, as you very well know—offer little in the way of economic security, social position, or educational opportunity to the single woman. You will certainly wish," she said almost sternly, "to choose immigration as a domestic servant over poverty, social ostracism, and unemployment, which are your options in your own homeland. You will certainly wish to choose immigration over subjection to male domination, which is so taken for granted. And you will opt for independence over being ground down as a woman."

Now Anne's pink lips parted and she seemed to breathe, for the moment, the free air and blessed opportunities of the Canadian North West. And to think it beckoned to her!

As the result of another question, Mrs. Mountjoy was asking, "How is this financed? The money—which it would take for a woman to make such a move—is advanced either by the prospective employer or the British Women's Emigration Society. The debt incurred is cared for very simply: It is usually discharged by the employer withholding up to one-half of the monthly wage, to keep until his investment is repaid, or to send to Canadian authorities designated to collect loans on behalf of the immigration agencies."

"How would one go aboot getting work?" Anne asked, trying to keep her interest from showing in her voice.

"The association has a standard application form," the commanding woman confided. "It is in the form of a contract. Then, there are lists of job opportunities available, and they work on both ends, getting worker and employer together. You may be sure it is well overseen. The Y.W.C.A.—Young Women's Christian Association—takes a very active part in all of this."

Anne and Tierney were impressed by this piece of information.

"Tell us," Anne asked, "aboot wages. What may one expect to receive in the way of pay?"

"First of all, let me mention that a maximum work day of ten hours is set. I know you will be impressed by this, considering the longer hours women work in your factories, and at jobs that have no appeal for them. Here, you will be putting your womanly skills to work and need not fear that you are unqualified. A minimum wage of fifteen dollars a month is offered, and an overtime rate of fifteen cents per hour is also set. Clear enough?" Ishbel Mountjoy looked carefully around the circle of women before she continued.

"Let me read a typical contract form, in part: 'I shall have every Sunday evening free after half-past six, unless a different arrangement has been agreed upon. I shall be addressed as 'Miss' and be referred to as 'housekeeper.'"

And now it was the turn of the raggle-taggle group of women to look impressed, and they looked at each other and nodded solemnly before turning their attention back to Mrs. Mountjoy and the continued reading of the contract.

"'I shall have the use of a suitable room one evening a week in which I may entertain guests until ten o'clock . . . comfortable lodgings shall be provided for me by my employer . . . I shall be privileged to enter the house by the front door . . .'"

"But what if a place is unacceptable, not what it was represented to be?" a hesitant listener asked. "After all, you can't really know until you get to a place whether you want to stay and work there."

Confirming nods could be seen all around the group, which had now swelled to a dozen women, with a few males listening disgustedly for a few seconds and moving on, shaking their heads and tapping their foreheads.

"Either party may terminate the arrangement, the contract, at any time simply by giving two weeks' notice. As you see, everything to make for a satisfactory situation is being cared for. This is very important—a point that has helped many to make the decision to sign up. You'll be interested to know that hundreds are responding, here and in other European countries, and we shall continue to spread the word until every need is met, on both sides of the ocean. Not only the men needing wives and the households needing domestic help, but the girls and women needing desperately to have a choice about their future.

"Let me ask you, seriously, ladies: Do you *have* a future, as things are now? If not, you may view this opening as God's hand of guidance for your life."

Ishbel Mountjoy was invoking powerful forces here. But it seemed to have the desired effect. Women took deep breaths and seemed relieved of some worrisome uncertainty—whether or not the Almighty would look with favor upon such a project.

"Transportation . . . travel—" The fact that it was such a huge undertaking, and at such a distance, put an edge of fear into the voice of the inquirer who had probably never been farther from home than the distance from Scottish croft to Aberdeen streets.

"All cared for by the Society. All one has to do is sign up, arrange to meet me here at a designated time, and the rest follows automatically. Now, any more questions?" Mrs. Mountjoy was all business . . . pleasant business. It seemed she believed in her Society and its objectives.

"What about the weather?" The questioner seemed to have settled the weightier problems and now honed in on secondary problems.

All heads lifted from their pamphlet reading, and all eyes waited for the answer. Everyone had heard stories of the prairies, the blizzards, the dust storms, the mosquitoes! If you knew anyone who knew anyone who knew anyone who had contact with an emigrant in the territories, you knew about these legendary problems faced by pioneers in the West.

A light laugh issued from the otherwise businesslike, rather stern mouth of Ishbel Mountjoy. "You see me before you. I've lived through all seasons there and have survived in rather fine fashion, wouldn't you say?"

The doubt on several faces may have persuaded Ishbel Mountjoy to bridle a bit and add, "Your own highland weather would cause many a delicate female to cringe, and we're not expecting women of delicate sensibilities to respond to the challenge of the Canadian West. This is for the woman with the heart of an adventurer. The woman of courage, strength, determination, and even humor. For every woman who quits, a thousand stand ready to take her place. *And* her man."

Again that reference to marriage. And it may have had the desired effect, for several women brightened. Well, marriage was the least of Tierney's thoughts! In fact, she had determined, when Robbie Dunbar sailed away, that she would never consider marriage again.

But a pioneer, a woman of adventure! As a lone star braves the night's overwhelming darkness and endures, so Tierney responded to the challenge of the tremendous odds presented by the speaker. Was challenged and, in her heart, cried out a silent but vigorous "Aye!"

Glancing at Anne to see what her reaction might be to all of this, it was to see Anne's lips parted slightly; she was breathing quickly as though having run through a troop, her color was high as though she had walked through a gale, and in Anne's eyes something flickered that Tierney recognized as a glimmer of that same star that had risen on her own dark horizon.

Anne's eyes were the exalted eyes of one who explores untraversed regions to mark out a new route—a true pioneer, a dedicated adventurer.

Were Tierney's eyes any less expressive? Surely Anne saw her own commitment mirrored there as the girls looked searchingly at one another. If what Ishbel Mountjoy had set out to do was instill in her hearers a sense of well-being, power, and importance, of being in charge of their own future, she had wonderfully succeeded where Tierney Caulder and Anne Fraser were concerned.

"Be on this spot at noon three days from now," Ishbel Mountjoy said, striking while the iron was hot, "with whatever you wish to take with you—no more than two bags each, please. Now, who wants to be first to sign up?"

All right, girls—time to ascend."

Tierney and Anne looked at each other, stifling grins. Through the gloom of the ship's hold where they were quartered, amid the scuffle and scurry of preparing to go up on deck, in spite of the heavy odor of too many bodies in one space—the girls found occasion to laugh. Ascend, indeed!

No matter the moment's disarray, no matter the occasion's emergency, no matter the situation's aggravation, Ishbel Mountjoy kept her poise, kept her standards. Her good English schooling and training never forsook her. Canadian she may have become, but English she would remain until the day she died. Where Ishbel Mountjoy went, there went a little bit of England. And there went propriety.

"I can imagine," Tierney had said one time to Anne, shaking her head in unbelief at the woman's magnificent aplomb in the face of some emergency, "the ship goin' doon and the billows risin' over our heads, and Mrs. Mountjoy strictly insistin', 'One at a time, girls, one at a time.'"

Ishbel Mountjoy was the perfect choice to represent the British Women's Emigration Society. Not only could she give a lucid explanation about why a move to Canada was advantageous, painting an attractive picture of all it had to offer the downtrodden, abused, discouraged, and neglected females of the British Isles, but her very appearance and demeanor spoke of solid Victorian virtues. Wherever the name of the good queen was invoked, there went morality, excellence of character, modesty, decency. And there went Ishbel Mountjoy.

The group Mrs. Mountjoy had managed to assemble—with the help of others who had spread themselves over England, Ireland, and Scotland—was a motley crew, about forty-five females in all; there were farm girls, slum girls, impoverished girls of a slightly better "class"; girls from families with too many children to provide for them properly; girls whose parents had died, leaving them no alternative but to seek refuge with reluctant relatives.

There were those among them who could not rightly be called "girls," being more advanced in years, though still single—for one reason or another marriage had passed them by. There were several widows who had been left with no means of support, women weary of serving as scullery maids or laundresses in the homes of the favored and titled. But all, regardless of age, were in good health (or represented themselves as such, desperately fearing being turned back because of some illness or disease), and were, in normal times, full of life and the sense of adventure. It couldn't help but spill over from time to time.

But after several days at sea with the ship wallowing in the grip of a storm, even the healthiest among them appeared peaked, pale, and wan. Some suffered the miseries of severe seasickness, and with facilities for personal grooming limited, were in considerable disarray of body, not to mention mind and spirit.

There were some three hundred females quartered in a space that would have been overcrowded with one-third that number. And yet they considered themselves favored; men, they understood, were in a hold below where farm animals had been kept previously, and the air, what there was of it, was noxious. For eating purposes, they understood, there was a large table in the middle of the hold, but so wretched was the food, the men from the kitchen dare not come in lest they be mobbed, even killed. Standing at the door, they literally threw chunks of meat to the sweating, swaying, cursing pack of men; they tossed in potatoes, cooked in their jackets, deposited cans of water at the door, and fled.

"Good catchers and tall fellers get most of the grub," one poor, thin young man had conveyed to Anne when a lull in the storm had allowed groups of emigrants to "ascend" for air and exercise.

Eventually a delegation of men had insisted on seeing the captain. "We'll take over the ship and turn her back to Liverpool," they threatened, "if things don't improve."

Word seeped into the women's compartments that the captain, recognizing the problem and the desperation, had chosen fifty men, given them free passage, and put them to work preparing decent meals, feeding the starving horde, and cleaning the toilets. Even the women benefited from the improved menu.

Today, feeling better, and the weather being conducive, the women and girls had bathed themselves, in a limited fashion, washed hair for the first time since leaving land, and were looking forward to going up on deck to dry it.

With Mrs. Mountjoy's businesslike order, "Assemble for ascending," the girls jockeyed for position at the foot of the ladder. A pained glance from the eye of their leader reminded them of their manners, and with a sigh they obeyed the injunction of their morning devotions, led by Ishbel herself: "In honor preferring one another."

As the girls were preferring one another, stepping aside as graciously as they could to allow for a peaceable lineup, awaiting the command to "ascend," Tierney's thoughts flew to Binkiebrae and home. Her heart was still raw from the painful separation from family and loved ones, her thoughts were still full of the memories of that wrenching leave-taking and the probability of never seeing James again.

"Maybe," she had offered between tears and sobs, "you'll come oot to Canada after a while, James. Could it be, d'ye think?"

"Na, na, sister, never think on't. I'm fer Scotland. And Phrenia, she'd never agree t' leave her folk. See, it's like a game of dominoes—one after the other, leavin'. Someone has tae stop it, or Binkiebrae will be a ghostly place. Na, na, it's guid-bye fer all time, I'm thinkin'. Onless ye coom back, and I dinna think ye're aboot to." And James's eyes, too, puddled with tears, tears of which he was not ashamed.

According to Anne, her farewells had been more subdued. Angry at first, flatly refusing permission for her to go, her father had found himself helpless in the face of Anne's adamant preparations, short of locking her up. And how would that end? With her continuing with her plans when she was eventually loosed, with nothing gained in the end by him and his demands.

"Go then!" he had finally agreed wearily. "But what I'll tell the master I dinna ken." It seemed to be Paul Fraser's chief concern.

"Tell him he dinna own me. Tell him," she added recklessly, "he dinna own any of the Frasers." Paul had growled and shifted uncomfortably, obviously dreading the reaction of the MacDermotts.

Anne's brothers, Pauly and Sam, when they saw her determination, confessed they would miss their only sister, wishing they were bold enough to go with her.

"Ye'd have to be a lass," she had told them. "This plan isna for laddies. Find yersel' somebody that'll pay yer way, and ye can work it off. A sort of indenture, I guess, tho' not sae long or binding. The debt could be paid off sooner, and ye'd be free to make yer own way, get your own place. Think on't!"

The brothers promised, with true longing, to "think on't," and gave their sister a hug and kiss, something they had not done in all their lives, to her memory, until this moment. It meant something to Anne; she found herself, at times, thinking "on't" and rejoicing over the separation more than regretting it. It had been a sweeter moment than any she could recall since the death of her mother, and it did much to wipe out the years of her brothers' carelessness and unconcern.

The actual moment of their leaving Binkiebrae had been marked by the turnout of most of the small hamlet, embracing, waving, with a few tears making their unaccustomed way down the craggy, wind-worn faces of friends and neighbors. Robbie Dunbar's family had told her, with regret, "We dinna know whaur Robbie be, Tierney. We havna had time to hear from 'im." And it was true; there had been, as yet, no communication from the absent sons; it was too soon.

Tierney and Anne turned from the warm show of affection to climb aboard the cart. Looking over the heads of the assembled group they could see a lone horse and haughty rider—Lucian MacDermott.

Before touching heels to his mount and whirling away, Lucian's malevolent gaze met the startled eyes of Anne. His lips curled in a sneer, his slitted eyes glittered, and he touched his hand to his forehead in a mocking salute. Anne shivered, her gaze caught in his, like that of a snared bird. His presence—towering and menacing—was more threatening than words could have been. Anne's last impression of Binkiebrae was of impending doom.

"Quick, settle doon, and we'll be on our way," Tierney ordered under her breath. "An' forget him; he can't reach you or touch you, ever again."

With more than a hint of hysteria Anne dragged her eyes from Lucian's hypnotic gaze. At the last his sneer changed to something resembling a smile—a mocking, twisted smile, a smile of . . . what? Disdain? Superiority? Promise? Surely not a promise. And a promise of what? In a day's time she would be forever beyond the long arm of the MacDermott clan. *Wouldn't she?*

Tierney and Anne prepared to settle themselves among turnips, not as odorous as the onions of the earlier trip when they had met Ishbel Mountjoy and established their future, but equally dirty. Carefully spreading sacks, they protected their best and finest clothes against starting the journey in a state that would call forth correction or condemnation from the leader of the group. Mrs. Ishbel Mountjoy was to meet them at the designated place and take charge of them from then on; they planned to meet her in satisfactory condition.

What a whirl of activity it had turned out to be! For girls who had never been farther from home than Aberdeen, the world opened amazingly to new faces, new experiences, new speech. Their own speech began to show change almost immediately.

"Girls," Mrs. Mountjoy had said, looking around the circle of faces in her charge and having listened to the distinctive rolling burr that marked their manner of talking, "it'll be to your advantage to make an effort to drop the colloquialisms—the regional dialect expressions—from your talk and to discontinue rolling your r's. It makes it difficult, at times, to understand you. I'm sure, knowing the problem, you'll work on it."

And the Scotswomen, astonished that their manner of speech was strange in any fashion or hard to understand, made an attempt to speak more like Mrs. Mountjoy, herself the epitome of all things acceptable, the judge of all things unacceptable.

Upon reaching the ship, they were joined by a group of girls recruited from London, Liverpool, and other cities, and they saw, for the first time, Pearly Gates of the vivid little face, thin figure, and disreputable clothing. If these were the child's best garments, Tierney and Anne had thought, noting her particularly, how dreadful had been the rags she left behind. No wonder she was taking off for greener pastures—England obviously had not been kind to Pearly Gates.

Aboard the *Lake Manitoba,* making up their beds, Tierney had found herself next to the girl, a mere waif of the streets, she supposed, and had introduced herself.

"I'm Tierney Caulder, from Binkiebrae, near Aberdeen," she said, and added, "seems we're to be bunk mates. That's my friend, Anne Fraser, up there above me, makin' up that bunk for hersel'. She's also from Binkiebrae."

"I'm from Lunnon," the wisp of a girl had said, holding out a small, clawlike hand, "and me name's Pearly Gates."

Only Tierney's kind heart kept her from repeating the name and exclaiming in amused tones, "Pearly Gates!"

"Laugh if y' want ter," Pearly had sighed, as though reading her thoughts. "Most people does. I have a bruvver named Garden; he gets as much fun poked at him as me, though he looks sharp at people when they do it, and dares 'em to laugh at 'im. Gets in lots of fights, me bruvver Garden. Me muvver's got a new babby comin' any day now, and me favver says he's goin' ter call it Heavenly, no matter if it's a boy or a girl. I guess I should be grateful he dint name me lych-gate."

"I guess so! Pearly—it's really verra . . . nice. Your favver . . . father must have a rare sense of humor."

"Oh, he's a real card, me favver is. Especially when he's in his cups."

"Is he in his . . . cups often?"

"Often, and always when a new babby is born."

"I imagine," Tierney said, trying to be sensitive and yet friendly, "ye will miss sich good humor, as well as missing your father and mother, Garden, and, soon now, Heavenly, o' course."

"And Thelma and Winifred and Maisie an' . . . about eight more. Yes," Pearly said, "I s'pose I'll miss 'em, about like they'll miss me. Among so many it's easy to fergit someone." Pearly sounded a bit forlorn, as though loneliness in the middle of a crowd was a common thing.

"Weel," Tierney said, not yet correcting her speech to any marked degree, "ye'll just have to take on Annie and me. We'll be yer family, if ye want."

It was the only invitation needed; Pearly Gates attached herself to the two girls, particularly Tierney. In an instant Tierney gained the sister she had never had until now, though Annie had come close.

Pearly Gates, not quite certain of her age ("older than Garden, younger than Jack"), was probably no younger than Tierney, but in size she was indeed a "wee" sister. Even the poor food the ship's galley provided—and it was better for them than for many of the others, Ishbel saw to that—was received gratefully and almost greedily by Pearly; so poor was her condition from the beginning that she actually began to show signs of improvement. Her color was better than her London pallor, her dull eyes brightened, and most important of all, she seemed to relax and enjoy herself to a degree unequalled by the others, most of whom complained rather bitterly, at times, about numerous miserable aspects of the voyage. Yes, whatever Pearly's lot had been up to now, the poor fare and harsh conditions of the ship were an improvement.

Now, standing in line, waiting to "ascend," the three girls huddled in conversation, running their fingers through their damp hair occasionally, impatient to go up on deck.

"Your name, Pearly," Anne said, returning to the conversation begun earlier and laid aside, "I was wonderin'—why don't ye change it? This would be the time, when ye're leavin' one place an' goin' to another."

"Why not!" Pearly responded quickly. "I'd like that!"

"What name do ye like? Ye could take yer pick, ye know."

"It'd have to be me last name . . . I don't mind the Pearly part, and I'm used ter it. Yes, I'll change me last name."

"But that's yer family name," Tierney reminded. "Ye'd lose that tie wi' yer family."

"Don't matter," Pearly responded stoutly. "They won't miss me none, and since none of 'em can write, and me only a little, we won't be keepin' in touch."

"Well then, how about Smith. Isn't that a good English name?"

"Smiff!" Pearly sniffed. "I'm gonna get me a name that's all mine . . . there's too many Smiffs now."

The order to "ascend" being delayed for some reason or other, Tierney asked, "What name did you have in mind?"

"You'll laugh . . ." Pearly said, looking around cautiously as though about to reveal some great secret.

"Na, na. Promise!"

"Well then—Pearly Chapel."

Though the chattering around them didn't abate, there was a small pocket of silence around Tierney and Anne. You could almost hear them thinking—*Chapel?*

Pearly drew closer and spoke earnestly. "See, I went to this chapel fer a year or more . . . made a big difference in me life. If I call meself Chapel, I'll always remember them good times."

"What chapel was that, Pearly?"

"The Meffodist Chapel. Somebody invited me. . . . I was glad to go, wif noffing much else to do that meant anyfing. That's when . . ." Pearly's little face glowed, and she faltered in her account of the chapel and its affairs.

"You dinna need to tell us if ye dinna want," Tierney said kindly, while Anne put a spontaneous arm around the girl.

"I don't mind. Fact is, I sorter like ter tell it. That's where me life changed—at the Meffodist Chapel. Me heart, I mean."

"I see," Tierney said, not seeing at all. Anne looked equally baffled.

"Yes, changed. Changed from noffing to somefing. You see, that's where they told me about how Jesus loves everybody, even me. That's where I believed it. That's where *I got saved!* And that's me testimony, see?"

"Saved?" Tierney repeated weakly. It was like no term she had heard in Binkiebrae's small kirk.

"So I love the name Chapel. Or," Pearly said, her face ashine under her wet hair, "I could call meself Christian. I have a right to that name, I bin told. Pearly Christian. How's that?"

"It seems to me," Tierney said cautiously, "that Pearly Christian, though it's nice, verra nice indeed, might get ye a few raised eyebrows, same as Pearly Gates. Not from me, o' course," she hastened to add.

"Or me," Anne added quickly.

"Well, then," Pearly concluded and just in time—there seemed to be indications that the line was about to move—"I'll be Pearly Chapel. It'll always remind me of the love of those people, and what happened ter me because they cared about me. Chapel—that's a posh name! I'll hafta tell Mrs. Mountjoy to change me name on her list."

And now, at last, Mrs. Mountjoy was ready to maneuver her "girls" up the companionway to the deck above.

"Girls—commence ascending!" she commanded, and Pearly Chapel's story was discontinued for the time being. But Tierney, for one, found herself unsettled in her mind and wondered about it. What was there about the pinch-faced girl and her cheery "testimony" that was so captivating?

Drying her abundant auburn hair in the warm sun, rocked hypnotically by the surging seas, Tierney thought on her future. Thought more seriously than she had thought before. She and Anne, yes, and Pearly too, were at the mercy of Ishbel Mountjoy and the British Women's Emigration Society. But surely, with the Canadian government back of the plan, it could be depended on. Mrs. Mountjoy seemed, in all ways, a rock of Gibraltar, a paragon of all virtues a woman would strive to have in her life. Added to the attraction of those virtues was the one thing Tierney desired most of all: freedom to be herself, freedom to make her own way, freedom to succeed or lose by her own merits. It was a heady opportunity for a poor Scotch lassie; it was worth taking a chance on.

Mrs. Mountjoy had continued daily—after devotions were completed—advising, explaining, extolling the wondrous works of the Society.

"You've gotten in on a marvelous opportunity," she had said that morning. "It's true that single women are more enthusiastic and adjust better than childbearing women. For them, pioneering is hard; they often submit to it at the will of their husband. The 'reluctant pioneers,' we call them. You have made your own decision; you go into it with an open mind. And for you all the details have been worked out; for you there will be no heavy burden of anxiety over facing another long day's journey across the wilderness over mostly trackless ways.

"That is indeed difficult, and women who undertake it are to be admired; they pay a great price to follow their men into uncharted territory. But for women like you, full of zest and enthusiasm and the confidence that the Society brings, it can and will be an adventure. Each of you will have a fabulous story to tell, some day.

"Even now, you can begin to consider your options and choices, deciding what appeals most to you personally. Let me share one opportunity with you." Here Ishbel adjusted her spectacles and read from the *Regina Leader Post:* "'Wanted—Housekeeper for Canadian bachelor, age thirty-nine, on his own homestead, quarter section, near school, five miles from town, offers permanent position if suited. Apply Box 223, Gray Wolf, Sask., state starting wages, particulars, nationality.'

"Now, isn't that challenging? But if not, there are many more open doors. Requests keep coming in to the Society and, once in Canada, we'll have access to current openings."

At the reading of the advertisement there had been considerable tittering from her listeners, some blushing, a few frowns. "Of course," Mrs. Mountjoy concluded, folding the paper, "this is just one letter. There are countless homes across the territories that are simply begging . . . waiting for you to come and fill a need. Be assured that you will, each of you, find the place best for you. The Society will see that you are satisfactorily settled, and they will be available for any further needs you might have."

"And how can that be," Anne had muttered in Tierney's ear, "when they are far from us, and farms are miles apart, and roads turn to ice? And that bachelor—I thought we would not be goin' anyplace whaur there's no woman."

"This all started oot as a matter of puttin' our trust in the Society," Tierney reminded the cold-footed Anne, who hadn't regained her composure from the moment she had glimpsed Lucian MacDermott when they were departing Binkiebrae. "The same gumption that got us oot o' Binkiebrae will get us oot o' any miserable spot we might get in."

"I certainly hope so," Anne replied grimly. "As for me, I'm no' goin' tae take any place like the Madam read aboot this mornin', I can tell you that. No single men. . . ."

"Ye're reet, Annie. Girls are no' placed where there's no woman in the home," Tierney consoled Anne. "It's one o' the rules. What Mrs. Mountjoy read is a marriage proposal, and wasna addressed to the Society."

Anne's spirits seemed to lift, as though a great load had been taken from her shoulders.

"O' course!" she said, much brighter now and clearly relaxing. "We'll be happy as newborn lambs. Reet?"

"Reet," Tierney confirmed, with a hasty glance toward their leader to be sure their Scot's interpretation of "right" had not been overheard.

"I thought," Pearly, who had been listening, said doubtfully, "lambs was dreffully weak little fings. I thought wolves got after 'em."

"Not in Binkiebrae Scotland!"

"But in Canada maybe?"

8

Having quickly gotten their "sea legs," the Mountjoy girls, as they were called, thoroughly enjoyed the ocean trip, at least as much as was possible considering the distinctly inferior food, lack of water for personal cleanliness and the washing of clothes, crowded conditions, and too many hours in the gloom of the hold where they were billeted. Youth, and a natural ebullience, triggered their sense of adventure, perked their interest in this new experience, and lifted any depression caused by farewells.

It was a time of getting acquainted; after all, they would be together for weeks, probably months, as they crossed an ocean and most of a continent, eating and sleeping in close quarters, sharing their most intimate moments. Hardly a secret would be kept hidden by the time this was all over and everyone scattered to their assigned place. In a few cases friendships were made that would endure across the years and through many exigencies of life. In a few instances there was bitter feuding and antagonism, and enmities were made that also lasted a lifetime.

A sewing project occupied a good bit of time. To Norma, a settled, placid, mature young matron, was given the responsibility of entering Madam's cabin and using the sewing machine provided for the occasion. With a helper, Norma ran up the side seams of the skirts that had been cut and labeled at some previous headquarters in England. Those who had no such garment in their wardrobe would be hand-sewing the remainder of the seams and the hem. The costs involved would be paid from the emigrant's salary, added to the amount already due the British Women's Emigration Society, as arranged, and promised by the girls themselves as they made their "X," if nothing else, when they signed on.

Though Tierney already had a serge skirt, Anne did not; and neither, of course, did Pearly, who actually had so little that it was an embarrassment to her new friends, though Pearly herself was cheerful about it.

In fact, so cheerful was Pearly that others, of a more pessimistic nature, grumbled and complained about her; some went so far, in their gloom, to ask her to hush. Pearly was never squelched for more than a moment. One of her favorite testimonies was through the singing of a hymn; her choice usually spoke to the problem better than she could in her fractured English. Surprisingly, Pearly had a good voice, sweet and full at the same time.

When she understood that Tierney and Anne and others, with their own wardrobe obviously poor and insufficient, found hers to be pathetic, she burst into song. Naturally it was one she had learned at Chapel. To Pearly it took care of the situation, and there was no need for fretting.

Children of the Heav'nly Father
Safely in His bosom gather;
Nestling bird nor star in heaven
Such a refuge e'er was given.

God His own doth tend and nourish;
In His holy courts they flourish.
From all evil things He spares them;
In His mighty arms He bears them.

"I guess that's good enough for me," Pearly said, twinkling a little. Her eyes, wide and purple as pansies in her small, rather peaked face, smiled easily, and she radiated great good humor. "If the heavenly Favver cares for the little sparrer," she added, "He'll look after me, won't He?"

No one resembled a sparrow of the street more than bird-frail Pearly; if the thought gave her comfort, so be it, Tierney and Anne agreed.

"But you haff to wear more than fevvers," someone pointed out. "Did y' ever see a sparrer in a serge skirt?"

Pearly cocked her head, more like a sparrow than ever. "The King's daughter," she said brightly, "is all glorious within."

"Hmmmph," was the frustrated reply, while another doubter said, "Not the queen's consort; you're not his daughter. Everyone knows he's dead and been dead too long to be your father."

"Oh, not Albert," Pearly said with a trill of laughter. "I mean the one who 'dopted me. Abba Favver, see?"

"No, I don't see," the questioner said crossly. "Can't you speak plain English, you little cockney? Abba? Abba? Sounds like baby talk to me!"

"Maybe it is," Pearly responded spunkily. "Cos I fink it means daddy."

The questioners and doubters, now surrounded by several listening, sometimes amused girls, shook their heads and marched away, muttering.

Pearly was more grieved about the confrontation than she had let on and shared with Tierney her regret over how she had handled the conversation.

"I guess I should keep me mouf shut when I don't know any more about the Bible than I do," she said, sighing. "I want to tell uvvers how I feel inside, in my heart, but it's hard to put it in proper words. You know . . . it's better felt than tellt."

Teirney laughed at the odd phrase and put her arm around the drooping shoulders. She didn't understand, either, but wouldn't hurt her new friend and sister for anything.

"If ye feel ye jist have to say something," she advised, "jist toss it out there, like chicken feed, and let the chicks pick up what they can."

Pearly brightened at what seemed a splendid idea. But she did attempt to use more wisdom than she had formerly. If it dulled her bright testimony a little, still it shone like a light in a dark place to the unbelievers in the ship's lower deck.

"I am . . . the door, by me . . . if . . . any man . . . enter in . . . he shall be . . . saved."

Flushed and victorious, Pearly looked up at Tierney from her reading lesson, her finger in place so that she could continue in a moment or so.

Saved. There it was again—that strange word. Tierney looked into the charming little face at her side, aglow with some inner satisfaction. One almost had to believe, listening to her, watching her. But believe what? That Pearly was *saved?* It didn't make a lot of sense to Tierney.

"Why did you read that, Pearly?" she asked rather tensely. "I mean, why did you begin yer readin' there? If you can't read very weel . . . well . . . how come you chose that verse? Was it jist by chance?" Surely Pearly wouldn't choose a verse to purposely annoy her! Why did she keep harping on being saved!

"No," Pearly answered promptly. "It's one of me favorites. I have it marked, see? It's marked 'number two,' see?" And Pearly tipped the Bible so that Tierney could indeed see a childlike figure 2 scrawled there in the margin.

After several days with Pearly in almost constant attendance, Tierney was becoming accustomed to this strange girl's "testimony" and so continued cautiously.

"I see. So, if there's a 'two' there must be a 'one.' Reet?"

"Reet . . . right," Pearly said, correcting herself and Tierney too. "And it's prob'ly me favorite of all. Do you want me to read it?"

"Na, na," Tierney said, so hastily she forgot herself and her pronunciation. "That's all reet . . . right. Dinna worry aboot it."

Pearly's enthusiasm faded for the moment. But it would return; there was no denying the reality of her "Meffodist" experience. She had learned to say "Methodist," but the correction had not dimmed her testimony.

Pearly had such a bright mind and was such an imitator that her ways were changing more quickly, it seemed, than for any of them. She listened avidly to Ishbel Mountjoy, and her speech was clearing and refining wonderfully as she imitated that paragon of all things English. She watched Tierney and Anne and soon mimicked their small ways of thoughtfulness with each other, their kind concern for those around them, and once in a while a smidgen of their Scottish speech turned up in her speech. She read—to the best of her ability—her small Bible and incorporated its teachings into her life and ways as she could.

Pearly's attempts at reading were the result of her association with the Methodist Chapel. She had trouble, often, with the words and sometimes with their meaning. Tierney, therefore, sat by her side to help her. But when it came to the scriptural meaning, she found herself truly at sea. With actual waves tossing the ship and Pearly spelling out some worrisome Bible verse, Tierney's body was no more tossed than her heart.

The Bible seemed to be the only reading material available. With their belongings pared to a minimum, few girls had dared include a favorite book, considering it the extra baggage Mrs. Mountjoy had declared must be eliminated for the sake of space. "Be practical when it comes to packing," she had said. "Try and imagine a day's work in a kitchen or a hotel. Try and imagine yourself in a garden, or feeding turkeys and chickens, and bring what's appropriate."

Chickens, Anne knew, demanded a "practical" gown, and she and the others had been guided by Ishbel's suggestion; their garments were, hopefully, suitable for the life of a domestic in the wilderness of the area called the North West Territories, soon to become, legally, Alberta, Saskatchewan, Manitoba.

To newly "saved" Pearly, her most precious treasure was the Bible the Chapel had given her, with the wish inscribed in the flyleaf that she "grow in grace, and in the knowledge of our Lord and Saviour Jesus Christ." Pearly would as soon have stayed behind herself as leave her Bible.

At the urging of the Chapel friends when they told her goodbye, Pearly not only kept up her reading lessons but writing lessons as well. One of the girls eventually loaned her a slate, though heaven alone knew why or how she had brought it along. On this Pearly could practice to her heart's content, erase, and begin again.

Stopping by one day as Tierney and Pearly sat hunched over Bible and slate, Mrs. Mountjoy nodded her approval, both of the slate and the Bible.

"Study to show thyself approved," she had quoted, "a workman that needeth not to be ashamed," and, having disseminated her wisdom, moved on, like a ship under full sail.

"It all makes me feel like such a gowk, such a lack-wit," Tierney admitted to Anne after one session with Pearly. "I wish to heaven there was some other readin' material. I'm gettin' weary o' all this Scripture. How coom we never heard these verses afore . . . before?"

"I dinna know," Anne admitted. "But since it's her own wee finger pointin' them oot, and her own sweet voice readin' 'em, we canna help but admit they're in the Book, a' reet."

"All right," Tierney corrected automatically, and Anne dutifully repeated it.

The girls had agreed to help each other where their speech problems were concerned. Occasionally, when talking to Mrs. Mountjoy and using words such as *afeart* or *muckle* for *afraid* and *much,* they noted the briefly closed eyes, the pained expression as though the hearer were suffering, and recognized the need to change those particular words' pronunciation.

Yes, they were *all* learning, not only Pearly. As Pearly practiced her reading and Tierney supposedly tutored her, more learning was taking place than was intended; Tierney had just absorbed a verse from the Bible that—try as she would to forget it, work as she would to ignore it—would stay with her forever: "I am the door: by me if any man enter in, he shall be saved."

"The serge skirt, whether black or blue, is the mark of the Society's army of domestics," Mrs. Mountjoy was explaining one day as the girls gathered on deck in a sheltered spot to work on the skirts. When someone finished hers, she was assigned to help another girl, a laggard, perhaps, or one who had been indisposed and was badly behind on her assignment. With luck and industry, they would march off the ship clothed in their dark serge skirts and white waists. God grant that it didn't rain, with the impressive sight covered by cloaks and capes that were ill-matched and would never give the impression that the Society hoped for, and Mrs. Mountjoy in particular.

"You will always be decently dressed in a dark serge skirt and waist," she was exhorting—again—as she meandered through the seated group, pointing out a puckered seam here, frowning over careless stitches there, "and a good, white waist. Plain white for workdays, trimmed, with good taste, for social occasions. We cannot have you turning up on the prairies in colorful habiliments, in ill-fitting attire, in outlandish costumes. No, indeed! It's imperative to get the 'uniform' completed. It's important that we all epitomize the dignity of the Society."

Ishbel Mountjoy glanced oppressively at three rather garishly dressed females whose previous means of livelihood were under suspicion. So tight-knit were the three that Tierney and Anne had named them Winken, Blinken, and Nod. The names had taken hold, and as the three became better known, were shortened to Winky, Blinky, and Noddy. Winky and Blinky had taken the nicknames with good humor. Noddy, red of face and spluttering angrily, had demanded the use of her proper name, which was Lucretia.

"I'd rather be Noddy, if ye ask me," Anne had offered in an aside to Tierney. "How can ye shorten Lucretia? I'd hate to be called Cretia, for heaven's sake, and with the way these girls play around with names, it'll happen, you'll see. Lucky for us that there's no possible way to shorten Tierney and Anne."

This day Winky and Blinky were seated side by side, sewing diligently, each hemming a portion of a hem that had been turned up and pinned to the correct length. Lucretia, scowling over a knot in her thread, sat at their elbow, a part and yet apart, which seemed to be her usual place.

Turning from her cold glance at the three questionable "ladies," Ishbel continued with her advice. "All of you must be decent and dignified," she said firmly. "You probably have no idea how much your appearance affects people. An experienced eye can look at an individual and tell at a glance if she is quality or upstart, one of the respected class or the swinish multitude."

Mrs. Mountjoy was graphic in her description. Her listeners, some of them, heard with glazed eyes and slack mouth, startled by their options—swinish multitude!

"How you present yourself, as noble or ignoble, will decide how you are treated, whether as a person of some breeding or as a . . . a mushroom."

Again Mrs. Mountjoy's choice of words boggled the imagination of her hearers, having the result of diverting the attention of the very ones she wanted most to influence. While a few looked impressed, most of the girls had trouble hiding their grins.

Weary of the same old tirade, Anne—safely obscure in the back row—leaned toward Tierney and whispered, "Who does she think she's takin' to the backside of beyond—the Duchess of Binkiebrae? Ha! We're all jist a bunch o' hewers o' wood and drawers o' water—"

Anne, as well as Tierney, had been helping Pearly with her Scripture reading. Tierney almost choked, highly amused at gentle Anne's impatience and quotation, and went into a coughing spate that disrupted Ishbel's current discourse.

That lady looked sternly down the line, drew a deep breath, sighed, and wisely changed course.

"Now," she rapped out in commanding tones, "we'll engage in the morning's calisthenics. Fold up the sewing and lay it aside. Now—stand, please! Get in formation! Formation, if you please!"

Lagging interest sharpened; one thing could be said of Ishbel Mountjoy—she brought things alive; she was impossible to ignore. Like her or despise her, you paid attention.

Young bodies, having been cooped up far too long and having been bent in close attention to sewing for more than an hour, ached for activity, and the girls obeyed with alacrity. Lining up, a few feet began marching in place. The invigorating sea air blew severe hairdos into halos of wisps and curls, and a touch of color began to tinge cheeks pale from life too long below decks.

"All right, now!" Ishbel sang into the wind. "Straighten your shoulders! Lift your head—that's the way! Pull in your er . . . your *mid-section*! Fine, fine! Shoulders back! Chests *out!* Not *that far!*"

Ishbel, thoroughly dismayed at the enthusiasm of her charges, hastened to see to it that the exercises, as all else, were done chastely.

"Decently and in order!" she rapped out now. "Never forget: decently and in order."

Ishbel glared around the group now standing perfectly still and totally quiet, not daring to look at each other lest laughter erupt; the wanton display of their "chests" had been the subject of more than one lecture. "It's imperative," Ishbel warned them, "that you not taunt and tease; no lady would be found lowering herself thus. Remember, while many of these men you'll be meeting are bachelors legitimately looking for a wife, some of them are married men, long separated from their families. A Society Girl is supplied to *help* conditions on the frontier, not provoke them."

Hilarity at the time of lectures had incurred the dreadful wrath of Ishbel Mountjoy more than once—life was serious! their undertaking was of great consequence!—an experience the girls wisely wanted to avoid repeating at all costs, and the remainder of the time went smoothly.

At last, the moderate and restrained (after all, sailors were watching) calisthenics were called to a halt, due more to the exhaustion of Ishbel Mountjoy than her charges, and the girls were dismissed. Like naughty schoolgirls they trooped below deck, whispering and giggling, invigorated by the sunshine, the exercise, and the entertainment unwittingly provided by their leader.

"Prepare yourself," a flushed, worn and weary Ishbel, her nerves sadly frazzled, couldn't refrain from shouting down the ladder after them, "for ten hours a day in a sweltering kitchen, or an icy one!"

Obviously feeling much better about things now, the intrepid leader mopped her face, picked up her instruction manual, and sought her cabin and a return to peace of mind. Her final thought was not a cheerful one. In spite of all she would do to prepare them, some of them were meant as lambs for the slaughter; it was inevitable.

Dear Robbie . . .

Tierney settled herself at a rather rickety table, having first shoved aside numerous items stacked there—the room was small for the number of occupants it housed—spread the small book of blank pages open before her, licked her pencil, and began.

Here I am in St. John's, Newfoundland, Canada. I wonder if you landed here too. If so, your heart thrilled, as did mine, as you entered the harbor—completely land-locked, it is, being entered by a short passage known as the Narrows. What a sight! Did you, too, feel like a dwarf before those high beetling cliffs? Many are the ships berthed here—from New York, Australia, Liverpool. And of course Glasgow—home, sweet home—will we ever see it again?

Wherever you are, Robbie, I know you are thinking of me, as I think of you. What hopeless thoughts they are! Knowing I may not . . . probably won't . . . ever see you again, still I long to pour out my heart to you. Knowing you probably will never see this journal, I'm writing it anyway. It helps me just to "talk" to you in this way. Though I sent a letter to James, it isn't the same. He can write me in care of the Society in Toronto, for we shall be there for a while as our assignments are being made, and you could too, if only you knew it. But you don't even know about this contract I've signed, and the change my life has made. No doubt you think of me back in Binkiebrae, perhaps on my hilltop, while here I am, in Canada. What a miracle.

So ignorant of where the other one is—it's so sad, Robbie—but there, I promised myself that this shall be a pleasant journal (or long, long letter), with no need to tell of any dark and desperate days. Or talk about dreary things. I trust I may be able to keep that vow.

Perhaps you stayed here in St. John's and went to work; there is plenty of activity going on. Perhaps you are just a stone's throw from me even as I sit here in this hostel. As we girls walk about the streets, do a little shopping, and a lot of looking, I find myself watching for you everywhere I go. Many places, you could have found employment. There are pulp and paper mills here, several factories, and fish, fish, fish, everywhere. Cod and whale oil are manufactured; codfish is dried—there are great cod-fishing grounds here. You can believe me when I say, and perhaps you already know, that certain parts of the town don't smell good! You could have worked in the fish at home, Robbie, but I remember you dinna . . . I mean did not, want to.

And oh yes, sad as it makes me, skins of the hair seal are sold here in great numbers, to be made into leather and fur abroad.

All this and more I have learned as I've walked around town, asked questions, listened, and read the local paper.

So happy are we to have our feet on dry ground again that some of the girls have expressed the secret wish just to stay here. It is so fresh and new and bustling, surely there would be work here for us. Some are weary of traveling and dread the trek across the continent. What a huge land it is! We are barely on the edge of it.

But we cannot stay here, much as we might like to do so. We are pledged to the Society, and we must keep our word. After all, they paid our way over here and have a lot of money invested in us.

If we didn't want to work, we could marry! Yes, already the lack of marriageable women is obvious. Some men have come here—from far away, perhaps the Territories—because they hear ships are bringing single women. Why can't they understand that we came not on a bride ship but as workers, domestics? I, for one, am fiercely determined to make my own way. Me—marry? Oh, my Robbie, how could anyone else appeal to me? Am I not, in my heart, pledged to you? But I hasten on.

Anne, in particular, draws the stares of hungry-hearted men like moths to a lamp. Lucian MacDermott isn't the only one to press after her. But her experience in Binkiebrae has made her fearful of any and all attention; she flees from it, has no patience with it.

Let me tell you about some good that came out of the voyage, Robbie. I studied and read almost continually, there not being much else to do. One of the women, a governess back home, said she'd help with my studies. Oh, how I benefited—see, I know how to use and to spell that word. Binkiebrae school gave me, as you, a good education insofar as it went, but I want to know more. I shall keep on reading, writing, and spelling, for I find I love it. Perhaps I shall settle where there is a lending library; how I would like that! Of course Mrs. Mountjoy keeps after us all the time about our grammar, and the way we speak in general, and it actually helps, keeping me, at least, aware of my speech. Maybe, Robbie, doing so well myself, I'll be able to hire on with some family as a teacher of small children. Trouble is, both Mrs. Mountjoy and the governess say it's my pronunciation that is so bad that at times I'm hard to understand. I canna seem to shake all my accent, probably never shall. I'll say "dinna" and "canna" all my life, I expect. Ah, well, there could be worse habits.

Back to the account of our landing. There was much milling and stewing around the dock when we reached it, some girls taking a seat on their baggage, others with nothing on their mind but ogling the surroundings, seeing how they are a great deal different than the "old country." There was some righting of hats that had been tipped by the crush and straightening of skirts that had suffered this first day's test. Even the weather cooperates with Mrs. Mountjoy, not daring to disobey, and each girl had put on her serge skirt and white blouse, with her cloak flung over her arm lest the clouds spill their contents before we could get under cover and we all got off together, as planned. Anne and I stayed close to each other, careful not to be separated. . . .

"We look like penguins," Anne whispered to Tierney, aware of the stares of the great host of people either leaving the ship or gathered on the dock. For truly the sight of so many women dressed alike did arouse considerable curiosity.

But it was a sight that was recognized for what it was, by certain people. Male people.

As the girls stood, en masse, on the dock, and Ishbel distractedly saw to the conveyances that would transport them to the waiting hostels, one could see—like bees hovering around a bouquet of flowers—a circle of masculine beings. To a man their eyes were fixed on the girls, looking them over much as they might examine a herd of dairy cows about to go on the auction block.

"Look at those men," someone said in a low voice, and all eyes turned to the circle of males. Some, perhaps, were there because of curiosity; others, it seemed, were there to do serious business.

"What are they lookin' at?" someone asked uncomfortably.

"Us, silly. We are goods on display, dressed in these 'costumes' of ours."

"Us? Whatever for?" was the innocent question.

"Because," an impatient voice murmured, "we're single, and they know it."

"Oh my goodness! You mean these are bachelors?"

"Probably. I know the world is in terrible condition, sinful and all that, but I hope married men have better sense than to hang around a dock lookin' over a bunch of females!"

Most of the girls drew together into a close-knit group, casting glances over their shoulders, unsure whether to seem pleased or angry or unconcerned. Anne and Tierney stayed close together, one with her back turned to the circling men, the other peeping over her shoulder and giving a report of what was happening. Pearly hovered nearby.

"You'll never believe this," Anne said, looking beyond Tierney's shoulder. "Or maybe you weel."

"What? Tell me!"

"Winky, Blinky, and Lucretia are sorta steppin' awa' from the rest o' us and are talkin' amongst themselves as if no one else was around. Wait a minute! One man is makin' a move in their direction!"

"What else! What else!"

"He's taken off his cap and is holdin' it in front of him. He's a sma' man, with a big moustache . . . has on a suit—sort of a dandy type, I'd say."

"And?"

"And they're talkin'. That is, he's talkin' with Lucretia. Winky and Blinky are walkin' up the dock a bit, turnin', comin' back—"

Tierney and Anne weren't the only ones watching the little scene unfold. Mrs. Mountjoy, hurrying back from her distant responsibilities, saw the interchange between an unknown man and one of her charges.

"Oh, oh! Mrs. Mountjoy is stoppin' dead in her tracks; she's spinnin' around . . . she's stompin' her way over there."

Tierney could stand no more. Turning, she too watched what was happening.

Ishbel, flushed and determined, had Lucretia by the arm. Interjecting herself between the two, she spoke to the man. He seemed to blink in the face of her comments, then spoke briefly, and all could see it was mildly, but with a certain defensiveness. Ishbel seemed to be giving him a piece of her mind, speaking scathingly, then turned accusing eyes on Lucretia, giving her arm a shake, and turning the two of them back toward the group. Marching firmly, Ishbel hurried the reluctant Lucretia along. Turning her head toward Winky and Blinky, Ishbel called, and all the girls heard: "Miss Beamer! Miss Daggs!"

"So those're their names," someone murmured, as Winky and Blinky moved languidly in the direction of the Society group.

"You have my offer," the lone man called, lifting his voice above the commotion and confusion around him. Ishbel ignored him and marched on. As they joined the group, the girls could see that Lucretia was in no way cowed; rather, she was flushed angrily. Yanking her arm from Mrs. Mountjoy's grasp she turned deliberately, looked back, and twiddled her gloved fingers in the direction of the man who had caused all the ruckus. Then, as though nothing had happened, she joined Winky and Blinky.

"What was that all about, do y' suppose?" Tierney wondered aloud.

"Robbie, it was as we feared—that man was after a wife. Or that's what Mrs. Mountjoy told us. Winky—Miss Beamer—said he had come all the way from somewhere up north, figured he'd get in his request before the girls was all 'doled out.' What a thing to say! It makes me feel cheap. Have we come this far just to be deceived? Will our opportunities be real ones?

"It truly would seem so, for Mrs. Mountjoy was very angry and told the lot of us to keep to the letter of our agreement. 'You are not,' she said, 'to be thrown out like hunks of meat to a ravening pack of wolves! Now behave yourselves, and everything will work out well for you.' I find myself quite believing her, Robbie. Hunks of meat, indeed!"

The ranks of the Society girls were depleted by one, come morning. Putting her pillow under the covers and plumping it up, Lucretia had taken her bag, slipped out a window of the hostel, and taken her silent departure. If Winky and Blinky knew about it beforehand, they weren't saying.

Mrs. Mountjoy was white-hot with anger. "What a way to repay the Society," she gritted to the girls as they gathered for a morning session. "You may be sure we will find her. No matter where she is, we'll find her. Not that we want her back," she said darkly, breathing hard, "no, not at all. But we *will* have our money. She is legally obligated to pay that debt. If any of the rest of you think you would be better off making your own plans, slipping off and finding a job or a husband on your own, I'd think again if I were you. That man

may have been looking for a wife, and then again, maybe not."
Winky and Blinky looked a little uneasy at the very idea.

"Girls, listen again to what you promised and signed, of your own free will—"

And Mrs. Mountjoy read the contract aloud.

"Now," she said, folding the paper and putting it away, "plans are all made for the train trip. Get your gear together, ladies. In a few days we will be in Toronto, where you will be given assignments from the head office, and from there the division will be made—some to go here, some there. But all of you, *all* of you, to the Territories. Now, step lively—"

Alberta, Saskatchewan, Manitoba—which would it be?

They had been in Toronto less than a week and already most of the girls had been placed and were gone.

"It isn't that places aren't available," Ishbel Mountjoy explained to the remaining women, of whom Pearly, Anne, and Tierney were three. "It's the length of time it takes settling each girl to her satisfaction. With your cooperation, things should hurry along."

Ishbel sighed; apparently the end of the trip was no more smooth than the rest of it had been.

The trip from the east coast of Newfoundland to Toronto had been a novel experience for the girls, most of whom had never been on a train before. But the novelty wore off quickly. Resting poorly, washing scantily, eating haphazardly, eventually brought frayed nerves, just beginning to recover from the torturous sea voyage, to the breaking point. At the slightest provocation, it seemed, hot words were exchanged, tears flowed, and fisticuffs, in one instance, were barely averted, before the entourage arrived at its Ontario destination.

In spite of all that, Ishbel reported to her superiors that the trip, in the main, had been the best, the most successful, of any she had yet undertaken. And she agreed, with only a brief hesitation, to do it all over again just as soon as the final girl was situated, and she felt free to leave. To be a female left in a strange city, among people she didn't know and who yet had the authority to send her whithersoever they pleased, would be a frightening experience; Ishbel understood this. Ishbel Mountjoy, for all that she may have seemed like a martinet, truly cared about the future of the young women she had wooed away from their homeland; she would not desert them now.

Yes, Ishbel would return to the British Isles and would do her best once again to "liberate" helpless and hopeless females. She knew that Europe and Britain offered little economic security, education, or social position to the single woman. Shame! No wonder it wasn't terribly difficult to persuade girls to choose immigration to Canada over unemployment and poverty, even social ostracism in their homelands. Poor darlings! Ishbel counted the hardships she went through as learning experiences that would help her do a better job next time around.

So Ishbel lingered in Toronto, prodding, advising, encouraging, until each girl was settled, and, hopefully, settled to her satisfaction. Every once in a while there was a hitch, and someone became picky, balky, sorely trying the patience of Ishbel Mountjoy and the estimable Miss Dobrie, who did the prodding and advising, but little encouraging. Still, she got the job done when it came to placing the girls.

Though they were nearly last, Tierney and Pearly would be no trouble to place; they had dragged their feet over signing on for one reason only: Anne.

Anne's experience with Lucian MacDermott, wrongly or rightly, had left its mark upon her. Every home situation that was presented to her was studied minutely, and if the possibility of trouble was so much as hinted at, Anne refused the job. In this way she had turned down an opening for a "mother's helper," because there were two young men in the family. She had dropped like a hot potato a request for a domestic to keep house for a widower and his three children, because the only woman in the house was his aging and bedridden mother. As frissons of doom played up and down her spine, Anne shivered and handed back the application form and stumbled, trembling, from Miss Dobrie's presence.

Finally the three girls could hold out no longer. Miss Dobrie, feeling greatly responsible, and frustrated over this particular situation, was looking with more and more coldness on what she called their "fussiness."

Pearly was called, once more, into the small room that was an "office" and heard an offer that she could not immediately fault, outlined to her with supreme patience by Miss Dobrie, considering Pearly's previous shilly-shallying.

"It's past time, Miss Chapel, to make your choice. Now," Miss Dobrie offered almost wheedlingly, "this one seems ideal, does it not?"

Still Pearly hesitated, wishing, secretly, that Anne's case might have been settled first.

Slowly she spelled out the terms of the agreement: "Dairy farm near Sask-a-toon . . ."

Miss Dobrie, a buxom female with a highly colored face, tightly corseted and creaking at every movement, retrieved the paper from Pearly and read speedily and rather sharply, her patience at an end: "Dairy farm near Saskatoon. Companion needed for housewife. Mainly housework, some outside chores.

"They have agreed, of course, to the Society's stipulation regarding pay, as has been outlined for you already by Mrs. Mountjoy. They also stipulate that you shall have every Sunday evening off after six P.M. If you work overtime, you shall receive the fair sum of fifteen cents an hour.

"Well, Miss Chapel, what do you say? Eh?"

"Where is this place?" Pearly asked, her pansy-purple eyes innocent as she stalled for more time.

"On the prairies, of course, where most of the girls have gone or will go. About thirty miles from the hamlet of Red Fife—

named for their wheat, no doubt—and about seventy miles from Regina. Does that mean anything to you?"

"No, not really. What I mean is, is it in Manitoba—"

"Saskatchewan. That's where Regina is—originally called Pile of Bones—Saskatchewan."

"Pile of Bones," Pearly repeated, fascinated in spite of herself.

"No matter; you probably won't see Regina once you pass through on your way to Red Fife. Someone, probably Mr. Belknap himself, will meet you. This is," Miss Dobrie inspected the paper in her hands more closely, "an English family. You should feel right at home with them, I expect. Any more questions, Miss Chapel?"

Pearly's mind seemed to be a blank. The great moment was upon her; the reason she had left London. Now, this minute, her future hung in the balance, for happiness or despair. All it required was her signature. Suddenly Pearly was very glad she had prayed about it; from the beginning she had prayed about it. Anne or no Anne, she would delay no longer; it had a right "feel" to it.

Drawing a deep breath, Pearly took the paper dangling before her, noted the line marked with an X that Miss Dobrie told her should have her signature, licked the pencil handed to her, and painstakingly wrote her name, ending with a flourish. Yes, this was the right place.

"You will take the train to Regina," Miss Dobrie said, "and ride with the mail from there on out to Red Fife.

"Now I suggest you work on your wardrobe if any of it needs laundering or mending. You will be apprised of the departure date and time. Next!" Miss Dobrie, triumphant once again, yodeled the command.

Dismissed, Pearly made her way to where Tierney and Anne awaited, curious, a bit anxious. Pearly told them all she knew about her assignment, which was only what Miss Dobrie had said.

"A' reet," Tierney said firmly, turning to Anne. "One of us is settled. Now we know what to look for, what to hold out for. Whichever one of us is next must insist on Saskatchewan."

The girls had already determined to stay as close together as possible, so that, perhaps, in case of some emergency—God forbid!—they could be available to each other. At least they would not feel totally deserted and alone knowing someone else was not too unreasonably far away—like at the tundra, the gold fields, the north woods!

Hearing of the plan, Ishbel Mountjoy had said, "Don't be silly, girls. It'll be well nigh impossible to be anywhere near each other; this is vast territory, and you have waited too long to have a choice. You'll have to take what's left. Tundra indeed! Where do you think you are—the Yukon?"

Ontario may have seemed like civilization compared to the Yukon, but the girls weren't convinced. Even in the "settled" east, their hearts had turned cold at their glimpses of the domiciles of those settlers as seen from the train windows—small dwelling places, slapped together with whatever material the land allowed, *lonely.* All of the domestics had grown strangely silent as they went, ever deeper and wilder, into more isolated areas. The train had hooted its brave way across plains, through dense woods, past land-locked lakes and sloughs, always with homes scattered, separated from each other by many miles. If a house were within hailing distance of the train track, householders would sometimes step outside to wave. As the train pulled away, the settlers looked indescribably desolate, growing smaller and smaller until, like a splinter tossed on an ocean, they disappeared.

And all this before ever the travelers reached the prairies that were famous—or infamous—for their vastness and loneliness!

Seating herself, eventually, before the battered table and Miss Dobrie, an equally battered employee of the British Women's Emigration Society, Anne braced herself, determined to hold out if it took her last breath: She would not, *would not,* submit to signing on for a place where there was any possibility of male dominance or abuse.

After once again explaining her mindset where men were concerned, Anne added, politely but firmly, "Then too, Miss Dobrie, it has to be in the territory of Saskatchewan."

"My dear Miss Fraser," Miss Dobrie said frostily, weary from a day's haggling and dealing, "what gives you the option of choosing where you'll go? You've dallied too long as it is. We are doing our best, so no, my dear, you'll have no favors. Saskatchewan? Why is it any more special than Alberta or Manitoba?"

Because Pearly will be there, Anne came near to explaining; instead, she looked mutinous, said nothing, and set her chin stubbornly.

"All right, let's see what we have here," Miss Dobrie said, picking up a sheet of paper. "Well now, harumph . . . if this isn't something. It so happens," Miss Dobrie looked almost disappointed, "that the place Mrs. Mountjoy personally selected today to bring to your attention, is in . . . I find it hard to believe . . ."

"Yes?" Anne's lovely face took on a most becoming pink tinge, and Miss Dobrie had an instant understanding of the problem Anne might face where unscrupulous men were concerned.

"Yes?" Anne prompted, her lips parted, her eyes dewy, her expression eager.

"Saskatchewan." The word was dragged reluctantly from Miss Dobrie.

"Good!" Anne almost chortled in her satisfaction. "Now tell me aboot the people—who they are and a' that."

"Mr. and Mrs. Schmidt," Miss Dobrie read, and Anne stiffened.

Maybe she expected too much. How she could presume to think there would be a setup with women only, in the wilderness of the territories, took more faith than Anne could honestly muster. And yet she had hoped. *Mr.* Schmidt.

"Franz Schmidt, age sixty-eight; Augusta Schmidt, sixty-three. This is a small farm, as farms go on the prairie. I suspect it's not true prairie at all but near the bush line, perhaps partly in it. The nearest hamlet is named Hanover—sounds German to me, perhaps a settling of Germans. Should be a community of good thrifty people."

"Why do they need a domestic?" Anne asked, curious about this couple in spite of her caution.

Miss Dobrie read, "'Augusta Schmidt laid up with rheumatiz,' is what someone has written here. 'Help needed for farm chores, as well as usual household tasks.' Well, there you have it, Miss Fraser. Now what can you find wrong with this one?"

Anne thought about it. A man. But an old man—safe as a butterfly, hopefully. Anne suddenly had a great feeling of relief. How wise it had been to have Pearly pray!

"I'll take it," she decided. "How about wages, time off, and so on?"

Miss Dobrie went over the details; everything was in line with the rules and regulations of the Society. "Now then," she said, hurrying on before the temperamental Miss Fraser could change her mind, "sign right here."

"Saskatchewan!" Anne reported blithely to Tierney and Pearly. "And Pearly, please thank God for me. It's verra good o' Him to gi' me jist the kind of place I need. *And* in Saskatchewan!"

"Call unto me, and I will answer thee," Pearly quoted wisely. "But you can thank Him fer yourself. Y' know that, don't cher?"

"Oh my, no, I couldn't," Anne, accustomed to a ritual of prayer rather than spontaneous conversation with the Almighty, insisted. "I wouldn't know how to go aboot it. Besides, I don't know Him that weel. And anyway, ye're the one who asked 'im."

"Well, I'll thank 'im, but you gotta learn to do yer own askin' and thankin'. No tellin' when ye'll need Him. I won't always be with yer, y' know. You jist have to—"

"I know, I know," Anne said quickly. "You've told us many's the time. When I'm gone awa' from ye, and ye're no' there to pray fer me, then maybe—"

Pearly shook her head. "I'll be gone, gone to Red Fife, and ye'll be in this Hanover place. But God'll always be nearby."

"Now, Tierney," Anne continued, happy to leave the subject of her need of prayer, "ye'll be next. Jist see to it that ye stay in Saskatchewan. Did ye ask Pearly t' pray?"

"Miss Caulder!" came the ringing command.

"Now, Miss Caulder," Miss Dobrie began, after Tierney had seated herself. "I trust you won't expect to be placed in a specific part of the Territories. We're getting down to the end of the list, you know. You are bound, by your signature, to take one of these."

And a large white hand indicated a few sheets of paper spread before her.

"I know," Tierney said, interested now that Anne and Pearly had been settled. "Tell me what you have for me, Miss Dobrie."

"Let's see now. We'll just take this first one here. Name of Ketchum. Chicken farm, it says. Thousands of chickens. A crew of men to cook and wash for. It all seems straightforward enough, strictly housework, laundry, meals, that sort of thing. Pay and time off all in line with our policy. Oh yes, one small boy."

"There's a Mrs. Ketchum?" Tierney asked.

"Of course. Would we consider it, otherwise?" Miss Dobrie was offended, sniffed, and brought herself to continue. "Lavinia Ketchum. No problems there, as far as I can see. Now, Miss Caulder, it's down to the wire. What do you say—will you sign?"

Tierney signed, as anxious to get about the task as Miss Dobrie was to send her to it.

"Thank ye, Miss Dobrie," Tierney said politely, turning to go. At the doorway, she turned back. "Ah, where is this Ketchum place?"

"What do you know," Miss Dobrie said wonderingly, all unaware of Pearly Chapel's prayers, "Saskatchewan."

11

Not yet fully understanding the extent to which they had been cast on their own resourcefulness, not knowing how truly alone and self-dependent they were to be, still Tierney, Anne, and Pearly felt the first riffles of uncertainty concerning their future, and because of it, clung together as long as was possible. The train ride was the last leg of their journey.

Their destination was not Regina, after all, but a place called Saskatoon; it sounded almost Scottish—Saskatoonie! From here, their paths would diverge—to a chicken farm nearby, to Red Fife and a dairy farm, and to Hanover and a German couple on yet another farm.

It was all thanks to Pearly's prayers that their postings were not far distant from each other. And it was amazing, to say the least, when one took into consideration the size of the territories and the distances hungry landseekers would go in order to obtain a place of their own. Like tiny ants separating and scurrying across a huge park in all directions, so the emigrants parted ways somewhere along the way—often at Winnipeg—to trek to the remotest places, each following that glimmering lodestar—property!

Free land! Would the world ever see the like again? The offer was a magnet that drew men and women sick of poverty, yearning for freedom, and actually fleeing from all parts of the old world with its custom of landed aristocracy worked by tenants.

Any man who was the head of a family or who had reached the age of twenty-one could apply for the coveted 160 acres—the filing fee was ten dollars—obtaining full title at the end of three years if he had cultivated part of the land and done some building. He filed on the free, quarter-section acreage, built his houses and barns, and cultivated according to the terms of the Dominion Land Act, and counted himself blessed. Never mind that first buildings, more times than not, were built from the turves—that upper stratum of soil bound by grass and plant roots into a thick mat—of his own land. Though unspeakably crude, these soddies, as they were called, offered immediate shelter to man and beast and, of great importance, qualified as buildings and satisfied the land office's requirement.

Cattle did well on the nutritious prairie grass, as did sheep, the difficulty being to keep them and not lose them into the grass that swallowed them up, should they stray. As yet there were few if any barbed wire fences around property; there were more important things demanding immediate attention, such as getting ready for a prairie winter, and there were many other things of more importance on which to spend one's small hoard of money. Still, cattle flourished, tethered securely, or guarded by a child of the family. And when it was discovered that the quick-maturing wheat, Marquis and Red Fife, could be grown with wonderful results on the grasslands, the area that came to be known as the Prairie Provinces was on its way to becoming the bread basket of the world.

It was this land, this stretching land, that unrolled endlessly before the emigrants as they entered it, went through it. The panorama was staggering in its scope and beyond expressing. Those who invaded it, to subdue it, seemed far too puny to make any impression on it.

Awed into silence by the magnificence and simplicity of the land, the girls could only shake their heads over the huddle of soddies—house and barn and chicken house—that were the only sign of man, the mighty conqueror, in the boundless, pathless sea of grass that stretched from horizon to horizon. One man was to write home: "I lined up my stakes to my quarter-section, hitched up my oxen, sunk the blade in that virgin ground, and got going. I went most of a half mile without a break, then stopped and looked back. There was my furrow, the first furrow ever, stretching away behind me for half a mile, straight as a gun barrel."

"Oh, I do hope," Anne said tightly, staring out at the loneliness and solitude, "I don't have to live in sich as that," and she pointed to a particularly sagging soddy, beside which a cow was tethered, its voracious appetite making no dent whatsoever in the bounty of fodder flourishing all around it.

"It could eat forever," Anne continued, watching sourly as the munching cow faded from sight, "until it blew up and exploded, and you'd niver see that it had made even so much as a dent in all that grass."

"I hardly think we'll live in sich as that," Tierney reassured her friend concerning life in a soddy. "Surely sich people couldn't afford—or need—domestic help. Now see, away over there on the skyline, a square lookin' blot on the landscape? That's a hoose."

Lonely it stood, with never a tree or a bush to soften its bold invasion of the land's simplicity—grass, grass, and more grass. But its outline alone cheered the quaking hearts of the newcomers. Perhaps, in this infinity of grass, a small spot of normalcy would be found for them.

"I dinna ken," Anne continued uneasily, "whither I can adjust to sich as all this."

And indeed it was a far cry from the sea and hills and cozy crofts of home. In that place, small in comparison, land was hard to come by, and most of it was well populated, at least where the girls had lived. Such loneliness as this! Could they exist in it?

"Weel, whatever it is, and wherever, I'm ready to get there," Tierney declared, dabbing futilely with her grimy handkerchief at yet another soot spot on her waist, a waist that had been pristinely white when they had boarded the train three days before. So much for arriving like "queens of the kitchen."

"Though how I shall abide bein' buried up to me chin in this wilderness o' grass is beyond me," she finished grimly. Tierney, for one, had come, seen, and now rather passionately rejected the prairie.

Perhaps Pearly came closest to saying something pertinent. With her small vivid face soot smudged, pressed against the window, she murmured, "If then God so clothe the grass, which is today in the field, and tomorrow is cast into the oven; how much more will he clothe you, O ye of little faith?"

Rebellious at heart now that the great mystery of the west was being unravelled before her very eyes, still Tierney was respectful of God's Word and said nothing. But her tightened lips, to anyone watching, spoke for her.

At one stop, a hamlet no more than a clearing in the prairie's grass, with a few outbuildings and a small building serving as store, station, and post office for those fortunate enough to live within driving distance, the girls took the opportunity to leave the uncomfortable, sooty, *smelly* car, as they had numerous times before, to walk beside the train, stretch their cramped limbs, and enter, curiously, the town's main building.

"Doctor?" the proprietor was repeating to one of the travelers with a small child in her arms. "No, ma'am. There's no doctor here. Not much else, neither. But it's comin'. It's comin'! Folks are puttin' in the plow almost as soon as they step foot on their homestead and gettin' a crop the very first year. Ain't that sumpin? Course it's probably potatoes first thing, but it gives them sumpin to eat and even sumpin to sell. That's why the railroad is so great, and it's also why all the first settlers get as near the line as they can. Yes sir . . . ma'am that is . . . we expect that in a year or so you'll see this place flourishin' like the . . . the cedars of Lebanon! Wouldn't that be sumpin? Not a tree in sight now! P'raps I mean like the rose o' Sharon. We do have roses—wildroses—them little sturdy bushes bloom like crazy at a certain time of the year. Anyway, p'raps then we'll have a doctor. Till then we are all mighty careful not to have any kind of accident. And, o'course," he said with a wink, "we pray a lot."

Even as he spoke, certain pieces of farm equipment were being unloaded from a boxcar and, with much effort, loaded onto a couple of wagons that had been drawn up close.

"That feller," the loquacious storekeeper continued, nodding in the direction of the activity further along the line, "takin' delivery of a plow, is still livin' in a tent. For him, farmin' comes first. Could be because our growin' season is short and he wants to make hay while the sun shines. Ha! But, as you see, he's gettin' delivery of that precious Prairie Queen plow, prob'ly ordered it before he ever came, and here it is. That's the train for you. P'raps the first sod he turns over will go into makin' a soddy for his family. That's his wife a'settin' there in the wagon. No doubt she," the man chuckled agreeably, "wanted to get out of the tent and come to town."

Another woman approached the travelers and silently held out a tray of something that resembled small tea cakes. Her square face spoke of European beginnings, or perhaps it was the babushka wrapped around her head and tied under her chin. She smiled openly and said something that could be taken for "You buy." A small sign, which someone had printed for her, read "3 for 10 cents."

Face-to-face with the prairie entrepreneur, Pearly dug around in the knitted bag hanging over her arm, came up with three cents, and looked helplessly at Tierney and Anne. They hastily went in search of a few coins, and the smile on the broad face of the woman was as rewarding as the few bites of sweet concoction she placed in their hands.

"You . . . live . . . here?" Pearly asked loudly, as though the poor woman were deaf. Whether or not she understood the words, the homesteader caught the meaning, for she turned and swept her hand over the panorama of sky, land, and the grass that moved

silently and continually as though in response to some heavenly orchestration.

"Mine," she said. "Mine blace, mine hoosban," and she pointed to a man helping with the loading of the plow. The pride of ownership was in her eyes. Tierney turned away with her own eyes misting. Such dedication, such determination, such satisfaction. Was it possible to know it?

The difference, she said to herself, *is that she's doing it for herself and her man. My problem, our problem, is that we have no stake in this place nor in any place. We're rootless.*

Surrounded by the rooting and grounding of grass as countless as the sands of the sea, still the girls were without roots themselves.

It's like home all over again, Tierney thought despairingly. *We're no better off than in Binkiebrae.*

And yet—here they were. To go back was impossible; there was one way only, and that was ahead, embracing the future, whatever it was. She wished, now that she was here, that she could be as certain as Pearly was.

Tierney studied the prairie, letting her sight go as far as vision would take it. Was it possible that Robbie Dunbar was out there someplace? He could be ten feet beyond the town's boundary and, if stooping or sitting, would be as lost to her as when he was on one side of the ocean, she the other. Could she, even for Robbie, settle for the prairie? She remembered her passionate avowal of faithfulness, that she would go with Robbie Dunbar at a moment's notice "to Timbuktu."

But surely Timbuktu, wherever it was, was not so starkly treeless! Letting her eyes sweep in a circle, Tierney found not so much as a sapling struggling for life. It was as though the grass had laid claim to the land. Man, that indefatigable, stubborn creature, would find himself challenged, almost to the breaking point, to reclaim what the grass had held forever and would give up stubbornly. And for some, it would mean the breaking point.

In spite of that, still they came—the emigrants. Even now the hopeful, the dreamers, were climbing back aboard the train that would take them rushing across the virgin ground—wherein plow had never sunk, seed never planted, animals never domesticated—eager to meet the challenge of the land.

"Think of it," Pearly said as they made their way back to the train, catching up the last few crumbs of the homemade goodie, "we'll be makin' this our home, too. We can, and prob'ly will, marry an' settle down here, on our own property, and then we'll b'long. I mean b'long like we never b'longed back home." Pearly giggled. "We'll prob'ly raise the next generation of Canadians, and they'll truly b'long. Ever think o' that, girls?"

Yep, this's Saskatoon."

It was the conductor confirming their suspicions. Surely nothing this raw and rambunctious would be called Prince Albert or Regina—the other two burgeoning "cities" up this way, so named in honor of their dear respected queen and her consort.

Saskatoon, for sure and certain, was a frontier town. Among many fascinating sights, the tent city was perhaps the most striking. At one place the streets were lined with tents; like mushrooms they had sprung up as the settlers poured in. Arriving emigrants had left the discomfort of the train for the crudeness of a tent, seeking temporary shelter before scattering out across the prairie to their homesteads.

"It's the end of the trip for you," one man, a traveling companion of the girls, said, "and for me too, though the train goes on to Prince Albert—the true jumping off place. I'll be jumping off here, myself."

"An' will y' be settin' up a tent, then?" Pearly asked.

"Not settin' up a tent," the cheerful emigrant said. "Rentin' one. And I'll not hesitate to do so, neither. Them tents is more or less permanent here, I been told. They got wood floors and, as you see, the walls, for a coupla feet up, are made of boards. Only the top part is canvas. Somebody with foresight built those things, rents them, and is probably pullin' in a fortune, far more than the rest of us'll make grubbin' for a livin' in the land. Yep, they may look ramshackle, but they sure fill the bill for those of us tired to death of this train contraption. They shoulda called it 'strain'!" And the speaker—whiskery with several days' growth and ripe from infrequent contact with bathtub facilities—roared at his own humor.

"It looks like a forest of stovepipes," Anne commented, studying the tents as the train rolled slowly past.

"I'll get one of 'em for my family," the man continued. "The plan is to leave the wife and kids here, in comparative comfort, until I get my homestead located—I understand it's about thirty miles out there," and he waved a hand in the general direction of the west. "Thirty miles is a long and hard day's journey with a horse and wagon loaded with everything to build a house—"

"Homestead shack, they call them," a listening man chimed in.

"Then, when the *shack* is ready," the first speaker continued, after fixing the interrupter with a frosty eye, "I'll come back and get the family."

"And all the rest of the things you'll need," the second speaker said dryly.

Everyone within hearing distance turned and looked at him dubiously. Leaning back comfortably, he hooked his thumbs in his vest and drew deeply on a great cigar that added odorously to the closeness of the car, bringing several women's hankies delicately to their noses.

"I'm a real estate agent myself," he said, "and doing big business, I can tell you. This is a country on the move. Land is so simple to get, if people don't like their neighbor once they get settled, or see land they like better, they up, sell, and move. Yes, we're a nation on the move. Even the dear Lord must have trouble keeping track of all of us. But it's good business for us real estate agents, I can tell you. You really can't," he said shrewdly, fixing his eyes on several men listening intently, "make a go of it on 160 acres, you know; you'll want more. So, people either move or get the land next to theirs—how else do you think every little town supports two or three real estate offices? And it all puts the old blunt in my pocket." He puffed mightily, blowing cigar smoke toward the roof of the car, crossed his legs, put an arm across the back of the seat, and seemed a man pleased with himself and the moving world.

His listeners turned away with various degrees of distaste on their faces. It was the last thing they needed to hear right now: that they might ever move again! One and all turned their eyes on the town by which it, and a berry, were called—Saskatoon.

This sturdy settlement, growing rapidly, especially since the arrival of the train, had been founded by a group of promoters who called themselves the Temperance Colonists. The Northwest Territories were officially "dry," so the temperance angle was superfluous. Still it drew settlers who thought there would be advantages to living in a community where high principles would be respected. But the Temperance Colony could not acquire land in a huge tract because, in every township, two sections had already been retained by the Crown for school districts, and another two belonged to the Hudson's Bay Company. It made for a checkered layout and frustrated and foiled the Temperance Colonists.

The firstcomers settled on the east bank of the Saskatchewan River's south branch; eventually the train track reached them—a tremendous advantage that caused the east bank people of the little community, which was called Saskatoon, to rejoice over their rivals on the west bank, who were trainless—only a ferry accommodated their needs. Eventually the railway company moved the station to the west bank, a dismaying turn of events for the east-bank people. Now a bridge, being imperative, was built, and the people of both sides drew together in their objectives. A new name was suggested: Nutana.

Nutana, it was said by the Temperance Colony agent who suggested it, was an Indian word meaning "first born." But none of the Cree and Sioux of the area ever knew or used the word. The man was suspected of having an overactive imagination; Nutana's subsequent use became limited to a small area, and *Saskatoon* was officially chosen as the town's name.

"Weel, it's no Aberdeen," Anne said, staring out of the grimy train window, "but it's better than what we've been seein' across the prairies. Oh, that we could stay here!"

Missing the hills of home, Tierney responded with a shake of the head, "This is too flat for my likin'. Way too flat—"

"Not really," someone corrected her. "It just seems that way. The prairie has folds and creases and the likes of that, but yes, it seems as flat as a table from our viewpoint."

Tierney continued her remark for Anne alone: "Oh, that we would end up whaur there's braes and trees!"

"Is it Binkiebrae, then, that ye're longin' for, Tierney?" Anne asked kindly.

"Na, na, it's no' that. I guess I'm jist jittery aboot everythin' being sae new and strange. Nae, I'd no' go back, e'en if I could. 'Tis jist . . ." In her depth of feeling, Tierney had slipped back into the old, unacceptable way of speech. Ishbel Mountjoy wouldn't have approved.

Anne laid a comforting hand on her friend's arm. "I'm the same, Tierney. But I think we'll feel better when we're in our new places, and workin'. We're tired to death of this sittin' around, wonderin'-like."

What a relief it was, and had been all across an ocean and halfway across a continent, to have the British Women's Emigration Society in charge. Here was a strange town called Saskatoon and/or Nutana, growing to lusty maturity; here was a river called "Kis-is-ski-tche-wan," or "the river that flows rapidly," which, despite its shallow depth—seldom more than twelve feet—ran its tawny waters treacherously across the territory in a giant Y, to empty eventually into Hudson Bay. Both town and river, and much, much more, were as removed from the old world as the moon from the earth, in the minds and thinking of three uneasy girls. They felt quite cast adrift, though they had contracts in their purses and assurances concerning the employers that had been alerted to meet them.

Tierney, Anne, and Pearly made their lone way from the train—having left the Toronto office and Ishbel Mountjoy far behind—under the impression that a representative would be awaiting them.

Standing on the station platform, with busy life and busy people swirling around and past them, Pearly, Anne, and Tierney came to the chilling realization that, in fact, no one seemed to be looking for them.

After ten minutes or so of looking this way and that, hoping to catch the eye of someone on the search for someone else, they looked at each other with wide, questioning eyes. Had they misunderstood?

"Now what?" Anne asked uncertainly.

"We'll have to ask around," Tierney said with more calmness than she felt. "Stay here," she ordered, but when she looked back it was to find Pearly and Anne on her heels, as close as possible, and all three girls made their way through the crowd, which was, it seemed, thinning out.

Approaching the ticket window, Tierney asked, bravely, "Do you know the location of the British Women's Emigration Society?"

"Sure don't," a thin faced, thick-mustached individual said cheerfully.

Perhaps the girls' faces reflected their worry, for the man said, "Wait a minute, and I'll ask around."

Coming back to his window, he said, "Nobody thinks there's such a Society here, with an office, that is. Man back there says he's acquainted with its work, and young ladies pass through here all the time. I suggest you go to the nearest hostel and wait. You may be sure we'll send on anyone coming here to meet you."

The girls were hesitant, either to respond or to move.

"Tell you what," the man said kindly, "I'll get a horse cab to take you—it isn't far, but you might miss it, walking. And then, there's your baggage. So, see, you'll get to the hostel and be fine there. Man back there," and the speaker jerked his thumb toward the back of the station, "says it happens all the time. Says everybody but me knows about the domestics coming here regularly. Says they're going to change the entire northwest. Now *that* I'll believe when I see it."

The man guffawed and continued, "I'm a newcomer myself; that's why I didn't know, you see. But I ain't seen anything changing around here so far, except to get busier and wilder. Thought I'd make a change in it myself when I arrived; never thought I'd end up working in a train station. But soon's I get my feet under me—"

His audience's faces beginning to look strained, the man checked himself, called a youth, explained the need for a cab, and bade the reluctantly departing girls good-bye.

"You'll have to share a room," the clerk said shortly thereafter, when the girls had reached the hostel, as he studied the register in front of him. "And a bed."

"Do you ever have other girls from the British Women's Emigration Society?" Tierney, as spokeswoman for the trio, asked. "I mean, is there a chance someone will think to look here for us?"

"Oh yes. Yes, we have the Society's girls come here looking for someone, and yes, someone comes looking for them. Usually it's the family they're to work for. I suppose anyone driving in this far, looking for a domestic, wouldn't go back without finding her; it would be a trip—probably a long one—for nothing. If I were you I'd just sit tight and see what happens."

"Have you had," Anne asked in a trembling voice, "girls waitin' and no one comes for them?"

"Well, yes, I guess that's happened, too," the clerk said, while the girls drew even closer together in their concern. "But to my knowledge," he added kindly, "it hasn't been a problem. It has always worked out, I'm sure. You just arrived, didn't you? Perhaps you need to give it a little time—"

"Well," Tierney, the brave one, asked, "what did they do in sich a circumstance, the lassies left waitin'?"

"They went out and found work, I suppose. There's plenty of work, never fear. Some stay here at the hostel even when they're working. You can do that, you know. That is," he quickly reminded them, "if you have money. Fact is, we have such a young lady here now; she works as maid at a hotel, I believe. Maybe you'll run across her and she can give you the particulars."

Somewhat reassured, Tierney signed the register, took the key, and turned toward the stairs, the girls once again on her heels.

The room was small but clean. There was one narrow bed, at which the girls looked with disfavor. The cots in Binkiebrae had been narrower, but they had been designed for one, not more. As for Pearly, she was accustomed to tumbling five or six in a bed.

"We'll have to take turns sleepin'," Pearly offered, though after five nights sleeping on hard train seats, just who would go first and who must wait might be a problem. "I don't think this bed was meant for more than two people."

"We'll manage," Tierney assured her, feeling weary enough to sleep the night through though crammed together like sausages in a frying pan. "Now, I'm goin' to take off my shoes, put my feet up, and rest. Maybe later we can find this lass the clerk mentioned and talk wi' her."

"Me, too," Anne sighed, suiting action to words and unlacing her boots.

Off came the shoes and hats, laid aside were the capes and shawls. Each girl splashed cold water onto her face, washed her hands, grimaced at the weary, rather disorderly person in the mirror over the washstand, and turned toward the bed.

Like spoons in a drawer they lay, too weary to care. Sleep was immediate as the sounds of frontier commerce faded from their ears and the day's bright afternoon light faded from their eyes.

It was a pounding on the door that jolted them, all three, awake, and brought them to a sitting position. It took each girl a few moments to recollect where she was, and why. But the male voice calling through the door's thin boards finished the waking process.

"Miss Fraser! Miss Anne Fraser! Is there an Anne Fraser in there?"

Anne's hand went to her mouth; above it her eyes were wide with terror. A male voice, in a strange place, calling her name with authority—for a moment it seemed that Anne must faint.

"Anne Fraser!"

The girls looked at each other, faces flushed with sleep, hair tumbled, ears pummeled with the unexpected, insistent pounding on the door, eyes coming into focus in the small, airless room, the unfamiliar room.

"Anne Fraser! Anne Fraser!"

Tierney took one look at Anne's horrified face, from which the color was quickly receding, and swung her feet over the edge of the bed.

"Just a moment," she called out.

Fumbling among the puddle of shoes on the floor at the bedside, Tierney managed to sort out her own and pull them on. Laces hanging, she stood to her feet, trying to bring the whole situation into perspective—sleeping in a strange room . . . someone knocking on the door . . . Pearly looking befuddled with sleep . . . Anne with her hand over her mouth, her beautiful eyes filled with dreadful fear . . . someone demanding entrance.

With a quick instinctive move she brushed her hair back, making a fruitless attempt to tuck it into its accustomed knot on the nape of her neck, straightened her rumpled clothes, left the shoelaces dangling, and stepped to the door vibrating with another barrage.

"Yes? Who is it?" she asked, repeating it when her voice cracked, still heavy with sleep. "Who is it?"

"I've come for Anne Fraser. Is she in there? I understand she is. Open the door."

In spite of Anne's violently shaking head, Tierney unlocked the door and opened it.

Outlined in the doorway stood one of the most harmless appearing males Tierney had ever seen. Not much taller than she, but twice as wide, he stood with fist upraised, ready to knock again, if necessary, causing Tierney to flinch at first sight. His other hand held his cap, snatched from his head the moment his eyes fell on Tierney. Soft locks of colorless hair fell over his forehead. The face below, as round as a cookie and as innocuous, featured eyes like raisins above cheeks plump and pink under fair brows and lashes. His little mouth, set for another squall, was round and open, perhaps in astonishment.

"Anne Fraser?" he managed, strangely abashed for one who had hollered so manfully but a second ago.

"Na na. And who might ye be, pray tell?"

"Frankie . . . Frank Schmidt. My grandfather is Franz Schmidt; he and my grandmother, Augusta, have a paper here saying a Miss Anne Fraser has been hired to work for them."

The voice of the young man—for such he appeared to be—was soft enough now that the pounding and calling were over. He struggled to work his hand into his coat pocket—a coat that fit too snugly on his chunky frame—and withdrew a creased paper that he waved with a hopeful expression before Tierney.

Tierney hesitated . . . what should she do? A quick glance back showed Pearly and Anne still perched on the bed, faces turned toward the couple at the door, hair askew, clothes askew, expressions not far different—particularly Anne's. Though she had removed her hand from before her mouth, and the dismay was fading from her eyes, Anne was shaking her head rather violently from side to side and her eyebrows were drawn together darkly in an expression of fierce disapproval.

"I tell ye what, Mr. Schmidt; you go doonstairs and wait, and we'll be on doon jist as soon as we make ourselves presentable."

The smile on Frank Schmidt's face was cherubic. "Yah," he said, "I'll do that. Good day to you, ma'am." There was a hint of an accent in his voice, as though he were not too far removed from the old country.

Tierney closed the door, turned and faced the girls, and knew immediately she'd have to go to work on Anne or have her eventually left high and dry and alone here in Saskatoon when she and Pearly had dispersed to their respective places of employment.

"What a nice young man," she said cheerfully. "Did you see him?"

"Looked like a pudding to me," Anne said unkindly. "All suety like."

"Not at all. Verra polite and well-spoken. An' anyway, suety puddings are perfectly harmless."

"Ha! Who is he, anyway? Nae mention was made o' any grandson; I clearly specified no men!" Anne sounded as if the whole thing was an underhanded plot against her personally.

"Annie, Annie—doesn't it stand t' reason there'd be relatives? Once one member o' the family emigrates, others soon follow. And if the Schmidts are old, they'd need someone, o' course, to come to get ye. And who better than a young, strong grandson. Be sensible, lass!"

"I'm not goin' off into the wilderness with . . . with any strange man, I can tell ye that!" Anne declared, rising, nevertheless, from the bed and beginning the search under the side of the bed for her boots.

Pearly was at the washstand, dashing water onto her sleep-puffed face; there was no way she was going to be left behind in the room when there was drama going on below. Besides, they were in this together. Sink or swim, they'd do it together, if it were at all possible.

In spite of her determination to have nothing to do with this Schmidt person, as she kept muttering, Anne was attempting to bring order out of the chaos of her hair.

"My clothes," she wailed, "look like they've been slept in."

"As indeed they have," Tierney said firmly, "an' he'll understand that. He's not a picture of high fashion, himself. Looks like a farmer in his Sunday-go-to meetin' clothes. And looks like they might hae been slep' in, too."

With Anne drawing back, still muttering, lagging behind the others, the three made their way to the small room that was waiting room and parlor. Frank Schmidt was there; he surged to his feet, his small eyes twinkling above his plump cheeks.

"Good day, young ladies," he started politely, as though meeting them for the first time and wanting to do it properly. "My name is Frank Schmidt."

"Aye," Tierney said with a small sigh, "so it is. An' I'm Tierney Caulder, an' this is Miss Pearly Chapel, an' this," Tierney pulled Anne forward, "is Miss Anne Fraser."

Pearly and Anne nodded stiffly, Anne from her safe position behind Tierney.

"I been waiting at the station," Frank Schmidt said, "all day yesterday, and no one came. Nobody can tell for sure, it seems, chust when trains pull in. Yours must have been sidetracked somewhere, yah?"

"Yah, that is," Tierney corrected herself, "aye, we had several layovers, and so on. We never really knew why we were delayed. But," she said firmly, "we're here now, and Miss Fraser has a contract with—your grandparents, is it? Franz—"

"Yah," the burly youth confirmed. "My grandparents, Franz and Augusta . . . Gussie. They couldn't come, of course, the age they are, so here I am." His broad face beamed. "It's a full day's trip to Hanover. Wouldn't be much sense in startin' now; it's too late in the day. I been bunkin' in my wagon and will do so again tonight. I see you got a room and will be all right tonight. Yah?" Frank looked at the girls hopefully.

"Aye, we'll be a' reet for tonight," Tierney agreed, wishing Anne would speak up and take charge of her own arrangements. But Anne was stubbornly silent. She was, in fact, looking at the young man with hostile eyes. One bad experience, and Anne was ready to condemn all males, it seemed.

"Well then," Frank continued, "I'll be here about six in the morning—that too early?"

Now he looked directly at Anne for the first time. Startled, no doubt at her fresh, young beauty, the young man blushed and, for the moment, lost his self-assurance. Having proceeded thus far with a certain poise, in charge of the situation, he lost his equilibrium almost completely.

With the small eyes fixed wide and the color high in his round cheeks, he stuttered, "Six o'clock—will that be good, Miss . . . ah, Miss Anne?"

"I'm not a bit sure—" Anne began coldly.

"That'll be fine, Mr. Schmidt," Tierney said crisply, giving Anne a pained glance.

Frank Schmidt couldn't be blamed for looking confused. He stood, irresolute for a moment, then, twisting his cap, turned to leave.

"I'll be here," he said again, "at six. If you'll be ready, please—" He cast a rather desperate look at Anne and made his departure.

He was no sooner out the door than Anne said, "I'm not goin'."

"Of course ye are," Tierney said patiently.

"Not a bit o' it. Nae indeed," Anne said, sitting down on a horsehair sofa and looking mutinous. "Wi' that suety fellow? Never in a' the world."

"What's wrong with him?" Pearly asked curiously. "I thought he were a sort o' pleasant chap, meself."

"Well, you go then," Anne said crossly, then, seeing the stricken look on Pearly's face, added quickly, "I'm sorry, Pearly. I'm jist upset. I said no men, remember?"

"He's not much more'n a boy hisself," Pearly said and withdrew from the field of battle.

"Now listen here, Anne," Tierney said, "you've got to go. You're bound, more or less, to go."

"I dinna have to. I dinna want to."

"But Annie, ye do have to. Ye signed a contract, remember. Your word—"

"No matter," Anne said stiffly. "They broke the agreement—I said no men!"

"You dinna askit him—does he live wi' his grandparents? P'raps he doesn't."

Anne muttered, and admitted, "I ne'er thought o' it. But I dinna want to ride oot there wi' him."

"Every man isn't tarred with the same brush, ye know. Just because Lucian MacDermott—"

"Dinna speak his dirty name!"

"But it's true. Ye cannot blame Frank Schmidt for Lucian's sins."

"Are you sayin' you'll put me in that wagon and send me off alone wi' that strange man?"

"Annie," Tierney explained, still patient, "Pearly and I will be doin' the same thing, perhaps even yet today."

"You have to have faith," Pearly piped up, having been quiet long enough. "We prayed about it, you know."

"*You* prayed about it, you silly girl," Anne said with some heat.

Once again Pearly looked hurt.

"There's nae need to strike oot at Pearly," Tierney said quenchingly. "Get hold o' yersel', lassie." It was as near disagreement as they had come to on the entire trip. Tired, tense, weary, they were near to straining the dear, treasured bonds of friendship.

Anne burst into noisy tears. "Almost . . . almost I wish I were back in Binkiebrae!"

Tierney had little sympathy for her. "Aye," she said grimly, "and that's whaur Lucian is. Now listen, Annie. Try and remember what an adventure this was . . . an' is. Nothing ventured, nothing gained, reet? Coom now, let's go up and get yer things ready and clean up a bit; then we'll go oot and hae a bit of supper, and you'll feel better aboot it all . . . we'll all feel better."

Anne was persuaded to dry her tears and go back to the stuffy little room. The girls threw open the window, opened their bags, withdrew fresh clothes and, after a wash, donned them, whether wrinkled or not, and felt better for the doing.

Supper, after conferring with the young man at the desk, was taken at a hotel not far away. Counting out their few coins carefully the girls ordered discreetly. Their general mood improved along with the plentiful, warm food. Good humor reasserted itself, and even Anne managed a few smiles.

"Mr. Frank Schmidt," Tierney pointed out, "is as much like Lucian MacDermott as a spavined nag is like a blooded stallion—with Lucian bein' the spavined nag, o' course."

With this the laughter erupted until tears—of relief as much as hilarity—spilled over. It had been a long trip thus far, with tensions unlike anything they had experienced previously, and the girls little knew or understood the pressures they were under, and had been for weeks. Like a safety valve the laughter and tears flowed until, gasping and wiping their eyes and aware of curious glances from other diners, they managed to bring themselves and their emotions under control. It was a healing moment.

Perhaps it was Tierney's comparison of Frank Schmidt and Lucian MacDermott that settled lingering fears for Anne. But the next morning, as the girls stood shivering in the morning's coolness and a wagon lumbered up to them with the sturdy form of Frank Schmidt on the seat, Anne, though pale, was courageous.

Perhaps it had been Pearly's prayer. About to leave the room, with Anne's baggage and purse and cape and shawl in their hands and over their arms, Pearly had paused and looked at the others expectantly. Though tempted, Anne withstood the urge to roll her eyes skyward and said, instead, in an unusually humble voice, "Well, Pearly, we a' know ye're goin' to pray. So—why not get aboot it?"

And pray Pearly did. Never free to pray aloud in her London chapel among her more experienced companions, here, among "heathern," as she referred to them, she felt perfectly free, even inspired.

"Dear Lord, here we are, poor girls far from home. But You sees us, You cares for us, and You promised You would never leave us nor forsake us, that is—" Pearly took the opportunity to do a little preaching along with her praying, "that is, if we acknow . . . if we take Your Son as our personal Lord and Savior. Even if some of us haven't done that [two out of three, she might as well have pointed out], still You love us. Please help Annie to know this, deep in her heart, and to be willin' to look to You for the help she will surely . . . I mean she *might* need, along the way. Keep her safe in Yer care—"

Anne shifted, uneasy under the spotlight of prayer on her behalf and ready for it to be turned from her. Pearly caught the hint and finished with a flurry: "Now and forever, ah-men."

Bravely Anne nodded good morning to Frank Schmidt; bravely she hugged and kissed the two who had been her companions for so long and on so daring an adventure. Bravely she held, a little longer, onto that special one who had been her friend through trials and joys across the years, now to be separated from her for the Lord only knew how long.

Bravely she climbed aboard the wagon, stepping on the wheel hub, reaching for the man's hand stretched out to her, and heaving herself up onto the seat beside him.

Bravely she watched Tierney and Pearly toss her belongings into the back of the wagon; bravely she waved as the driver flicked the reins and urged the team forward, the wagon creaking and groaning as it got underway.

But bravery could not conceal the shaking shoulders of the small, hunched form as the rig rolled down the street, turned a corner, and passed from sight.

14

Long after Tierney had turned back to the door of the hostel, Pearly stood in the street, gazing at emptiness, her face a mask, an expressionless mask.

"Comin', Pearly?" Tierney called gently, touched that the new addition to the friendship was so moved by the loss of one of the group.

If Pearly heard, she made no move. From the other end of the street a wagon approached, soon to be upon the motionless figure.

"Pearly!" Tierney called sharply, and Pearly jumped.

Looking wildly around, Pearly shook her head as though clearing it of dreams, certainly of thoughts, and leaped for the boardwalk. Still she lingered, standing in the hostel's doorway, looking up the street that had taken Anne—and Frankie Schmidt—away.

Waiting for her, Tierney was puzzled. If anyone was affected by the loss of Anne, it should have been Tierney. She was, after all, Annie's best friend, had been for years. She was not untouched by the parting.

Risking repetition, she repeated, "Pearly?"

Pearly turned slowly, a light fading from her eyes. Surely her slim shoulders were drooping, surely it was a long sigh that caused her small bosom to heave.

Silently the girls made their way back up to their room. Small, it suddenly seemed vacant now that one-third of them was no longer in it.

Still silent, Pearly sat on the edge of the bed, gazing at the floor and her dusty boots. Tierney watched her for a moment, then took a seat beside her. With a start Pearly turned her small face, and a smile—was it forced?—flickered on her lips. She drew a deep breath, as though shoring herself up under a heavy burden.

"Pearly," Tierney said, "wha's wrong, lass? I dinna remember seein' ye in this frame of mind afore. What is it, lassie? Surely ye're not worrit aboot Anne. I'll be takin' off, too, p'raps afore ye do, and ye may hae to watch me go, same as Annie."

"I'm all right, Tierney," Pearly said, but slowly, and Tierney was unconvinced.

"I dinna know ye felt sae strong aboot our Anne," Tierney said, still probing. In her concern, her reversal to the Scots dialect was natural.

"Anne? Anne?" For a moment it seemed Pearly was disoriented. "Oh, Anne."

"Yes, Anne. Pearly," Tierney said, urgent in her concern, "coom on, lass, what's wrong wi' ye? Ye act like ye're in a dream or sum'-mat. Are ye feeling a' reet?"

Pearly was silent, as though thinking. Apparently she made up her mind, whatever the problem may have been. "It's nothing, like I said. I'll be a' right in a minute." But it was spoken dully, and Tierney was unconvinced.

Surprisingly, there was a knock at the door. Pearly started, hope lighting her eyes. Tierney saw, and puzzlement creased her brow. The knock came again.

"Who—?" Tierney muttered, preparing to rise to her feet.

Pearly beat her to it; with a bound she was off the bed and at the door. With a glad cry she flung open the door. With a blank look she stepped back, the glow fading from her face.

A total stranger stood there. Not much older than Tierney, the young woman smiled engagingly.

"Hello there," she said, in friendly manner, almost as though she knew them.

And in a way she did. Was she not in the great Northwest for the same purpose? Apparently she was. And did she not feel a true kinship with these newcomers? Obviously she did.

"I'm Fria Klaus," she said, and seemed to expect an invitation in, a member of the family.

But Tierney was cautious. Who Fria Klaus was and what she wanted was more puzzling than the odd behavior of Pearly Chapel. For now, to add question to question in Tierney's mind, Pearly had stepped back, face downcast, and had seated herself once again on the bed as though she had no interest whatsoever in the person at the door. A visitor, in the faraway and strange place in which they found themselves, someone come to see them personally, and Pearly couldn't be roused to interest? It was too much for Tierney.

Casting a frustrated look at Pearly, Tierney turned again to the young woman at the door.

"Yes?" she asked, still cautious. Could this innocent-appearing female be one of the clandestine group of white slavers about which they had been warned? It seemed most unlikely; the girl seemed as straightforward and natural as they themselves. She might indeed have been one of the British Women's Emigration Society girls—

She was indeed.

She spoke the magic word: Ishbel Mountjoy.

Relief washed over Tierney like a dash of rainwater on a hot and dusty day.

"Come in! Come in!" she said warmly.

Fria Klaus stepped briskly into the room and, at Tierney's invitation, took one of the two straight-backed chairs; Tierney took the other. Pearly retained her place on the bed; but she could not, now, express disinterest. Another Mountjoy girl! And just when they were so alone!

"Did the Society send you?" Tierney asked, hoping it were true, hoping someone was still looking out for them.

"No. Sorry! Once you leave Toronto with your contract in your hand, you are pretty well on your own," the stranger said, speaking with a definite accent, Germanic perhaps, perhaps Scandinavian; Tierney and Pearly were too inexperienced with other lands, other cultures, to know. It didn't matter. The girl was neatly dressed, in what seemed to be a dark uniform, and with a white and snowy apron tied around her substantial middle. She was a strong, plain-looking girl, with an open expression and a straightforward look in her eyes.

Tierney and Pearly looked at the newcomer expectantly, set at ease by what they saw.

"I came here about three months ago—"

"To work in Saskatoon?" Tierney asked, obviously finding it hard to believe anyone would come freely for that purpose.

"To work on a farm," Fria Klaus explained. Then, with a shake of her head, she added, "No one ever came to meet me."

"Hoots!"

Fria Klaus was taken aback momentarily by the unfamiliar exclamation. But she rallied.

"There was nothing for me to do but to find work, which I did, and I've been here ever since."

"You're the lass the clerk told us aboot—"

"Yes, and he told me about you. I understand your anxiety about not being met by someone; I understand completely."

"I guess so. And did no one ever coom to get ye . . . you?"

"Never."

"And didn't the Society do anythin' aboot it?"

"By the time I finally got in touch with them, I'da been dead of starvation if I hadn't gone ahead and taken care of myself. It turned out, finally, that the farmer and his wife who had contracted for me had serious problems; the man died, in fact. Of course the wife never gave me another thought. Well, it can happen. We're so far from headquarters . . . there's no quick way to get word to anyone or from anyone . . . it'll be wonderful when that new contraption—the telephone—begins to be used—"

"Oh, do ye think it ever will?" Tierney asked, awed. "In these out-of-the-way places?"

"Sure to," the girl said confidently. "I work, you see, in a hotel near here, and I get all the latest news like that. Salesmen are always coming through, and newspapermen, and so on. Oh, it's a great way to keep abreast of things. Now you—if you settle on a farm—will be lost just as if you were in the outback of Australia." The girl spoke with scorn for the ignorant peasant who had nothing better to do than waste talents and time on farm work. Tierney was immediately certain that Fria was a farm girl, finally feeling superior.

"We're both goin' to farms," Tierney said uncertainly.

"I thought there were three of you," Fria Klaus said, changing the subject.

"One of us has already gone—"

"To a farm, I'll bet."

"Weel, aye . . . that is, yes."

"Poor thing."

Pearly, for the first time, spoke up. "Why do you say poor fing? She went orf wif a . . ." Pearly seemed to falter, "a very nice young man. She's luckier'n us, I'd say. Here we sit, nowheres to go—"

"Better to sit here than slave on a farm," Fria Klaus said with disdain for all such.

"Tell you what," she continued. "Looks like you are not going to be met, same as me. I bet I can get you jobs . . . or," doubtfully now, "one of you."

Fria's eyes swung from Tierney to Pearly, and back again. Her expression seemed to speak for her: Tierney was her choice. Pearly was too small, too childish, too frail.

Pearly was all backbone; Pearly was all determination. "Not me," she said stoutly. "I've had enough of Lunnon to do me a lifetime, and I'm not stayin' in no town when there's a clean, wide farm to live on."

"What about you?" Fria asked Tierney. "Are you interested?"

"I dinna know; it's a little early to say, isn't it? This is only our second day here. Our employers could show up yet, couldn't they?"

"They could, I suppose," Fria said grudgingly, obviously having no patience with the system.

"Tell me," Tierney asked, "what happens to your fee, when you don't fulfill the contract?"

"Well, in my case, it wasn't my fault. They just never showed up. It was the Society who finally ran down the problem and informed me what had gone wrong. Of course they offered to find me a new place, but by that time I was at work . . . had to be or I'da starved to death."

"The fee?" Tierney probed.

"They think I owe it, because they paid my way over here. I dunno. I'm balking at paying it, you may be sure, since they didn't fill their part of the bargain. We'll see, I guess. In the meantime I'm working and happier about it than if the old geezer from the farm had showed up. Tell you what, you take another day; if no one comes by then, you'd feel free to do something else, wouldn't you? You'd almost have to, wouldn't you?"

"Aye—for sure," Tierney said. "We canna sit around and do nothin'. If there's work for only one o' us, we'll take it and pay our bills, and the other one will look for somethin' else. Right, Pearly?"

Pearly seemed lost in a dream. She started. "Oh! Yes, o' course," she said quickly. "But," darkly, "I want to be on a farm, meself. I haf to pray about it."

"You do that," Fria Klaus said briskly, rising to her feet. "Now, it's almost time for me to go to work. I'll check in with you tomorrow and see what's happened in the meantime. All right?"

"A' reet," Tierney agreed, and obviously gladly. "By the way, I'm Tierney Caulder, from Scotland, and this is Pearly Chapel from Lunnon . . . London."

The young women shook hands properly. Even Ishbel Mountjoy would have been gratified.

Shutting the door behind their newfound acquaintance, Tierney turned to Pearly, relief on her face and in her voice.

"Well, dinna tell me that wasn't ordered of the Lord, Pearly. To me it seems like a life raft thrown to a drownin' person. I dinna feel nearly so adrift—in this sea of grass—as I did a half hour ago."

Pearly, however, had allowed herself to fall back across the bed. Her eyes were shut, and her lips were moving.

Frustrated again, Tierney rose to her feet, watched Pearly for a moment, and turned away. Pearly was praying, she supposed. Finally, battling anxiety and, in spite of Fria Klaus and her encouraging words, more than half-worried—with Anne gone and Pearly in a passion of prayer—Tierney dug her journal out of her battered traveling bag, seated herself at the small table in the corner of the room, and commenced writing.

Dear Robbie,

Oh, how I wish you were here. I've just said good-bye to Anne, and that was bad enough. But now Pearly is upset about something or other. It's plain to see she is in need of divine help, for she has her eyes shut, and I suppose she is praying. She doesn't know the prayers of the kirk, Robbie, and just goes ahead and makes up her own. I declare it's enough to make me question the whole of my upbringing and teaching. Is there anything to all of this that she tells us—about Jesus, about prayer, about being saved?

I feel better just talking to you about it. Helps me look at things in the proper Binkiebrae way!

I declare I don't know about the future. It's truly rather frightening, Robbie. Here we sit in the midst of a prairie the size and strangeness of which you wouldn't believe, unless you are out there somewhere in all that grass. If you are I despair of finding you ever again. Not that I have any hopes of that . . . but my dreams won't let go of you. Oh, Robbie . . . Robbie . . .

Loneliness, worry, weariness overcame even Tierney's intrepid spirit. Laying her head on her arms, she let the tears come. Her slim shoulders shook, and the tears puddled on the open journal, blurring Robbie's name and obliterating Tierney's silent call to him. Robbie was as lost to her as the penned name disappearing in the watery stain. The realization caused a fresh outburst.

What a sight they were—Pearly, eyes closed, lips moving silently as she lay stretched on the bed, Tierney, lying across the table, weeping. And Anne? Anne saying—

Pearly sat up with a start; Tierney lifted her head, one final tear running down her nose.

"Open the door; let me in."

Pearly's eyes met Tierney's; a blaze lit those pansy eyes with something like joy. Tierney stared blankly at Pearly.

"Tierney, Pearly—it's me, Anne. Open the door."

It wasn't imagination; it was Anne. Anne, or a perfect impostor.

Pearly got to the door before Tierney. Fumbling with the latch, then the knob, she eventually flung it open. Flung it open to see Anne—big-eyed and white-faced—standing in the hall. Behind her, Anne's bags in his hands—Frankie Schmidt.

For a moment there was silence. Anne, drooping, tired, pasty-complexioned, seemed transfixed just outside the door. Frank Schmidt, his open face a mix of dismay and helplessness, peered over Anne's shoulder, wordless, at least for the moment. Anne's bags dragged in his hands.

Reaching the door a moment behind Pearly, Tierney could see Pearly's face directly in her line of vision, joyous beyond belief.

Tierney stretched her hand toward her weary friend. Pearly's hand was stretched—not to Anne, who stumbled into the welcoming circle of Tierney's arms, but toward the figure still standing in the hall, the square figure of Frank Schmidt.

What a flurry of gasps, of hugs, of comforting pats! One would have thought Anne had been gone for months rather than minutes—sixty of them, to be exact.

With considerable fluster and flutter Anne was transported across the floor and to a chair. Here Tierney, clucking and murmuring wordlessly, seated her friend, removed her hat and helped her off with her gloves, first taking from her grasp the small case she clutched.

Pearly was, in a way, doing the same for Frank Schmidt. She indicated that the traveling bags should be set aside; then, with sympathetic face and gestures, she urged the robust young man toward the other chair.

There they sat, like twin statues, one on either side of the table: Anne, whose dazed look was being replaced with a shamefaced expression, Frank Schmidt continuing to seem more bewildered than anything.

"Weel . . . weel . . ." Tierney began, standing before the two of them, her hands clutched before her, threatening to wring helplessly and disclose her surprise, perhaps her dismay.

Anne—back? Now what in the world could Tierney do or say to persuade her to "do her duty"? The future—for herself as well as for Anne—gaped blankly before her. How could she leave for her own appointment if Anne were still here, alone, helpless, hopeless?

Pearly was direct, as she was apt to be. London had held little softness of character or ease of circumstance for Pearly Gates; Saskatchewan had done nothing, at least as yet, to bring change into the basic personality of Pearly Chapel.

"Whatcher doin' back here?" she asked bluntly, but not unkindly.

At this Anne burst into tears. Frank Schmidt raised his pale blue eyes to the ceiling and sighed deeply.

Tierney hesitated, torn between rushing to her friend's comfort or urging her toward stiffening her backbone. What should it be—approval or correction?

While Tierney fluttered in the throes of indecision, Anne sobbed, ever more noisily, Frank's eyes closed in longsuffering, Pearly acted. Pulling out a handkerchief she offered it to Anne.

"Now buck up, lassie," she said practically, borrowing a familiar Scots' word to do so. "How can we help yer if y' don't stop that puling and tell us what's the matter?"

It was well done. Anne, lost in her misery, was jolted out of it. "P–puling?" she repeated, raising her eyes while sniffing into the handkerchief.

"Me ma said it was 'grizzling' when the babbies did it—whimper, that is. Now come, lass, surely yer knows why yer done it, come back, that is, and in such a short time. Did Mr. Schmidt here do or say sumfing to upset yer?" Pearly was badly fracturing her English once again; Ishbel would have been dismayed, perhaps scandalized.

Anne fidgeted, Anne flushed.

"Weel," she wailed, finally, "I canna bring meself to admit it . . . again. I'm jist a coward, that's a' I am! I jist canna make myself do what I know I should . . . ought to do."

There was no reason; there was nothing new. Tierney realized it was as she had feared: Anne was still in the throes of obsession

where men were concerned, even such a seemingly unobjectionable man as Frank Schmidt. She sighed massively. What to do!

"We hardly got beyond the edge of town," Frank Schmidt said now, "when she burst into tears. I noticed plain enough that she had been shakin' and sobbin' silently, but I thought she'd get ahold of herself right enough, once the good-byes were all past. I thought she'd start thinking ahead to the next thing—her job, and her responsibilities. To my grandparents." Now Frank Schmidt spoke grimly. It was plain to be seen he didn't hold with this shilly-shallying and that his patience was sorely tried. Still, he made an effort.

"Tell me, ladies, what is a man supposed to do? I been away two days now, awaitin' and alookin' until I found ya, then fiddle-faddlin' around—" Frank's speech was becoming more and more highly modulated, less and less reasonable.

Tierney could see the young man was getting worked up, as he had every right to do, but it wasn't helping the situation, which was serious.

"Please, Mr. Schmidt! Let's talk aboot this calmly—"

"Well, is she comin', or ain't she?" Frank asked. "I gotta get on my way, that's for sure and certain. My family will think I've run into trouble somewhere, and they'll be sendin' out a search party for me. Is she comin' or ain't she?"

The amber eyes of Tierney, the purple eyes of Pearly, and the small, light blue eyes of the young man, were turned toward Anne—despairingly on Tierney's part, who knew Anne well; questioningly and brightly on Pearly's part, ever the eternal optimist; and distrustfully on the part of Frank Schmidt, who obviously had his craw full of temperamental women, Anne in particular.

If Anne, Tierney reasoned, ever had thoughts of Frank Schmidt casting longing eyes on her or harboring lascivious thoughts toward her, she had certainly annihilated them. He looked on her with great disfavor.

"Weel, Anne?" Tierney said.

"I can't go; I can't!"

Anne sobbed; Tierney sighed; Frank muttered. Pearly, for some unaccountable reason, looked thoughtful.

It seemed, as the story began to come out, that the wagon had cleared the town, with the vast prairie stretching out endlessly ahead of them, before Anne spoke.

"This . . . this grass an' sky—does it jist go on and on like this . . . all the way?"

"Sure does," Frank Schmidt had answered cheerily, giving the reins a flick and urging the team to a faster pace. "That's what makes it such grand farmland. My grandfather has a homestead, and so does my father; and I'd get land of my own, but my Opa—Grandfather—wants me to take over his place." Frank sounded very satisfied with life, with himself, and with his future.

"And the reason I can do it," he continued placidly, "is because this grand land just seems next best to heaven, to me at least." Frank didn't know that, with each glad word, his listener was shivering more and more. What he said next sent a lightning bolt of fear and fantasy through Anne's heart.

"The next thing I need, for sure and certain, is to get me a wife."

To the young man's surprise, Anne had reached for the reins, yanked back on them, and gritted, "Turn back! Turn back, I say!"

The wagon had stopped in the middle of the road. Frank turned bewildered eyes on the fierce face at his shoulder.

"Hey! Take your hands offa the lines, willya?" Naturally he gave them a yank to free them from Anne's hands, at the same time speaking soothing words to the team: "Whoa . . . whoa . . . whoa there."

When the prancing, startled horses had quieted, Frank turned a perturbed face on the bundle of agitation and frenzy that was Anne Fraser.

"What's the matter with ya? You gone crazy or something?"

"I can't go on . . . I *won't* go on—"

And with that Anne had attempted to clamber from the rig. Only the firm hand of Frank had held her in the wagon.

"I'll take ya. Sit down, wildcat!" And with that, Frank had turned the rig around and, once again, made his way into

Saskatoon and to the hostel, barely an hour from the time he had pulled away from it.

With the telling, by Frank, Anne had squirmed but had not attempted to defend herself.

"Weel, Annie," Tierney said into the silence that fell in the room, "what're we to do wi' ye now?"

"I'll stay here. I simply can't go out into the wilderness, far from y' all and by mysel'. "

Anne shivered. Her fear, Tierney realized, was very real. Unspoken, probably for the man's sake, was the real reason.

"But Annie, what're we to do aboot the contract? Ye promised!"

Anne looked worried but mutinous. "Wha' can they do tae me?" she asked. "Throw me in prison? I canna be the first one to turn down an assignment. I'll worry aboot that when the time cooms."

"But what'll ye do, Anne? Money's runnin' oot—"

"There's the job at the hotel," Pearly said promptly.

"But there are men—" Tierney looked at Frank Schmidt apologetically. "There are bound to be men there, too."

Frank Schmidt looked more bemused than ever. "Men? Men?" he murmured with a perplexed air.

As simply as possible, Tierney tried to explain. Anne sat gazing unseeingly at her fingernails, as though she were far removed from the problem or they were talking about someone else. But Tierney knew it was painful for her, and embarrassing.

"So you see, Mr. Schmidt, she has a sort of . . . of a panic aboot . . . weel, aboot men in general."

"Poh!" the burly young man said disgustedly.

"You can Poh all ye want," Tierney said with some heat, "but we've got a real problem here. I dinna know how we'll solve it—"

"The hotel," Pearly pointed out patiently.

"That may be fine, for Anne," Tierney said, just as patiently, "particularly if the job should be doin' kitchen chores and things like that. But what aboot Mr. Schmidt, eh?"

Now Pearly showed some impatience. "Poh!" (Pearly was a great mimic; never having heard the ejaculation before, she would now undoubtedly incorporate it into her vocabulary. Her limited vocabulary, which was growing by the day.) "I'll do it. I'll trade wi' her."

Anne lifted her head and gazed at Pearly as though at a savior. Tierney blinked her eyes, thinking seriously. Frank Schmidt gazed admiringly at the spunky sprite of a girl who had, in a few words and at one stroke, solved all their problems.

"Fine with me," he said. "And my grandparents don't know the difference."

"But Pearly," Tierney said slowly, "what aboot yer own contract? What aboot . . . what's their name? Those folks from Red Fife—Belknap, wasn't it?"

"Belknap? Belknap?" Frank said slowly. "I don't know the name, but if they live at Red Fife, they're burned out. Fire swept through there a coupla weeks ago. They'd be lucky to survive, let alone need a domestic."

"Are you certain, Mr. Schmidt?" Tierney asked.

"Positive! Just ask the clerk at the desk . . . ask most anyone. They'll tell you about the tragedy at Red Fife. Everyone knows fire is one of the great hazards of the prairie. Seems someone's newfangled engine sparked, and before it could be stopped it had swept through the community, clear to the coulee. Take my word for it; there won't be no one from Red Fife comin' in for any help. May not even have a rig, or horses."

There was silence in the room.

"Weel, Pearly—"

"If Mr. Schmidt is willin', I'm willin'," Pearly sang out.

No one was able to explain the light that shone in the big eyes. One would have thought Pearly was actually happy, perhaps tremulously happy, to go with the sturdy young man Frank Schmidt out to a prairie homestead, there to work her hands red, her back sore, her frame weary, for fifteen dollars a month. One might even think, knowing Pearly, that it was an answer to prayer.

Finally, Anne had the grace to ask, "An' do ye mean it, lass? Are ye willin' to do this? I mean, is it a' reet wi' ye?"

Little mimic that she was, Pearly seemed to bubble her response, "A' reet? Sure, it's a' reet! If it's a' reet wi' Mr. Schmidt, it's a' reet wi' me."

Mr. Schmidt seemed to lose himself in those pansy/purple orbs as he blushed and murmured, hardly hearing himself: *"A' reet!"*

16

Caught up in the little scenario acting itself out before him, Frank Schmidt murmured the Scottish "a' reet," only to change it hastily to "It's all right with me."

"All right" it may have been, but his expression indicated it was superlatively all right. Frank Schmidt was relieved, and massively so. Strange, come to think of it: Here was the lovely face and curvaceous form of Anne Fraser about to be withdrawn from his intimate world, and his expression, as he contemplated the stick-thin form and elfin face of Pearly Chapel who would substitute herself for Anne, was one of supreme satisfaction. The one—Anne—seemed a woman in all ways, the other—Pearly—a child by comparison.

But Pearly was no child in ways that matter. Her small face glowed; she actually *bustled* as she went immediately to the task of folding up her clothes and repacking her shabby bag with her meager belongings.

Anne watched silently, embarrassed and relieved at the same time. Tierney, more concerned with the legal and moral aspects of the transaction, looked doubtful. But what was there she could do? Both Anne and Pearly, who were the signers of the contracts, seemed content with the decision. Frank Schmidt, most concerned of all, was nodding, his round face reflecting his approval. "Are ye sure, Pearly—" Tierney began.

"Not a doot . . . doubt," Pearly said blithely, already casting aside the Scots she had picked up without effort. "In fact—"

Pearly hesitated, slanted a glance at Frank Schmidt, then continued boldy. "In fact, I were prayin' about it when they showed up, I were so sure it were my place to go and Anne's to stay."

Frank Schmidt blinked, then nodded placidly. "In all thy ways acknowledge Him," he quoted sagely, "and He shall direct thy paths."

You'd have thought the sun had come up. Pearly's face blazed with light and joy. She turned the full glow of her eyes on Frankie Schmidt, and words were not necessary.

Tierney felt a lump come up in her throat and, for a moment, battled with tears that threatened to spring forth. How steadfast and true Pearly was to what she believed! If one were to "get religion," Tierney acknowledged silently, one should get it like Pearly, having it consume one's life in every phase. Such personal devotion to the Christian walk made the kirk and its liturgies and formalities seem as a springboard to something vital and personal. Life in Christ, Pearly called it.

As if the lump in the throat were not enough, Tierney found her eyes misting. She was going to miss Pearly! Hardly having had time to get acquainted, still she was going to miss her most dreadfully. Suddenly she was filled with a small sense of panic. Why hadn't she been more responsive while it was possible? Why hadn't she taken Pearly's "testimony" more seriously? Who was going to pray now, when things were not going well? Tierney had grown to rely on Pearly's prayers and the consolation it brought to know a troubling situation had been placed in God's hands.

"Pearly," she said now, half anxiously, touching the girl's shoulder and turning the piquant face to herself, "there was a verse;

you said you had a favorite, number one verse. Tell me, Pearly. Tell me—what is it?"

With Frank Schmidt and Anne willing listeners, Pearly, sweetly and poignantly, quoted the Scripture that had comforted and kept her across a wild and restless ocean, a vast land, and an empty prairie, that gave her peace the entire time, and courage, not only through it all, but to face today and tomorrow.

"He shall feed his flock like a shepherd," Pearly, soft-eyed, quoted; "He shall gather the lambs with His arm, and carry them in His bosom, and shall gently lead those that are with young."

"Aye," Tierney breathed. "He shall gather the lambs . . . He shall carry them in His bosom. How comforting."

"And, Tierney," Pearly took time to say, earnestly, "He'll carry you like that, iffen you'll let Him."

"Aye; I won't forget. I'll try not to forget," Tierney promised, and she stepped back, but taking with her a promise and a pledge that would see her in good stead in the days and months ahead, whether she knew it or not at the moment.

What a day for tears it was! Pearly's cup seemed about to run over. Tears, of happiness and satisfaction, puddled in her eyes. She dashed them away, not ashamed before the gaze of the young man, who seemed to understand, as though it were perfectly natural for a prospective domestic employee to use Scripture and to talk about praying as though it were an everyday occurrence. One would have suspected the young man had been born into a home where Christian principles were important and the name of God revered, being often mentioned in prayer and praise.

"Can yer remember where it's found, Tierney; in the Bible, I mean? It's the Book of Isaiah, chapter 40, verse 11. Read it all, Tierney. It tells about people bein' like grass. Fits this prairie, I'd say, and makes y' think. Still, think of yerself as a lamb, will yer, Tierney, will yer?"

And Tierney promised.

Dressed in her "uniform"—the dark skirt and white shirtwaist—clutching her threadbare cape, Pearly turned toward the patient Frank. With alacrity for such a solid young man, he gathered up the bags and chattels that she indicated were hers and turned to go, Pearly at his heels, Anne and Tierney following.

Pearly paused. "Wait a mo. I better pray now; outside will be too busy and too public to do it prop'ly." She bowed her head; the others followed suit.

"Dear Favver in heaven, here we are now, about to part and go our ways. Fank You for Anne and Tierney and their kindnesses to me. Bless 'em, Favver, and lead 'em in the way they oughter go. And let us all meet again, in Yer time and place. Fank You, dear Favver. Amen."

Perhaps because of the prayer, perhaps because of the kindly, trustworthy-appearing young man and his solid ways, Pearly trotted down the stairs, across the foyer of the hostel, and to the street with no hesitation whatsoever. How different, Tierney thought, than the dragging steps of Anne and the reluctance she had displayed just a short time ago. Surely the One who answered prayer had guided them thus far and would continue to keep His good hand upon them, gather them in His bosom.

Even Anne seemed to realize the rightness of it all and clasped Pearly to her with warmth and gratitude; she had indeed been feeling guilty over her failure to keep her bargain. In the midst of her personal problem, she had given an uneasy thought or two to the elderly couple who needed help and who would be disappointed if no one showed up with their grandson's return.

Tierney folded the childish form to herself with some understanding of the Almighty's plans and purposes—far greater and more far reaching, far more personal than she had imagined—and blessed the day the little "Lunnon" waif had entered her life.

Pearly's belongings were stowed in the wagon, and she was gallantly assisted up onto the spring seat by a solicitous Frankie. The stalwart fellow lumbered around the rig and "ascended" (Tierney recalled Ishbel's word with a small smile) to take his seat, tipping it until wee Pearly grasped the iron handle at her side and clung on for dear life.

With a grand flourish of the reins and a vigorous "Ya, away my good fellows!" by Frank, the team stepped out briskly, down the same street they had trod just an hour or so ago, but with a new cargo.

This time there was no shaking of the shoulders on the wagon seat, no tearful sob, no air of dejection. Pearly's narrow shoulders were erect; her hat bobbed joyful cadence to the jolting of the wagon, and her smile, thrown over her shoulder to Tierney and Anne, was seraphic.

"I guess," Anne said a trifle defensively, "she's the one who is supposed to go. She seemed certain of it. Maybe," she added thoughtfully, "there's somethin' to this prayin' business. I mean somethin' more than liturgy, somethin' personal, maybe?"

"It certainly seems to work for her," Tierney admitted and waved as Pearly cast another glance back. "Maybe . . . maybe it would work for us."

Anne shrugged. Free of the despair of going to an unknown place with an unknown man, her burdens seemed not so great, after all. Let another fearsome moment come, however, and Anne, too, would have no alternative—now that Pearly had left her "testimony" to ring in their hearts—but to think seriously of the availability of an Almighty God.

Tierney and Anne stood alone in the street, watching the wagon trundle around the corner and out of sight, feeling more alone than they could have imagined. Was it just the absence of one, depleting their number by one-third, or was it a strangely vulnerable feeling of being out from under the covering of Pearly's prayers?

And yet Pearly had tried, earnestly, to instruct them in how to approach God, how to make Him an integral part of their lives, bringing, at the same time, the comfort and strength they so badly needed to face the days ahead. With the bright sunshine of another Northwest day pouring its light over and around them, Tierney and Anne were still groping their way through darkness in more ways than one. Had Pearly's brief time to "testify" been enough? Would there yet be a harvest from the planting she had done?

Nothing of this, of course, passed between the two girls; it may not have been definite, coherent thought. But the seed was planted, and stirring and struggling for life.

"There she goes," Anne said inadequately, from a tumultuous mix of feelings: guilt, that she herself had not fulfilled the contract, that she would be responsible if Pearly stepped into a hotbed of misery and abuse, and relief—great, sweeping relief—that it was not she driving off with a strange man, into an unknown situation, in a new and, in some ways, terrifying land.

"We'll probably never meet up with her likes again," Tierney added with a tightness in her throat and unexpected tears stinging her eyes. "She's a rare one, she is. Somehow, I think, we willna lose touch. After all, she's not impossibly far awa'. Thirty miles, did he say?"

"That's from here, where I'll be," Anne reminded practically. "An' if they coom to town for supplies, as they're bound to do, and Pearly persuades them to let her coom wi', I, for one, will get to see her. Knowing summat o' my plans, that I'll be workin' here, she'll surely look me up." Anne slanted a glance at Tierney.

"Ye're remindin' me that I really have no idea where I'll be. That you'll be here in toon, or so it seems, and I—"

The unknown future stretched, blankly and darkly, before her, and Tierney, having come so far with fortitude and courage, faced the hardest part of all—the end of the journey and the purpose for which she had come.

If she found herself settled into a miserable situation, what could she do about it? On a farm she could be stuck many miles from "civilization"—if this raw Saskatoon town could be termed civilized—and with no one, no one at all, to whom to turn. Ishbel Mountjoy had washed her hands, so to speak, of the girls when they were placed; Anne, quite helpless herself in many ways, could offer sympathy but probably no real solutions; and Pearly, whom she was now recognizing as a tower of strength, would be isolated on a farm out there, somewhere, in the vastness that was Saskatchewan's prairie. And Robbie? Robbie Dunbar was as lost to her as though he had stepped off the end of the world.

It would be weeks, perhaps months, before she could hope to hear from Binkiebrae. She hadn't, as yet, given James an address to which to write. Once settled—out there, somewhere—and

finally able to finish and send the epistle she had been working on, giving James a return address, how would it get to a post office? How long would it take to cross this wilderness to a ship going to Scotland? How long would it take to hear back—back across the ocean, back across the wilderness, back to this unknown farm? In spite of herself, Tierney shivered. Isolation—she was beginning to understand the meaning of the word.

Though her future was unsettled, hopefully Anne was taken care of, and that was a relief to Tierney. With a job and a place to live, though she might be surrounded by strangeness and strangers, there would be one small place of familiarity and security for Anne—the hostel, which was already beginning to seem like an oasis in a desert of immense dimensions.

Knowing Anne well and loving her dearly, Tierney was unselfish enough to be glad it was Anne who was settled and she who must still face the unknown future.

When the wagon had disappeared from sight, when the very dust of the street had settled, when the last of Pearly Chapel had been seen, Anne and Tierney turned back toward the hostel and their room.

"At least," Anne said as they stepped inside—and Tierney appreciated the attempt to turn the conversation to something of a lighter nature—"we won't be so crowded in that beddie!"

"Pearly—wee lass—dinna take up much space," Tierney reminded, and thought, with a pang, *She scarce made a ripple under the covers but leaves a big emptiness in our hearts.*

"I guess," Anne said, "I must go and see aboot the job. Will ye coom wi' me, Tierney?"

"I'll coom," Tierney said, not certain it was a good thing to do. Anne must immediately learn to stand on her own two feet. Soon she would be as alone as the one clump of bracken atop Tierney's barren hillside back home in Binkiebrae. That bracken had bent and bowed to wind and weather and had remained unbroken. Anne, sprung from the same Scotch soil, so to speak, would demonstrate that same stern ability to adapt and endure. Tierney counted on it. There was no alternative.

Shaking their heads over the condition of their clothes, the girls, dressing to go to the hotel, settled once again for their serge skirts—which had survived better than anything else—and smoothed out their waists as much as possible. Still they looked wrinkled and limp, and they decided, sighing, to wrap themselves in shawls, pulling them neatly around their shoulders and clasping them in front and more or less covering up the pathetic waists.

Downstairs at the counter they asked directions to the Madeleine, finding it was not far away, a fine thing if Anne should be working nights, a finer thing when she would be working during blizzardlike conditions.

"Ye know," Tierney needed to explain to the clerk at the desk, "that I'm lookin' for a family named Ketchum to coom fer me. I dinna ken if 'twill be today or no'. I dinna like to gang sae far awa', in case they coom—"

The face of the clerk was becoming curiously strained, perhaps embarrassed. For not only had Tierney, in her concern, slipped into pure Scots, but she was speaking rapidly and rolling r's richly; the young man was obviously not comprehending what was being said to him.

"Whoa!" he said finally, stemming the flow of words. "Begin again, willya? I'm used to all kinds of people, from all kinds of places, with all kinds of languages and accents, but you've got me stumped for sure, lady."

Tierney paused, flushed slightly, breathed deeply, and apologized, and began again. But slowly. "I'm sorry. Now, sir . . . if you could be . . . on the watch . . . if you please . . . for a family . . . by the name of Ketchum. . . . They may coom . . . come . . . lookin' for me—"

"Of course," the young man said smoothly. "I understand plain English very nicely, you know. No need to treat me like I'm deef and dumb. Ketchum, you say? I'll just make a note of it. You'll be back after breakfast, I suppose?"

"Aye. We're actually goin' on . . . on business. But I guess we'll eat while we're there."

"Looking for work, eh?" the clerk said wisely. "Well, good luck. Ketchum, you say . . ."

"He certainly won't forget the name," Tierney muttered to Anne as they made their way to the street and turned in the proper direction, still smarting from her slip into "jargon," which Ishbel Mountjoy had often warned them against.

The Madeleine, a four-square, unimposing, two-story building, was, as reported, close by, not more than two blocks away. Anne and Tierney made their way to a dining room crowded with customers. The clientele seemed largely of the rugged, mostly male, variety.

"Yes, ma'ams?" A slim, middle-aged, thin-haired man stepped toward them. Dressed in dark clothes, with a badge on his lapel that, on close inspection read "Host," he exuded authority.

"May I seat you?" this paragon of propriety asked, rubbing his hands together.

Though neither Anne nor Tierney were judges of the patrician and aristocratic, even they could see that it was a serviceable room rather than elite. The floor seemed scuffed as if from heavy boots, the table coverings, though white in color, were oil cloth rather than linen, and the customers were of the hearty, hungry variety rather than the fastidious and fashionable. Still, there was a certain raw energy about the place, and a young woman—in serge skirt and with an apron cinched around her waist—was pouring coffee to a table of men seated near a window.

At the man's approach, Anne had stepped just behind Tierney's shoulder.

"Well?" the host asked, eyes turning a little frosty as he studied the two females standing before him in wrinkled clothes and having, truly, rather weary faces. To Anne's weary countenance was added distrust.

Suddenly Tierney, tired, and tired of it all, stepped aside, revealing a startled Anne, and simply waited for her to speak.

"Well?" the man said again, more than his eyes frosty by now; his voice also revealed his suspicions about these two.

Anne gulped, but managed, "I've coom . . . come aboot . . . about a waitress job. Can ye . . . you direct us to the proper person to talk to aboot . . . about it?" With each correction Anne's color rose and her eyes glazed a little more.

"The back door," the man said rigidly, "would have been the proper place to come. But," he added, more graciously, "I am the person to see. Step this way, if you please."

Anne gave Tierney an anguished look as they followed the stiff back of the dining room's "host." *I'd hae been better off wi' Frank Schmidt!* Anne was obviously saying silently. Tierney forced herself to ignore her. The time for action had come; there would be no more shilly-shallying.

The small room off the dining area seemed to be an office, and here Tierney and Anne were seated.

"I'm Mr. Whidby," the man said, having seated himself at a desk. "I have charge of the dining room and kitchen. You've come to the right place." The long face took satisfaction in the small moment of power. Watching, Tierney didn't have a good feeling about this Mr. Whidby. But Anne had showed herself capable of looking after herself back in Binkiebrae, and she could do it again, though Tierney hoped it wouldn't be necessary.

Mr. Whidby, as many others had done before him, was now assessing sweet Anne with half-closed lids. He obviously liked what he saw, which had nothing whatsoever to do with her ability to work.

"Ah, unfortunately," Mr. Whidby said, and he did indeed seem sorry, "there is no opening at the present time in the dining room."

Tierney's heart plummeted; Anne actually seemed relieved, in spite of her pressing need to get settled with a job.

"But—" Mr. Whidby continued, clearing his throat and twiddling with a pencil on the desktop.

Tierney's hopes lifted; Anne's face went still.

"—there is an opening in the kitchen." It was spoken regretfully. "If you'd rather wait," he added, looking hopeful, "until an opening for a waitress comes along . . . ?"

"Na, na," Anne spoke up quickly. "The kitchen will be fine, jist fine. In fact—"

Tierney was sure Anne was going to say "I prefer it," but Anne seemed to collect herself, stumbled a bit, and finished, "—I'm sure I'm better suited for kitchen work."

"You've had experience, then?" the surprised man asked.

"Well, hasn't every woman?"

"Oh, you mean general kitchen work, like in the home. I'm afraid," Mr. Whidby said somewhat superciliously, "restaurant kitchen work is a good deal different. But," he added, half-closing his eyes and studying Anne again, "you'll catch on quickly, and do very well. I, personally, shall supervise you." And again—that hand rubbing.

Rather than blanching, as Tierney had feared Anne would do, she flushed, and her eyes—those lovely eyes—glittered. Anne was fighting back. Hurray for Anne! Tierney cheered silently. Anne would work at the Madeleine, but Anne would be prepared.

"We'll go back and introduce you to the staff," Mr. Whidby said, rising. "If you wish, you may start right away. Ordinarily you'll work from six to six, or ten to ten. Just now they're preparing for the dinner hour, which will soon be upon us. A train arrives about then, and we usually have an overflow crowd."

Once again the man led the way, down a hall, to the back, and into a large, hot room abustle with activity. At least three women and two girls were busy at tables or bending over one of the three ranges lined up along one wall. A boy was bringing wood from the outside, plunking it down noisily into a wood box. Everyone turned momentarily to stare at the newcomer.

"This is cook," Mr. Whidby said, indicating a red-faced, hefty woman of forty or so. "Mrs. Corcoran. Mrs. Corcoran, this is . . . ah, what did you say your name was, young lady?"

"Anne Fraser."

Mrs. Corcoran reached a sweaty but clean hand toward her new help, and her fleshy face creased in a smile that seemed sincere.

"Welcome aboard," she said. "Glad to have you. Now, that's Maysie, that's Dora, and . . ." Mrs. Corcoran gave up on the

introductions. "Ah, shucks, you'll get acquainted as you work. This, though," and she indicated the merry-faced lad, "is Spalpeen. Not his name, of course—it's unpronounceable, some foreign concoction or other. Spalpeen seems to fit him."

Spalpeen grinned a gap-toothed smile, touched a hand to his forehead, and made a face at Mrs. Corcoran behind her back.

The girls couldn't hide the grins that lit their faces spontaneously.

"What's he up to now?" Mrs. Corcoran asked comfortably, reaching back, taking the towhead by an ear, pulling him toward her. "Your face will freeze that way if you're not careful. More wood, boy," she commanded, "and bring a bushel of potatoes while you're at it, if you've got all that energy to waste, makin' faces an' all."

"Yes, ma'am!" Spalpeen said smartly, and he sidestepped the pudgy hand that reached to smack him lightly.

"Too smart for his own britches," the cook and kitchen queen growled, but happily. "Just off the boat. Like you?"

"I guess ye could say that," Anne answered. "We coom from Sco'land—"

Perhaps it was the "Sco'land," but Mrs. Corcoran rolled her eyes and interjected, "What else! Scotland, of course. We have a Swede, a Hungarian, and a coupla Irish gals here; why not a Scottish lassie?"

Tierney was feeling better and better about leaving Anne at the Madeleine. She had no doubts about Anne's ability to work, and work satisfactorily, and now the work place seemed to be all they could want. Almost . . . almost, one could forget the slit-eyed Mr. Whidby. Surely the redoubtable Mrs. Corcoran would be more than a match for him, particularly here in her own domain.

"Lay aside your shawl, my dear," that round figure of authority was saying, "and we'll give you an apron, a big one that'll about swallow you up but will keep that nice skirt and waist clean. I'd suggest you save it for . . ." Mrs. Corcoran's eyes narrowed as she studied Anne's buxom figure emerging from the wrap's encompassing folds, "for the day you're invited to join the waitresses in the dining room."

Before Tierney turned away, to return to the hostel and a further wait for her phantom employer, she saw Anne settled at a dry sink with a paring knife in her hand and a mountain of potatoes at her elbow. A piece of the first one to be peeled was popped into the pink mouth, and Tierney remembered that neither of them had had any breakfast. Anne would find plenty to nibble on, for fresh bread was being withdrawn from a cavernous oven by one of the workers, and Spalpeen was lugging in a basket of carrots. Even as she watched, Mrs. Corcoran was pouring a cup of coffee, waddling with it to Anne, and settling it beside her. Never mind that Anne would much prefer tea; she was here, in the new land, and its ways would, without a doubt, soon be her ways.

But not completely. With the influx of domestics came their ways, their habits, their practices, their values, to shape and mold the new land into something unique. From the new mix would come—Canadians. Along with the hundreds, yea thousands, of females who would pour in from the British Isles came strong Victorian social values to become established as the norm for prairie society. Tea, coffee—typical of the blend of the new breed being established, rooted and grounded, in the virgin soil of the Northwest Territories.

Hungry herself, with no raw potatoes to munch on, Tierney took a place in the dining room and ordered tea and toast. She longed for a scone and vowed that as soon as she was settled in a kitchen again, those missing treats would be available once more, a breath of home and a satisfaction to a stomach grown flat and a body grown thin on fare to which they were unaccustomed, and to which they had not adjusted.

Always slim, Tierney was now bone-thin, a condition that was obviously unacceptable in the eyes of Mr. Whidby when he approached the table, rubbing his hands, studying her critically.

"Would you be looking for work too, Miss—"

"Caulder. Na . . . no, thank you. I have employment," she answered stiffly, liking neither him nor the rasping sound of his dry hands.

"Ah, well then, I won't put in a good word for you—above stairs. As a maid, you know. We have three dozen rooms here . . . a thriving enterprise." Mr. Whidby, an employee as much as anyone else on the floor, wouldn't be associated with anything second-rate, it was clear.

With a sniff regarding Tierney's reference to her "employment," Mr. Whidby moved on, to rub his hands at the side of a table where three ladies dawdled over pots of tea and their husbands took themselves off to whatever business had brought them here.

Tierney enjoyed her walk back to the hostel; there was no sense in going anywhere else. Though she would have enjoyed acquainting herself with the town and wandering through its marketplace and shops, she had no money to spend. And always on her mind and worrying her considerably—her future.

Where oh where was Mr. Ketchum? Would she, too, have need to find work here in town? It had no appeal for the Binkiebrae girl who saw, looking up, a sky larger and bluer than any she had ever known back home, and which satisfied her homesick soul with its vastness. But, strain her eyes as she might, she could not see, anywhere at all, the hint of a hill or even a bulge that might indicate something other than flat, flat, flat earth. How could a Binkiebrae girl survive without her hills? The flatness of the land, as much as anything else, made Tierney realize just how removed she was from all that was dear and familiar.

Entering the hostel, it took a moment for Tierney's eyes to adjust. When they did, it was to see a tall, thin, kind-eyed, rather pale-faced man rise from a chair in the parlor, to step toward her uncertainly.

"Miss Caulder? I'm Will Ketchum."

18

"Oh!" In spite of the fact that she had been waiting for him, in spite of the long, long trip with this very moment in mind, Tierney was momentarily taken aback.

What had she expected? Some vague notion of a Binkiebrae farmer or fisherman, with high color, sturdy build, rough clothes? Here was a man more like a teacher or a merchant—certainly a gentleman—finely dressed, though simply, with something about him that spoke of "quality" even to the untrained eyes of the Scottish lass.

"Miss Caulder?" the well-modulated, perhaps educated voice, said again.

"Aye. That is, yes," Tierney said, flushing a bit. "And ye are—"

"Will Ketchum, as I said. If I'm not mistaken you have a contract similar to this one." And the man unfolded a paper he had been holding; it did indeed bear the crest of the British Women's Emigration Society.

"Aye, of course."

It was then Tierney glimpsed the small boy standing half concealed by the man, clutching the man's leg and peeping around shyly.

"This," Will Ketchum said, pulling the tot around and forward, keeping his hand on the small shoulder, "is my son, William. We call him Buster."

"How old is he? How old are you, Buster?" Tierney said, speaking directly to the boy who now stood before her bravely. Sturdy, neatly dressed, clean, shining haired, his cap was in his hand in exact imitation of his father.

Shy though he was, he answered properly, "Free. I'm free."

The man didn't seem to consider it necessary to repeat the child's age, correcting his pronunciation. Tierney, somehow, liked that.

"Shall we sit, Miss Caulder?" the man asked, indicating a settee and some rather worn plush chairs. Across the room the clerk, head bent assiduously over his books, took in every word.

"First," Will Ketchum said, "let me apologize for my delay. I started out in plenty of time, but one horse went lame. I finally made arrangements to leave him at a homestead along the way and use one of theirs.

"It's the way of the homesteader," he explained. "I may have opportunity to do the same for him someday, obliging or assisting in some equally important manner. If not for him, there'll be others needing help in one of a hundred ways. Pity the poor settler who lives in total isolation. Our nearest neighbor," he said, after a pause, "is eight miles from us."

He sounded as if Tierney might as well begin her stay among them by understanding the situation. And true enough, it was startling. Even after so long a time and having seen so many lonely homesteads, Tierney was startled to realize, finally, that it was happening to her. She blinked, making an effort to keep her face from any overt sign of dismay. Eight miles! Too far to walk during her few hours off, that's for sure!

Isolation. Again the word, and the reality, raised its head, and it wasn't a pretty one.

"Even so," Will Ketchum said, pursuing the subject rather doggedly, "we manage to get together with other folk for certain occasions. Even now one of our neighbors—if thirteen miles away can be called a neighbor—is with Mrs. Ketchum . . . Lavinia."

"Is Mrs. Ketchum . . . *all right?*" With care and forethought the "a' reet," came out correctly.

Mr. Ketchum hesitated. "Mrs. Ketchum is . . . with child. Yes, she's all right. But there are the chickens—so many chickens; it's a chicken farm, you know—the pigs, a cow to be milked. But even more than those reasons—I don't want her to be alone. Anything can happen, and does, from time to time. It's a fearful thing to be alone and far from help in time of emergency."

The speaker's face was a little grim as if he had specific situations, even tragedies, in mind but, out of thoughtfulness, refrained from speaking of them to the newcomer.

"Like snake bite—" Tierney offered, half-strangled at the very thought of snakes.

"Canada has very few snakes," Will Ketchum reassured her, "and we've seen none as far north as our area. Other than garter snakes, that is."

"North . . . we're not going south from Saskatoon, then?"

"No, we are about thirty miles to the north. In fact, our place borders on the bush. You've heard of Canada's bush, I suppose?"

"Aye." Tierney didn't think it was the time to burst out with, "And it sounds grand tae me! I've had aboot all o' this pancake I can take!"

"I had this opportunity," Will Ketchum was explaining, "to take over a homestead that was going to be left vacant. This family wanted to sell . . . couldn't take the isolation, the work, the emergencies. They lived in a soddy, of course, while they settled in. I guess it was too much for the missus, perhaps for all of them."

"And ye?" Tierney couldn't help but ask, anxiously.

"Oh, we don't live in it, not now. About the first thing I did, as soon as weather permitted, was to build a frame house. Buster here was a baby when we arrived, and the soddy was so crude; I couldn't bear for Lavinia and the child, my son, to live for long like that. One has to admire people who do. Have you ever been inside a soddy, Miss Caulder?"

"Na, na. I dinna have the opportunity."

"You haven't missed anything, that's for sure," Will Ketchum said, and the grimness was obvious now. "But," he continued, "there are many gracious, well-bred women who submit to such an indignity, as Lavinia did, and do it quite willingly, perhaps even cheerfully. However—" Will Ketchum hesitated, then continued, "my wife's health hasn't been quite the same since those months. It was winter and we were so terribly shut in; one could almost say it was traumatic . . . a very trying time. Buster, though," and he smiled down at the rosy child, "survived, and thrived. One in every five children," he added soberly, "doesn't make it. At least those are the statistics I've heard. There are many, many graves dotting the prairies. We've been fortunate—"

Perhaps he noted Tierney's shiver; perhaps his finer instincts told him he'd gone too far. At any rate his face cleared, and he said, more lightly, "We have a substantial home now, Miss Caulder, and that's one of the reasons—that, and my wife's, er, condition—that we need domestic help at this time. We are so grateful you've come. And come such a long way . . . Scotland, I understand. As if I couldn't tell by your accent." And a glimmer of fun touched the finely molded, slender face.

"Aye," Tierney said, nodding. "A toon called Binkiebrae."

"Binkiebrae. As strange on the tongue as some of our names hereabouts: Buffalo Pound, Elbow, with its nearby Eyebrow Lake, and Findlater, to mention a few. Even Saskatoon sounded strange to an Easterner."

"Is that what you were?"

"Mrs. Ketchum and I are from England, originally. At least we were born there and came over with our parents, who settled in Ontario. Eventually," he said a trifle wryly, "we found it too tame, or at least I did. I suppose you'd say I have the heart of an adventurer. It was either Saskatchewan or the Yukon. Lavinia—and I don't blame her—vetoed the Yukon. So here we are."

Master and maid looked at each other companionably. The little give-and-take had done much to allay Tierney's anxieties, and she felt ready to leave when Will Ketchum pulled a watch from his pocket and glanced at it.

"I suppose we better get on our way, Miss Caulder," he said. "It's going to be a long, long day. We'll only make it if we get right on the road and keep at it steadily. At that, it'll be dark when we arrive, even though the days are getting long and dark doesn't really settle until almost 10 o'clock. Later on it'll be close to midnight. Makes for short nights. That's good, I suppose, when one considers the amount of work that has to be done while the weather permits."

That workload, Tierney thought—already a little sympathetic—accounted for the definitely worn look on the man's face, a face that was, she judged, more patrician than common.

Will Ketchum—with a brief acknowledgment of his responsibility for Tierney's hostel bill—paid it, while Tierney went to the room to throw her possessions into her bags. She turned to find him at the door, ready to carry them downstairs and to the wagon.

Following that lean back, shoulders already bowing from heavy work, Tierney realized she was following a total stranger and leaving the only security she knew—the hostel itself, and Anne—with no hesitation.

Anne! Tierney stopped in her tracks. There would be no way of saying a proper good-bye to Annie.

"I'll be jist a minute," she said and turned aside to the desk, where she requested a piece of paper and a pencil. What was there to write except that her employer had come for her, urged getting on the road immediately, and that she must leave Annie to her own devices? She couldn't, Tierney realized with a stab of regret, honestly and comfortingly assure her friend that she was leaving her in the hands of God and would pray for her. *Pearly—where are you when you are needed!*

"Mr. Ketchum has come for me," she scribbled, "and—"

Turning to Will Ketchum, she asked, "Where can my friend write me?"

"Our post office is Fielding—"

"Eight miles from the hoose," Tierney recalled.

"Ten. It's the nearest neighbor who is eight miles from us."

"You won't be gettin' mail verra often then," Tierney said, and she added that important bit of information to her note.

About to leave the only familiarity she knew, Tierney had to restrain herself from reaching to the clerk, gripping him by the hand, and bidding him an emotional farewell. Instead, she folded the note and handed it to him, with no trace of the emotions she was feeling. It would have helped . . . it would have spelled *finis* . . . if Anne had been there and they could have experienced a normal leavetaking.

"Will ye please see that Miss Fraser gets it?" she asked. Then she turned away, closing the hostel door behind her and feeling a loneliness she hadn't known since her good-byes had been said in Binkiebrae.

As soon as she was out of sight the clerk opened the note, read it, refolded it, and went about his day as though Tierney Caulder had come and gone and made no impression on Saskatoon whatsoever.

19

The groaning complaint of the wagon as they rolled out of Saskatoon and headed north sounded final, very final indeed. With every turn of the wheels, the last thing that resembled familiarity was left behind. There was only prairie ahead; prairie, prairie, and more prairie. There was no reality but prairie.

It was a very large wagon. All her life Tierney had been accustomed to conveyances designed for much smaller loads than wheat. Though it was early July and threshing time was a couple of months off, a few ancient kernels danced on the wagon floor in cadence with the jiggle of the rig, in a crazy rhythm all their own.

High above, Tierney was perched on the spring seat, which tended to slant toward the heavier weight of Will Ketchum at her side. Sandwiched between them, looking up occasionally to study her face, was Buster; it was a right squeeze.

"I'd have brought the buggy," Will explained, "which would have been more comfortable, in some ways—except that its seat is even narrower—but it would have meant one of us had to hold Buster. This way, he can get down into the back of the wagon, move around a little from time to time, play with some things we brought along, and lie down and take a nap when he needs to."

Sure enough, there was a small bed of blankets below their feet, and a few toys lay scattered about, doing their share of rattling with the vibration of the rig.

"Then, too," he continued, indicating the boxes in the rear of the wagon bed, "I needed to get certain supplies, and the wagon allowed for that. There are a lot of things we can't get at Fielding. It has a basic general store and of course a post office, but other than that, there's not much. Certainly no luxuries—"

"Luxuries?" Tierney couldn't help but murmur. To a "puir Scottish lassie" it sounded wonderful but too good to be true.

What would be counted luxurious on the frontier? Most anything, Tierney presumed, considering the distance it had to be shipped by train, dragged by Red River Cart, drayed by wagon, hauled in one way or another.

"You wouldn't call them luxuries, in most circumstances, in ordinary times," Will Ketchum explained, while Tierney searched the horizon for some form of life and Buster casually swung his feet back and forth.

"The chocolate creams, first of all," Will Ketchum said, enumerating present luxuries. "Just a little treat for my wife, something she loves and can't buy locally. And washing powder. Ordinarily you wouldn't think of washing powder as a luxury. But here, where most all soaps are made by hand—lye and lard and ashes, not a pleasant mixture to mess with—that case back there of fifty half-pound packages of Roseine Washing Powder will be just as welcome as the five-pound box of chocolates."

"Fifty!" Tierney marveled, at the same time conjuring up the unending wash days they represented. Wash days in which she would play a big part; perhaps, with Mrs. Ketchum not well, the entire part. One thing about wash day on the prairie (in her mind's eye Tierney could envision long lines of clothes flapping briskly in the wind and sun), garments would dry in no time at all. Except in winter . . . what did one do with wet clothes in winter?

Her thoughts were interrupted when Mr. Ketchum moved the reins into one hand, and, with the other, reached into his coat pocket and withdrew a small box.

"Medicines . . . drugs . . . these are things we can't get in Fielding, except perhaps a basic cough syrup. This," and he held up the package, "I was afraid might break back there in the box, rattling around with the other stuff." And sure enough, urging the team into a trot, the boxes shifted and clattered as the wagon increased its bouncing over the grassy clumps of the prairie.

"We are so far from a doctor, you see. With Lavinia's delicate condition, I'm concerned she won't have the proper care. Someone recommended Dr. Barker's Blood Builder. The three B's of birthing a baby." Will Ketchum seemed to have trouble twisting his tongue around the wordy description of the item in his hand. "Have you heard of it?"

"Na, na. But then, everything back home is different. There's muckle . . . much here that's new to me."

"It says here," Will Ketchum flourished the box, "that a few bottles, taken in the spring, will prepare the system to stand the heat and corrupting influence of hot summer days."

"Cor . . . corrupting influence?" Tierney managed. It sounded dreadful.

"And ward off sickness. I admit it seems unbelievable, but modern science is coming up with some great advances. Such as ether, for pain. Would to God it would be available for Lavinia when the child is born."

Will Ketchum spoke with some vehemence, and Tierney felt certain his wife had experienced a difficult birth where Buster was concerned.

"When is the new babby due?"

"In the dead of winter. Probably means getting myself to Saskatoon in a snowstorm, if she's to have a doctor. There's none at Fielding—you haven't officiated at the birth of a baby, have you?"

Will Ketchum's voice quickened with hope. "Ah," he said, deflated when Tierney shook her head, "it was a dim hope.

"Buster was born just before we came, and Lavinia's mother was there, and a midwife too, so we haven't lived through this isolated-birth experience before. But we've lived through two winters on the prairie, and I am, by now, very familiar with them . . ." Will Ketchum's voice faded away, but his tone was grim and his face just as grim.

"This is another reason it will be such a comfort to have you with us." Will turned his gray eyes on Tierney, and they were full of gratitude. "Can you imagine pulling out in a sleigh or cutter, in the dead of winter, roads more than likely snowed in, heading for town, never knowing just when, or if, you'll get back, and leaving a woman in labor, alone?"

No wonder the man wanted medicine to build up his wife, assuring good health for her and the child. Tierney reached for the small box and read aloud from the wrapping, "'Physicians tell us that one in every twenty persons is infected with poisonous microbes.'"

One in twenty—infected. Tierney shuddered, hoping earnestly that she was among the fortunate nineteen.

"It is universally conceded," Will Ketchum said thoughtfully, having just read all about it, "that 75 percent of the diseases with which the human family suffer today are produced by poisonous germs in the blood. If that's so, then this blood-builder might work miracles of a sort. It's to be hoped, anyway. Certainly it's worth the seventy-five cents I paid for it."

"Seventy-five cents!"

"It's a large bottle. It also says that taken in the fall it braces the system to stand the blasts of winter. Spring or fall, it's effective."

"The corrupting influences of hot summer days . . . the blasts of winter." Tierney, bemused by the words and the thought, quoted the nostrum's promise and pledge and wondered why she didn't feel more relieved and encouraged than she did.

The wagon rolled down the road, a road on which the grasses flourished almost as freely as across the unbroken prairie beside and around it, and Tierney, between bounces, tried to concentrate on the miraculous properties of this blood builder and cleanser.

"It says it will cure scrofulia," Tierney reported cautiously, uncertain what scrofulia might be but not liking the sound of it, "and cancer. And rheumatism, especially that arising from mercurial poisoning. It cures eczema and other skin diseases that arise from the impurity of the blood. And nasal catarrh—ol' Fenway, back home in Binkiebrae, could hae used some o' this!—and acne or pimples, chronic ulcers, carbuncles, boils. It is a 'true specific for syphilis'—" Tierney stopped abruptly.

"Well, anyway," she continued faintly, "it's . . . it's a powerful remedy, and listen to this—it says it's 'purely vegetable.' I never knew," she finished thoughtfully, thinking of all the tatties and neeps she had consumed across the years, "that all those healthy things were in vegetables."

Buster, who had been squirming for the past five minutes, obviously wanted down. With one hand his father lowered him from the wagon seat, and the small boy made his tottering way toward the boxes at the rear.

"There are both ginger wafers and lemon wafers back there, and he knows it. Son," Will Ketchum called, twisting on the seat, "see that tin box with the pretty lady on it? Bring that here; Miss Caulder will open it for you. Take some for yourself, Miss Caulder, and hand me two or three, if you please."

Nibbling the crisp, sugared cookies, they jolted along in companionable fashion. Buster, sitting on the wagon bottom, clutching a cookie in one hand and, in the other, a small, wooden toy wagon—much like the one in which they rode—was nodding his head sleepily and seemed destined for a nap, whether he wanted one or not.

"Back to our Fielding store," Will Ketchum said, reverting to their earlier topic of conversation. "We're fortunate to have it, I guess. Other settlers have to go much farther for much less in the way of supplies. Not to mention the post office—what a blessing that is. One disappointment of this trip is that we aren't going by Fielding, and Lavinia will miss having mail from her family.

"Yes, we manage to keep body and soul together, with the flour, sugar, tea, oatmeal, and such as that which the Fielding store carries. When the railroad finally reaches us—right now there's only the main line through to Prince Albert, and it doesn't branch off—we'll be much better fixed. Town should grow, too. In the meantime we make do or get friends to bring things for us when they go to Saskatoon. We simply have to go once in a while, though it ends up being a two-day trip."

Tierney immediately thought of Anne. But would she, a domestic, be given the privilege of taking two days off to go to Saskatoon? She doubted it; Anne would have to survive by herself.

"Did you," Tierney asked, "coom into Saskatoon yesterday?" It would seem so, the amount of shopping he had done.

"Yes, yesterday, late. It's hard, almost impossible, to be at the station exactly when a train arrives—it can be delayed by so many things—and so we didn't make the proper connections with you. I'm sorry about that. Then, I wasn't sure where you'd be, and I knew we couldn't start back until today, so I did the buying. This morning I tried to locate you at the Madeleine, and when you weren't there, checked the hostel. Both are near the railway station and many newcomers or overnighters stay at one or the other."

"An' of course, that's where we were—the hostel." No mention of Pearly and her trek yesterday, much like this one, to an unknown destination. Where was she now? As lost, in the swirling grasses, as a single grasshopper.

"So I concentrated on the supplies. We try to keep a pantry that's well stocked. Some homesteaders," Will flicked the reins on the backs of the plodding team, hurrying their gait, "aren't as blessed as we are—as soon as we got the chicken investment under way, buildings erected, stock in and all, we were productive. Others have to live on little or nothing for a while, until a crop is harvested. Often they make do on what the land has to offer."

"An' that is—"

"Largely rabbits. And *large* rabbits. Even gophers. Not so large maybe but plentiful." Again that flicker of fun in the gray eyes. Tierney had an idea that here would be a man of grace and humor, given a chance. But even now, as short a time as he had been here, the work, the care, and the deprivations—having begun to bow his shoulders—were wearing away his zest for fun and frolic. One didn't laugh at the inconsequential; one didn't cry at the inconsequential, either, Tierney felt quite sure. Did one learn to become stoic? Tierney wondered, and dreaded that it should happen to her.

Buster had conquered his moment of drowsiness and had crawled under their feet, turned, and was facing them. He had resumed his unblinking study of Tierney's face. Finally he asked, "What's your name?"

"I told you her name is Miss Caulder," his father said patiently.

"I mean, her *name* name," the child pursued.

Will Ketchum cocked an eye at Tierney, awaiting an answer.

"My name is Tierney. It was my gran'mither's name an' her gran'mither's name."

"I have a grandmother. Her name is Gramma."

"And does she live with you?"

There was more than casual interest in Tierney's question. She knew so little about the Ketchums. What she had seen thus far, she liked. Would there also be a grandmother or other relatives on the homestead? Perhaps she was trying to stave off the lurking fear of loneliness, or alone-ness, that the very grasses—in their ceaseless, meaningless motion—conjured up.

"My gramma lives in the bush. She does, doesn't she, Daddy?" The gray eyes, so like his father's, swung anxiously from Tierney's face to Will's, seeking confirmation of his brave statement.

"Indeed she does."

Immediately, though her vision was filled with flatness and grass, Tierney's soul was filled with a longing for *bush.* Never having seen it, she yearned for it—shrub, lone tree, berry patch, bracken, something other than grass.

"It's not far—that way," Will Ketchum said, pointing ahead, northward. "We see no sign of it in Fielding and thereabouts, but it's about as close as you can get and not be there. It begins rather suddenly. First there are some miles of scattered growth, then it thickens, and before you know it, you are into the heart of it.

"Saskatchewan—or the area that will soon be termed the province of Saskatchewan—has two major geographic areas: the lakes, streams, and bogs of the north, which some people call the Canadian Shield and is mostly covered with forest, and the plains region, where we are located. These areas are sort of spliced across the middle by the bush, or parkland—"

"Why isna there trees here, then?"

"Drying winds—"

Tierney's hand flew to her cheeks; already it seemed dryer than normal.

"—light rainfall, extremely cold winters—"

Tierney, caught up in the telling, found herself shivering. In the hot morning sun, she shivered.

"—fierce snowstorms late in spring and drought in the summer; those are the reasons. Oh, you'll find water and green growth here and there, in the coulees. We'll stop at one for a rest and a lunch."

"Why," Tierney couldn't help interjecting, "would y' choose the prairie rather than the parkland?" Binkiebrae had not been bush, by any means, but neither had it been flat, stretching, endless. Its braes called to Tierney's homesick heart. *Robbie!* Tierney turned her thoughts quickly from the stab of pain the memories evoked.

"It's a matter of choice, I guess. The prairie is so compelling—accommodating so many people—and is so fertile and productive. In the bush there is all that chopping and removing of trees; even then a farm is riddled with sloughs and such, making the acreage for crops much smaller.

"But that's where Lavinia's folks live—in a place called Bliss."

20

Bliss," Tierney murmured. "It sounds heavenly."

"Not necessarily," the narrator said decidedly. "Bliss isn't a description—except perhaps to a fortunate few who have actually found it there—but simply a name chosen by the first settler, in honor of himself. Furtnagler Bliss, I think he was, and folks didn't want to call the place Furtnagler. Just kidding!" he amended hastily, catching a glimpse of Tierney's astonished face. She'd heard enough strange names here, it seemed, without adding Furtnagler to the list.

Tierney's laugh mingled with the sound—almost under their wheels—of a meadowlark, both carefree . . . for the moment. But winter—what would it bring, for the bird, and for the domestic? The one could leave at will, and would. The other—Tierney sobered, knowing she was bound here by contract and by circumstance.

At least she wouldn't be in a soddy! They were passing the sagging remnants of one, deserted and forsaken, and it looked bleak beyond believing. Accustomed as she was to small crofts, often thatched with straw, still the soddy seemed unbearably crude, a hovel of a place.

"Poor folks. Froze out the first winter, I understand," Will was explaining. "The man tried to get to town for supplies, couldn't make it, turned back, and they nearly starved to death before a chinook, and a reprieve, rescued them. They lit out for civilization—Saskatoon, that is—before winter closed in again."

"Are they doin' a' reet, then?"

"To my knowledge, they are. As many folks leave as stay, it seems, or at least go to town. There they become good Canadians, opening stores, taking jobs at whatever comes along, helping in one way or another to build the nation. Some, a minority, are desperate enough to go back where they came from.

"By the way," he said, as though he hadn't thought to mention it before, "did I tell you I took eggs to town yesterday? We have thousands of chickens, you know, and they are laying well right now. I'm a little foolish, maybe, insisting on a chicken farm, being so far from the railroad; but I'm not the greatest farmer, don't feel drawn to it. We raise enough for our own flour and grain to feed the chickens and animals. I don't count on much of an income from the eggs, just enough to keep us going. What will make us cash money is when it's time to butcher. I like to wait until frost, so they won't spoil before I get them to the depot—send them off in time for the holiday markets. How are you at butchering?"

"Weel, of course I've . . . that is, ducks and geese, and occasionally a hen—" Tierney remembered those offerings brought in by Anne from time to time, and her heart gave a lonely pang.

Will Ketchum grinned. "Don't worry about it. When that time comes, I hire help."

And so the morning passed, Tierney learning about the new land to which she had come and to which she had, willingly and by her own decision, committed herself, Will Ketchum a ready narrator. He seemed to have a balanced opinion: seeing the problems but still enamored of the possibilities.

Noon came and with it a stop at a coulee in order that the horses might be watered and graze on the grasses by the stream that still flowed quite freely in its shady depths. After unhitching the animals, Will removed one of the boxes from the wagon, dug around in it, and handed Tierney a tin cup.

"Here. Get yourself a good drink and give one to Buster. We'll not build a fire and wait for tea, I think. The cool water will be refreshing. As soon as the horses are rested a bit, we'll go on."

He produced a box of crackers and a slab of cheese. "Ever make cheese?" he asked, quirking an eyebrow in Tierney's direction. "Well, you'll learn; Mrs. Ketchum learned and is quite proud of her success."

Other than cheese and crackers, there was only another helping of cookies, the tin box growing lighter by the bite. With the last one, Will turned the box upside down, shook out the last crumbs for the ants, and handed it to his son.

"He's a great gatherer of frogs," he warned. "Sadly, they don't live long when he gets them home, but they're a change from grasshoppers."

"He plays with . . . grasshoppers?"

"Watch." Will waited until an especially fat grasshopper settled on a blade of grass nearby, snatched it up, closed his fist around it, and commanded, "Spit tobacco, spit tobacco, spit!"

He opened his hand; the grasshopper leaped away. In his palm was a brown stain.

"What . . . is . . . that?" Tierney asked in a strained voice.

"Well, it ain't tobacco juice!"

Tierney grimaced, and Will threw back his head and laughed. Buster, watching, laughed, too.

"You do it, Miss Caulder; you do it!" the child demanded.

Tierney cast a desperate look at the father, but Will was blind to her plea. "It won't hurt you," he said. "Kids have been performing this minor miracle as long as kids and grasshoppers have coexisted on the prairie."

At last the ghastly performance was over. Tierney, none the worse for it, felt, actually, a small sense of accomplishment. Certainly she'd never be afraid of grasshoppers again. But she wiped her palm on the grasses on which she was sitting, later washing it thoroughly in the stream, and didn't feel free of grasshopper "spit" until she did so.

Among the green growth at the edge of the stream a certain small plant grew, catching her attention. None taller than a foot in height, amid its grasslike leaves bloomed a small, clustered, blue-violet flower; its six petal-like segments were star-shaped, with yellow centers and sharply pointed tips. It was beautiful in its daintiness. It was brave in its choice of bed, with the intimidating prairie grasses above and all around.

"What are they?" Tierney asked, enthralled.

"Actually they're not grass, though the leaves look grassy, but a member of the iris family," Will explained, taking a handful of them from Buster, who had laid aside his frog tin in favor of other pursuits.

"Put some water in your cup, son," Will suggested, "and we'll take the flowers home to Mama. They might live," he said in an aside to Tierney, "and they might not. But, fresh or wilted, Lavinia will appreciate the effort. She loves beauty." A spasm crossed his face, a face unremarkable except for its unremarkableness. "And she loves coulees . . . we visit them far too infrequently. Sometimes she goes with me when I go for wood, or, in earlier days, water. Though we've got a well now and water is sufficient for the first time since we came, we used to take barrels to the nearest coulee, fill them, lug them home—for drinking, washing, everything."

Comfortable they might now be, Tierney realized, but the Ketchums had paid a price not figured in dollars and cents. First the soddy . . . then the lack of water . . . whatever else they had been called upon to endure. Tierney was devoutly glad that it was in the past and she would reap the benefits of their sacrifices.

"Now this," Will said, pointing to a foot-high plant with a lovely greenish shaft of small, spiky flowers, "if I'm not mistaken, is camas. See," he said, pulling one, "it has a bulbous root. People who don't know, sometimes mistake it for the prairie onion and eat it to their own harm. It's definitely poisononous. But," he thrust the bulb near Tierney's face, "it doesn't smell like an onion. That's the clue."

"I'm sure I shan't be eating prairie onions," Tierney said decidedly. "Or . . . will I?"

Will gave a shout of laughter. The little side trip down into the depths of the coulee was good for him; he seemed to have left his troubles above, on the prairie.

"You never can tell," he warned. "Now this looks like the coneflower. The Indians make great use of many of these plants . . . they make a tea from the leaves and centers of the flower of this particular one.

"Well, enough nature study," he said, rising from his knees in the grassy growth. "Actually, I've imparted to you just about all I know; it's too late in the season for buttercups and too early for goldenrod."

It was just a matter of minutes on Will's part to hitch the horses, while Tierney gathered up the remnants of their lunch, packed the box and put it in the wagon, and rounded up the reluctant Buster with his tin of frogs and his cup of flowers. Climbing in, she clung to the seat while Will maneuvered the wagon up the steep bank, away from the small "oasis" and up onto the windswept "desert" again.

But it was no desert. Southeastern Saskatchewan and Alberta did indeed have their semiarid areas and were dominated by short grasses and sages, their shallow, spreading roots readily absorbing the little rainfall and their small leaves helping to conserve moisture despite the scorching sun and drying winds. But here, as in most of Canada's grassland, rainfall, though light, was not insignificant, and the grass grew to about four feet.

Tierney looked at Buster, intent on play in the bottom of the wagon, and shuddered, realizing his small stature would be completely enveloped by grass if he should roam away. Once surrounded by grass, losing all sense of direction, what hope was there? More than one story of lost children had seeped out to sober prospective settlers; only the desperation of their situation drove them to come ahead anyway, no matter the cost, taking a chance on the very lives of their little ones. The grasses in summer, the blizzards in winter—it was a fearsome place, especially for children who might be lost in them forever.

The prairie was demanding too much of her attention! But what else was there? For miles and miles, in all directions, it stretched, even, it seemed, to infinity. What a relief it was, almost a hysterical relief, to see another wagon approaching. Tierney watched it come as one would watch for Christmas or for the dawn, her attention focused solely on it until it pulled up alongside.

"Hello there," the unknown driver called, having first hollered, "Whoa!" To have passed without stopping and drawing together in some sort of camaraderie was unthinkable; Tierney could see that.

"Hello, yourself," Will called jovially. "Name's Will Ketchum, from over Fielding way."

"Oh yes, I've heard of you. Chickens, right?"

"Right. Just took a batch of eggs to town. This here," he indicated Tierney, "is our new help—Tierney Caulder, from Scotland. Back there is my son, Buster."

"How do you do, ma'am," the hat came off, and the man, though seated, actually managed a bow. "Dilbert Short here. These creatures in the back"—three pairs of eyes in three blond heads were peering with interest over the side of the wagon—"are the D, E, and F of our family—Damon, Ellery, and Florence. The A, B, C's are home working under the supervision of the wife. These'uns need to have some shoes or they'll be using their feet as snowshoes come winter. Too bad kids couldn't have feet like rabbits! I'm taking a calf to pay for 'em."

Sure enough, tied to the back of the rig was a brown-and-white yearling, dusty and weary, but game. Even as they watched, it dipped its muzzle into the growth at its feet and tore up and began chewing a mouthful of grass.

Buster, standing on a box in order to peer over their own wagon, was saying nothing but was holding aloft, in one hand, a thrashing frog. The eyes of the three in the Short wagon grew as large as saucers.

"Got 'im at the coulee," Buster managed, shyly but proudly.

"Can we stop there, Dad; can we?" D, E, and F chorused.

"Plan to," the father said, without turning around. Then, addressing Will, he remarked, "Say, I'd like to come over sometime when work is scarce—ha ha—and see your operation."

"Glad to have you. I think you are south of Fielding? Come on through Fielding, about ten miles to the north . . . anyone in town can tell you."

Reluctant farewells were said on both sides; duty called, and there was no time in the middle of the day for the finer facets of life, earnestly though they beckoned the lonely in heart.

"Short," Will Ketchum said, as they lumbered on. "Dilbert Short. Good man, I've heard. Too bad there isn't time for socializing. It's one of the hardest prices we pay."

And so saying, leaving a nostalgic trace in the air as they went, they proceeded homeward. Buster went to sleep on the floor of the wagon, the loosed frogs hopping around him until they too became sluggish from the afternoon heat. Tierney's head drooped, and she dozed fitfully on the wagon seat, waking once to find her head resting on the shoulder of the uncomplaining man at her side. Apologies seemed unnecessary; explanations were not needed.

If truth were told, Will himself might have dozed off without any problem. Unless, of course, there came a branching of the dim trail they followed, and the beasts took it, leading off into unknown and frightening emptiness. As it was, the team trudged on doggedly, and the reins lay slack in Will's hand, and he too found his head nodding from time to time.

There was something about creatures that honed in on the familiar; lost in a blizzard, horses had, at times, taken a snow-blinded driver home as straight as an arrow.

Even Tierney recognized the increased measure to the horses' gait; even she could see their pricked ears. She looked inquiringly at Will.

"Home," Will said briefly. "Just over the rise. And the horses know it."

I wonder, thought Tierney, *if his heart and breath quicken as the horses' do?* Certainly the man straightened his shoulders, ran a

weary hand over his face, and seemed to be more alert than he had been.

"Almost home, Buster," he said, and the child roused himself, to rise and cling to the edge of the wagon box, anticipating home and Mother and the end of the trip.

The supper hour was over and the shadows of the day were growing long when, over the horizon, Tierney could see the tip of the windmill. Next, not far from it, came the outline of a tall, narrow building—the house Will and his wife had erected, allowing them to move out of the soddy at last. Around and behind it were grouped what seemed to be several small buildings, granaries, perhaps, or storage sheds, and a barn that was, in spite of all improvements, made of sod. Finally she located the long, shedlike building that she presumed housed the "thousands" of chickens.

As they pulled into the yard, a low cacophony of sound could be heard, unrelenting, unchanging, that she figured out was the sound of a thousand and more chickens conversing with one another or perhaps lifting their complaints to the sky. That it was muted, she was to understand later, was due to the lateness of the day and the fact that common sense—if chickens had such—and more likely Mother Nature herself, alerted them to the futility of their loquaciousness.

With a bang that carried to them as they turned in at the gate, the screen door closed behind the form of Lavinia Ketchum. She stepped to the edge of the stoop at the back door of the house and shaded her eyes against the sun's final rays.

In spite of the smile that lit her face and the small, tentative wave with which she welcomed them, Will, in an undertone, almost as if he was speaking to himself, muttered, "Something's wrong."

The Lord certainly knew what He was doing when He substituted Pearly for Anne at the Schmidt farm. And not entirely for Anne's sake, who so dreaded being placed where there was an unknown, suspicious-appearing man. The elderly Franz she was prepared—grudgingly, it's true—to accept, but the sturdy, manly form of his grandson—never!

How auspicious then, that the very person Anne looked on with apprehension, Pearly found so satisfactory.

Jolting across the prairie, a sapling at the side of the massive trunk that was Frank Schmidt, Pearly's overflowing heart poured out, the entire trip, in paeans of joy. Everything, it seemed, pleased her.

"Oh, look!" she exclaimed when a hawk soared overhead, when a patch of prairie flowers appeared, when the wind blew the grasses in a magical display of syncopation and synchronization, back and forth, silently, as though swept by a Master's hand. She sang it when a covey of prairie chickens flew up, almost from under the team's hooves. She warbled it when the sun, sinking at last, wrapped itself in folds of pink and silver and rested there on the horizon a while.

"Oh, listen!" she exclaimed when a lark sang, when, at a coulee at lunchtime, a frog croaked unmusically and bees hummed over a bed of blue-eyed grass flourishing daintily at the stream's edge. She trilled it when, not far from the road, a ground squirrel chattered shrilly, accompanied by a sharp jerk of its tail, and slipped into its burrow.

The stolid, stoic Frank was bemused by her life and liveliness. She was the perfect match for his matter-of-fact, ponderous mind and body. Frank thought slow . . . he moved slow.

Pearly, in turn, was captured by that very deliberateness. While she had a lifetime of uncertainties behind her, he seemed to typify reliability, good substantial values—and, best of all!—staunch Christian virtues.

Hardly able to believe it, at one point she rejoiced, apropos of nothing except perhaps that a four-legged creature—"gopher," Frank said—scuttled across the road in front of the rig: "Praise God, from whom all blessings flow; praise Him, all creatures here below!"

Immediately Frank responded with, "Praise Him above, ye heavenly host; praise Father, Son, and Holy Ghost!"

It was truly a litany of praise, lifting out over the silence of the prairie as sweetly as though a mighty choir had sung the ancient doxology.

Pearly's heart within her filled with an exultation over and above that of worship of her Lord. There was an acknowledging of the kindred spirit sitting next to her and a swelling of joy at the revelation. So certain was she, that she never doubted for one minute but what Frank recognized it, as she did.

At the realization of what was unfolding itself between them—as a flower, unresisting to the tug of the sun, uncurls itself fully to scatter its fragrance abroad—so the hearts of Frank Schmidt and Pearly Chapel opened at that moment.

Pearly's great pansy-purple eyes swung in wonder toward the light-hued but earnest gaze of the young man, now looking at

her with astonishment mingled with awareness. Unlearned in the ways of love as they were, simple as they were in all things, and innocent, it never occurred to either of them that anything might be improper, or that it was too soon, or that anyone—man on earth or God above—wouldn't approve.

Never a word was spoken. But Frank's hamlike hand reached spontaneously toward Pearly, and her small hand, not yet free of calluses, slipped happily into it.

And so they jounced and bounced over the prairie, homeward, as certain of their future as though it had been spelled out in frothy clouds in the vast blue sky above them. And, who knows, perhaps it had. Certainly heaven seemed to smile on them, the earth around them reflected only bounty and blessing, and the very breeze was pungent with promise.

And when, toward the end of the afternoon, the rig pulled into the grandparents' yard and Franz and Gussie came out to greet the newcomer, they saw a wisp of a girl, all hair and eyes, step down and turn toward them with a smile that superceded the written contract. In that moment the barrier of hired and hirer was erased.

"T'ank Gott!" Gussie whispered, all her fears laid to rest, all her hesitations settled over having a stranger in the house, an unmarried female around the bachelor grandson who was the apple of her eye and heir to the spreading Franz homestead.

There was no hesitation: Gussie took the London waif in her arms. "Velcome—you iss so velcome, mein liebchen," she said.

Pearly had come home.

She stepped into a simple house, as solid and substantial as its inhabitants. Here the delicious odors of fresh strudel made the ever-hungry Pearly heady with its unspoken welcome—it was so *homey.* Her hand touched the few family treasures scattered around the room, and it was a touch of loving possession. She pulled back the handmade lace curtains and looked out on a yard where trees had been set out and watered faithfully and a garden flourished under the prairie sun and rain, and felt the satisfaction of a home-owner.

And when she was escorted to the room that would be hers, and hers alone—a first for Pearly Gates Chapel—she burst into tears. But they were tears of pure joy. Frank, behind her and carrying her shabby bag, set the load down and, without a word, took Pearly into the shelter of his arms, patting her until her sobs abated. They were the happiest tears he had ever seen; they were the happiest sobs.

"Gott," the little mimic said through her tears, never realizing she was already adapting Schmidt ways and the Schmidt accent into her love- and family-hungry self, "iss so good."

Anne's tears were of another nature entirely.

She had come back to the hostel, after seven solid hours of work—she had started three hours late—to fold herself onto the bed and realize she was alone, tired, and afraid.

But she wasn't hungry. There was food, and in abundance, for the kitchen help at the Madeleine. And, to be fair, hard and steadily though she had worked, there had come a time when Mrs. Corcoran had put her hand on Anne's shoulder, turned her from the dry sink where she was still bent over what seemed to be an unending supply of vegetables, and said, "Come now, stop a while, dearie. It's time we all put our feet up and had a bite to eat."

Whether Mr. Whidby approved, or even knew, the kitchen crew ate exactly what the paying guests ate. "The workman is worthy of his hire," Mrs. Corcoran declared, and who among them, even Mr. Whidby, dared argue. Mrs. Corcoran did such a superb job, had so many admiring and satisfied customers, that no one interfered with her performance.

"Stick with me, dearie," she said to Anne, "an' you'll learn how to become a A-one cook one of these days."

Thereafter Anne had watched in fascination as Mrs. Corcoran had prepared, for certain customers, venison, elk, and even a bear steak. Pies, pies, and more pies were forthcoming—apple pies, gooseberry pies, lemon pies, even something called Saskatoon pies.

"Named for the town, or the town named for them?" Anne asked, wishing to sink her teeth into a decent scone or oatcake.

"It's like the chicken or the egg—nobody knows which came first," Mrs. Corcoran said comfortably, holding aloft a generous pie with one hand and turning it, and slicing off the extra dough with the other.

"Now I take this extra dough," she continued, setting the pie aside, "and roll it out, sprinkle it with sugar," and she suited action to words, "then roll it up, slice it into little rolls, and bake them. They are tasty snacks for the cook—the workman is worthy, remember—also, you can tell, from these little samples, before ever you serve the pie, if the dough is going to be good and flaky, or heavy and tough."

Mrs. Corcoran's pies were never tough. Neither were her buns, which were the result of pinching off portions of a rich dough, shaping them into tiny "loaves," and baking them, supplying individual, separate servings, crusty and tasty, to the diner rather than sliced bread. These farmers, Anne discovered, downed more bread than she would have thought possible. Some sopped up their gravy with it, many ate it with jam or syrup smeared generously all over it, some ate it with pudding, others even ate it with pie! Children, she was told, if hungry aside from meal times, sat down to a bowl of bread and milk sprinkled with a little sugar—if they were fortunate enough to have sugar—and perhaps a little cinnamon. What's more, they were happy with it.

No wonder, Anne thought with astonishment, they grew so much wheat! As for oats, the grain of her country, aside from the ubiquitous porridge for breakfast, it didn't seem to be much in evidence.

After a hearty supper of roast beef, mashed potatoes, and carrots (those she had spent most of the day peeling), something called cabbage slaw, some of Mrs. Corcoran's fluffy buns, and a piece of her delectable lemon pie, Anne was dismissed for the day.

"You've done enough for the first day," Mrs. Corcoran said kindly. "And enough for me to tell you'll work out just fine. Now scoot on home, wherever that is—the hostel, you say?—and take care of getting settled for the duration, for we'll be countin' on you. Be here at ten tomorrow and plan on working twelve hours—that's a normal day. You'll skip the breakfast hour and work through the supper hour. Sometimes it will be the other way 'round. Got it?"

Anne, weary, her back breaking, "got it" and was only half-satisfied. Would working on the Schmidt farm have been better, after all? Then she remembered again the ever-so-masculine form of Mr. Frank Schmidt and her aversion to men in general, and she felt she had made the only choice possible.

How was Pearly, poor chick, faring? Somehow Anne had the idea Pearly had been happy, even eager, to make the switch, riding off into the unknown expanse of the prairie with that . . . that *male.* As for Tierney, Anne hadn't seen her all day, and wondered what was happening with her.

She soon found out. Arriving at the hostel, she was stopped by the clerk and handed a note. Mystified, Anne went to her room—which was ominously empty—shut and locked the door, took off her shoes, lay back on the bed, propped herself up on a pillow, and opened the note, which was, she realized, in Tierney's handwriting.

Perhaps Tierney, too, had found a job and was at work. Then the emptiness of the room struck her. Not only were Pearly's things gone but Tierney's also. Heart thumping, Anne read what was, after all, but a brief scrawl:

Annie, I'm writing because Mr. Ketchum showed up (and his little son with him, so don't worry none) right after you left, and I'm going to my placement. Write me at Fielding, but remember that mail is not picked up very often, for I will

be ten miles from town. I pray [Tierney had scratched out the "pray" and added "hope"] *you'll be all right.*
Lovingly, Tierney

Weary, homesick, lonely, it was then Anne pulled a quilt over herself, curled into a ball, and cried herself to sleep.

22

What is it?" Will Ketchum asked, even before he embraced his wife. "Something's wrong, isn't it?"

"It could have been worse—"

"What is it, Lavinia!"

"The chickens—"

"What about the chickens?" Her husband was too impatient, perhaps, but it was their livelihood.

"Give me a chance, Will. Lemuel . . . well, Lemuel left the doors to one of the pens open, and some of the chickens got out."

Will Ketchum smacked his forehead with the palm of his hand. "That lackwit! I was afraid he would do something dumb when I hired him. But it's not easy finding one lone man, willing to work for little or nothing, and do it away out here. Where is he?"

"Well, that's the rest of it. He was scared, I guess. He quit and took off."

"Leaving me with no help whatsoever. What am I going to do? If I'd only known when I was in town!"

The eyes of husband and wife, after one brief pause, swung to Tierney. Still on the wagon seat, she was aware her mouth had dropped open and closed it quickly.

"I'll help," she said weakly, picturing herself thrashing through the grasses in search of escaping chickens.

"How long ago was this?" Will asked as he turned to help his son out of the wagon, then reached a hand toward Tierney.

Stepping out backward onto the wheel, reaching a foot for the hub, then jumping to the ground, Tierney sighed to note her dingy "outfit"—the serge skirt dust-covered, the white waist soiled—and was certain her face showed the same wear and tear. What a way to greet Mrs. Ketchum, who stood, neat as a pin in her calico dress and bib apron, on the kitchen stoop.

Several years older than Tierney, Lavinia Ketchum was as unremarkable, in a feminine way, as her husband. But she conveyed, somehow, the same strength of spirit that Tierney had discerned about her husband. Here was a pair who were, she was certain, the salt of the earth, though never considered diamonds, especially not diamonds in the rough.

Therefore she was not surprised when Lavinia said calmly to Will, "Come on in, wash, and have your supper, and you'll handle things better." Then she turned her attention to Tierney.

"Welcome, Miss Caulder. I'm sorry to have introduced you to our farm in the way that I did, but Will, here, understands me well, and had guessed that something had gone awry. Perhaps he expected it. Did you, Will?"

"I don't know about that," he answered, preparing to remove the gate from the rear of the wagon and retrieve the items he had purchased, as well as Tierney's things. "I suppose I've been a little suspicious of that Lemuel . . . he was too footloose. I wondered what he was doing way out here on the prairie, looking for work in a little burg like Fielding. He seemed shifty-eyed—"

"Come now, Will, you're dredging up things you didn't see before. You needed help; he needed work. It's about as simple as that. Anyway, he's gone. Supper's waiting. It'll be served up by the time you get the team cared for."

Buster was in his mother's arms, his tired head on her shoulder, as they turned toward the house, entering, as in all farm homes, through the kitchen.

The house, which Tierney had studied as they approached it, was tall and narrow, jutting up on the landscape like a sore thumb. Still, it wasn't a soddy, though she could see one nearby, obviously in use for one thing or another, perhaps as the domicile of the missing rascally Lemuel.

"Miss Caulder," Lavinia Ketchum said, "your room is at the head of the stairs. There are only two rooms up there, and you'll see that one of them is Buster's. He's been down here, with us, until now. It's a good time to make the change, while you're here, and before the new baby comes. Why don't you go on up, wash if you wish, then come on down, and supper will be ready. I'll feed Buster, if he'll eat, and Will can carry him up; he'll hardly know he's in a new bed, he's so worn out."

Tierney did as instructed, carrying with her the bag that contained what she would need to tidy her hair. Her own room for the first time in her life! A small room, simply furnished but clean, with a white coverlet on the bed and a colorful rag rug in front of it. Besides a dresser, there was a small table and one chair, and Tierney could picture herself writing to Annie this very night before crawling into that downy bed and dropping off to a much-needed sleep.

Will was drying his hands and face at the washstand when Tierney came into the kitchen again, and he was saying, "I see a few of them scrabbling around in the dust outside the run. All of them in that pen have probably been out, but some of them have gone back in, now that it's getting dark. I'm leaving the door open, hoping others will join them. I think there were a hundred or so in that pen, and there are fifteen in there now. Before I go to bed I'll go out and close the door. Those that are still out, we'll try and round up in the morning."

"It could have been worse, Will," Lavinia was saying as she filled a gravy boat.

The supper—fried chicken, of course—plentiful and tasty, was served at one end of a kitchen that was nothing more nor less than a lean-to on the side of the house. The main floor seemed to consist of two rooms, like the upstairs, probably the "living" room, and the parents' bedroom. Most of the living, however, would be done in the roomy kitchen.

Supper over, Will carried the sleeping Buster upstairs, followed by Lavinia. Tierney, very naturally, cleared the table, located the dishpans and soap, and found, to her surprise, that a pipe had been run into the house from the tank at the side of the windmill. Cold, ice cold, but the water in the kettle was hot, and Tierney soon had the dishes soaking and, weary though she was, took satisfaction in the familiar task. Worldwide, she realized—and found the thought a good one—women were washing their family's supper dishes—except in China, where they were washing the breakfast bowls, she supposed.

Before she was finished with the cleanup Lavinia had returned, showed Tierney how and where to put the remains of their supper, talked to her about rising time and breakfast, and explained what her duties would be—household tasks almost entirely, with some garden work, and sharing the care of Buster.

"That's it, more or less," Lavinia said, adding ruefully, "as you can tell, there is an emergency with the chickens, and that's the way schedules can change from hour to hour. I won't be much help where the chickens are concerned, I'm afraid—all that leaping around, grabbing, wrestling with the creatures." She indicated the small bulge below her apron.

"And anyway," she added, "one of us will always have to keep an eye on Buster. He's been warned many times about wandering away, and, as you notice, we have the grass cut way back in order to give us a good-sized clearing . . . but it's always a danger." Her eyes looked haunted as she spoke, as if the idea of her child lost in the grass was ever with her.

"But back to the chickens. You'll be needed, with Lemuel gone, to help round up what can be salvaged. Chickens are quite domesticated, it seems to me, and are drawn back to their pen oftentimes.

Still, some will have wandered into the grass, looking for bugs and so on, and may never be found." She sighed. "The situation could have been much worse, of course, and so we're grateful for small blessings. Now," she added, "tell me about yourself. Did you, for instance, come over by yourself? And do you have family for whom you'll be lonesome? We want you to feel at home with us, Miss Caulder, if you can."

Tierney took the straight-backed chair at the side of the table beside Lavinia Ketchum, feeling greatly relieved of the burden of strangeness she had been prepared to feel in such a lonely, out-of-the-way place. But she already realized that she would be busy, that Mr. and Mrs. Ketchum were not ogres, that the home was pleasant, the child lovable. What more could she want?

Robbie! The name sang in her heart, but like a dirge. The busier she would be, the better!

"My best friend came with me. Happily for both of us she has work in Saskatoon, not all that far away I realize, now that I've had a chance to see distances here—"

"We'll see to it that you get to Saskatoon once in a while," Lavinia said kindly, and Tierney's heart, broken and longing for Robbie a moment ago, filled with gratitude for this small thoughtfulness.

"But first," Tierney said, "willna ye call me by my name—Tierney? I'm nae used to bein' called Miss Caulder and have nae desire to get used to it."

Lavinia—features perfect as to size and shape yet missing beauty and individuality—smiled, and her face lit up. Her beauty lay in her kindness; her charm lay in her thoughfulness. "I love your accent, Tierney. Yes, I'll call you that, and thank you for asking it. I'd be pleased if you would call me Lavinia. Do you think the Society would mind? I know one of their rules is that we call you 'Miss Caulder'—did you understand that?"

"Aye, but I dinna know why."

"I think it has to do with allowing you your dignity."

"I dinna feel all that dignified." Tierney looked down at her skirt and waist and grimaced.

"Please round up what you need to have laundered, Miss . . . Tierney. There's no reason we can't take time tomorrow to freshen up all your things. Schedules aren't sacred around here, as I have already mentioned."

And so the two young women enjoyed a few minutes of pleasant talk. Tierney's lonely heart drank it in, and she felt assured that Lavinia Ketchum enjoyed it also. To think she, Tierney, had arrived to find—not only suitable work—but a friend. Or so it seemed at this juncture. Tierney wisely decided to retain some "dignity" after all and keep ever in mind that she was the domestic here, Lavinia was the homeowner's wife.

And so she became Tierney, as at home, and Mrs. Ketchum, soon to establish herself as a friend, became Lavinia. Tierney's newfound sense of the proper, however, demanded of her that she confer on Will Ketchum the title of Mr. Ketchum, and he, though he soon called her Tierney, did not persuade her to change.

Tierney's sleep was deep; she had come so far, and now something in her realized it was the end of the road and allowed her exhausted, anxious inner self to relax, perhaps for the first time since leaving Binkiebrae. The letter to Annie had been postponed.

Morning brought the usual breakfast preparations. Breaking fast was the same everywhere, only the food itself changed. But not much. Here, as in Scotland, there was a porridge of oatmeal. But here, as not often at home, milk was plentiful, even creamy, and toast was of bread, not oatcakes. And instead of tea—coffee. Tierney gallantly downed a cup but refused a second. With more of the cream and a teaspoon of sugar, it wasn't so bad, at that.

Her cotton dress was fairly new, having been made shortly before she left Scotland, but it was sadly wrinkled. Nevertheless Tierney took comfort in the fact that it was clean. And it was entirely suitable for the first call of duty—a chicken hunt.

Will handed her a gunny sack and tried to give her instructions. "I don't know how to tell you to catch a chicken . . . there's never been lessons in chicken catching, I guess. You just do what you have to do—chase them down, grab them, put them in the bag. If you have any luck and the bag gets heavy to lug, come on back and empty it in the pen." He had already reported that at least thirty chickens were now safe in the pen, which had been closed and latched.

"And be careful," Lavinia warned. "Keep your bearings at all times. If you lose your way, just sit down and wait. We have a bell, and if we think you're in trouble, we'll walk around, ringing it, listening for your holler. I'm sure, though, that you'll have no problem."

"Have you?" Tierney, big-eyed, asked. "Lost your way, I mean."

"Once, just once. I was looking for Buster who was, after all, asleep in the house. But I got panicky, and I guess I'd still be out there wandering around . . . or worse, if Will hadn't devised the bell scheme on the spot, and came clanging loudly after me. I heard, and moved toward the sound as soon as I felt confident I knew where it was coming from. The sky—" Lavinia shuddered slightly, as though recalling the barrenness of her surroundings, surrounded by grass and overhead the endlessness of a brassy sky with nothing recognizable on the skyline, "seems like a big bowl turned upside down over your head sometimes. So remember—the first minute you feel you're in trouble—stop wandering."

Once out of sight, following a couple of chickens that ran squawking before her into the grass at the edge of the clearing, Tierney, already hot, found her skirt a great hindrance as it caught and held in grass, thistles, and other weeds. Cautiously, well-hidden, she reached for the bottom back edge of her skirt, hiked it up between her legs, and tucked it into the belt at her waist. Clad thus in psuedo-pants, she resumed the chase, looking over her shoulder constantly to check on her position.

Perhaps the chickens played out before she did, but she found them, eventually, squatting helplessly, beaks open, and was able to snatch them up and stuff them, wings now flapping and voices raised in outrage, into the sack.

"Bird brains!" she muttered. "Dinna ken what's good for ye!"

The game of "search and snatch" was over before noon. Before returning, Tierney loosed her skirt, let it fall into place, and found herself no more wrinkled than before.

More than half of the lost fowl had been retrieved and dumped, complaining, into the pen. Here they made their immediate way to water and food, and told the others, perhaps, that it was a heartless world out there and advised them to appreciate it when they were well off.

"We're still missing a good half of them," Will said, latching the door for the last time. "I have an idea many of them will survive . . . we'll see them strolling out of the grass from time to time, looking for water. We'll probably catch more as time goes by. But for now, we'll call it a day." And he went his busy way, feeding, watering, cleaning pens. In his overalls and work boots he lost a little of his impeccable persona but not his dignity.

Dinner was at the noon hour, and Lavinia had it ready for them. First, Tierney took a basin of water and retired to her room, there to scrub herself down and cool herself off, noting that already the prairie sun had touched her nose with red and that the back of her neck burned; it would have been much worse if her hair, piled neatly on top of her head to begin with, had not fallen, in her mad dashes after the fleeing hens, to give some protection.

I can see, she thought, *why female settlers always seem to wear sun bonnets . . . perhaps I shall have to devise such a headpiece for the garden and all outside work, if I'm not to turn out as dark as an Indian.*

She'd seen some of these pathetic creatures as she crossed the territories and had sympathy for their nomadic situation, having been deprived, as they had, of their homes and livelihood and dissatisfied with being shunted to certain designated areas. For the first time she felt a sadness regarding the great migration—white man advancing relentlessly, red man pushed inexorably back.

"We'll take time after dinner to rest," Lavinia declared.

"Me too? It's . . . it's a' reet—all right—if you think I should keep on workin'," Tierney offered, well aware of the hours she was supposed to "do her duty."

"Tierney," Lavinia said, "we'll not stick relentlessly by the rules, if you don't mind. We don't expect you to work until the dot of ten, for instance, then quit. There will be days when we'll fold up after supper; there will be days we may sit and sew

together, or read, far into the night. But I assure you, we won't run over your time."

Tierney flushed. "I'm not feart o' that. Na, na, I jist want to do all that I should."

"I'll be free to tell you, all right? I think we shall get along very well, that way. Do you see any problem?"

Tierney shook her head and counted herself blessed. Oh that Pearly could hear how satisfactorily things were turning out for her. Oh that Pearly were here to express to her God Tierney's heartfelt gratitude. In the little Pearly had imparted before she left, she had somehow made it understood that there had to be some kind of reconciliation—was it confession of sins and acceptance of Christ as Savior?—before prayer could be meaningful and satisfactory. What was it Pearly had quoted in defense of her position? "If I regard iniquity in my heart, the Lord will not hear me." But wise, wise Pearly! She had followed this dire prediction closely with the message of hope and restoration she so loved: "If we confess our sins, He is faithful and just to forgive us our sins, and to cleanse us from all unrighteousness."

Impatiently, to drive all such thoughts from her mind, Tierney turned to the remainder of the day and the days following, falling into a pattern of work and rest that she found satisfying. The nights, too, fell into a pattern—drifting off to a much-needed and well-deserved sleep, but with a feeling that she needed to thank someone for the fact that, as Pearly had once maintained would be true, "The lines are fallen unto me in pleasant places."

Pearly nibbled the end of her pencil, staring thoughtfully out of her bedroom window. How to express to her dear friends how contented she was! And how, though they were greatly missed, to tell them that she wouldn't change her present circumstances or associations for anything!

Difficult as it was to tell, Pearly had an idea Tierney and Anne would be happy for her, rejoicing with her in her newfound state of affairs. They might even understand that it couldn't have been otherwise, praying about it as she had all across the ocean and the continent.

Across her line of vision a stalwart Frank moved, intent on lugging pails of water to the young trees that were and would—as the days and months and years came and went—change the landscape and the atmosphere of the Schmidt farmstead. Even to her loving eyes it was obvious that he was not the typical man of grace and elegance portrayed in books and magazines and newspapers as the ultimate in male pulchritude. Yet, to her, he was all he should be, and her heart was engaged, even though the words had not yet been spoken that would make their relationship binding.

Why hurry? Could one hasten the budding of the tree in spring, the hatching of an egg, the flowering of a rose? Only to its hurt, and the assurance that the result would be disastrous. Pearly was convinced that to everything there is a season—"a time to plant, and a time to pluck up . . . a time to weep, and a time to laugh . . . a time to embrace . . . a time to love. . . ." Pearly was convinced there was a God-ordained time to every purpose under the heaven. Such a conviction fostered peace and patience.

By faith Pearly saw her future here on the Schmidt homestead full of satisfaction and purpose, happiness and husband, fulfillment and children.

Her attention, sincere and rapt though it was, was childish enough to be drawn to the cuff of the sleeve on the wrist of the hand holding the pencil. The thrill was only slightly less than the one she felt when Frankie looked up, saw her through the window, and waved. (These were days of thrilling discoveries for Pearly Gates Chapel.)

The dress, one of three patiently and lovingly cut, sewed, and fitted by Gussie Schmidt herself while her "helpmate"—Pearly—put the house in shining order, was far and above all, her favorite of the lot. Not only was it the first, and never to be forgotten for that reason alone, but it was daintily made, with its turned-down collar, neat ruffles around the yoke in front and back and sporting serpentine braid; its skirt was full, with a wide hem; it was lined to the waist and girdle yoked in front. The color—oh joy of joys—was a sweet blue with small roses liberally sprinkled across its generous sweeping skirt and fitted bodice.

Pearly couldn't remember ever having had a new dress in her life. Her mum had frequented the secondhand dealers who sat in dark basements, sorting through bags of rags and castoffs, offering anything useable for sale for a few pennies. Whatever fit each

child of the large family was allotted to that one and always passed on when outgrown.

Dear Teerney and Ann—Pearly watched the ruffled cuff as it moved across the paper, and almost lost her place, so entranced was she with its beauty—*I am fine. How are . . .* Pearly paused. Spelling by sound dictated that "you" should be spelled "u," but she felt it was not quite right—*ewe?*

Pearly felt she had made a good start and was satisfied with it. Now, more laboriously, she continued, first licking the lead again in what seemed to her a businesslike manner:

The Schmidts made me welcum and I like it here very much. The work is not to hard. I have 3 new dresses, one with roses on it, one with stripes, and one with poka dots. I got yor letter Teerney and the one you sent on from Ann. Im glad she has a job. Yor job sownds good to. No I have not herd anything from my family in London. This is my family now. In Gods time Frank and I will marry. You will be at peece about this if ewe are praying for me as I hope ewe are.

Pearly was incapable of closing the letter without quoting Scripture. After serious thought, she inscribed:

Goodby to my fellow labourers, grace be with ewe. Pearly Chapel.

And though she knew it was a small epistle and not large, she couldn't refrain from adding:

See how large a letter I have written to ewe in mine own hand.

It was the best letter Pearly had ever written. It was her hope that Tierney, having read it, would forward it to Anne, saving her doing it all over again. Once was difficult enough.

Receiving the letter several weeks later, Tierney laughed and wept, missing Pearly but almost seeing her and hearing her London-street accent. She wasn't a bit surprised at the news concerning Frank Schmidt; she had suspected as much when Pearly had so happily and blindly climbed into the wagon with him. And knowing Pearly and her prayers, Tierney had no reason to think Pearly was mistaken.

Pulling an envelope to her, Tierney addressed it to Anne. Before she folded Pearly's letter again and enclosed it, she turned the paper over and wrote:

Dearest Annie, Enclosed you will find the first letter from Pearly. You will appreciate it, as I did, for it seems I can almost see her dear, sweet face and hear her happy voice. Work is going well here, as I have written you before. I wish you felt better about your work, but I am glad you are sharing a room now with Fria. I did like her so much when I met her, and it will keep you from being too lonely. Have you heard anything from home? I expect a letter any day now from James. I've been here 3 months. Can you believe that? Harvest is over, though we don't have a large one. Mr. Ketchum's main crop, he says, is his chickens. The nights are getting very cold here. I understand it could freeze any time. Mr. Ketchum says he may be making one final trip to Saskatoon before winter, and I can come with him. I have a little money now, but don't have any reason to spend much of it, though I do need some overshoes, Lavinia says. Perhaps I will be seeing you one of these days.

Lovingly, Tierney

The following week was a busy one. The weather had indeed turned freezing, and Will Ketchum deemed it high time to butcher his chickens for market. A quick trip to Fielding netted several workers, most of them teenaged boys, some of whom had worked

for Will before and knew the ropes of chicken sticking, bleeding, scalding, plucking, and gutting. Besides the chickens themselves, the feathers—or at least the small ones—would be garnered, packed into gunny sacks, and taken to town along with the frozen carcasses and sold for bedding.

When the job was completed, the chickens stacked in a shed awaiting transporting to the railway, Will announced at the supper table, "Well, girls, either or both of you ready to go to Saskatoon with me?"

He turned to Tierney. "Actually, the railroad is much nearer to us than Saskatoon. I could get my goods on a train about eighteen miles from here, at Hanover—"

"That's where my friend Pearly is! Eighteen miles? Oh—"

"Yes, but I need to come back with supplies for the winter. And if I take the chickens to Saskatoon, it may be I can sell them locally rather than shipping them back east, saving money and time. I did that last year and I think the same sources will buy again. So sorry about your friend Pearly; maybe you can see her another trip. This time it'll be Saskatoon. Now, how about it, ladies?"

Tierney's hopes soared. It had been a long three months without seeing more than a scattering of people who had stopped by. Twice she and Lavinia had taken the buggy and gone to Fielding for certain limited supplies and for the mail, but ordinarily Will went and they stayed home. She awaited Lavinia's response, fearing it would be negative on account of her pregnancy, now greatly advanced. There had been indications that all was not well, and Lavinia spent a great deal of time with her feet up, reading anything that was available, sewing some, sleeping a lot, thanking her lucky stars, she said, that Tierney was there to be a comfort and strength to her as well as carry the bulk of the household chores on her shoulders.

Now Lavinia was positive, though downcast. "I can't possibly go, Will. I can't risk jouncing all that distance over the frozen, rutted prairie. But how I wish I could! It would be such a great change. Next year for sure, though how I'll manage with two children to care for on that long trip, I don't know. I hope and pray," she said, looking at Tierney rather anxiously, "that Tierney is still with us. I'd be lost without her, that's for sure."

Lavinia, knowing the dearth of women in the territories, had threatened Will with blacking and bruising if he dared bring bachelors around the place while Tierney was there. Tierney, pledged to Robbie Dunbar now and forever, cared not a fig whether or not they came, to Lavinia's great relief and Will's disbelief. How any woman could stay true to a memory with flesh and blood suitors pressing their claim diligently, even feverishly, he couldn't see.

"Ye dinna ken Robbie, and ye dinna ken me," Tierney had declared stoutly when the subject came up, and Will respected her enough to leave it at that.

Perhaps because of Tierney's fierce hold on her devotion to someone named Robbie Dunbar, perhaps because she knew and believed in Tierney's trustworthiness, Lavinia had no hesitation in suggesting that Tierney go with Will to Saskatoon.

"After all," she said, "I promised her a trip back to see her friend. If she doesn't go now, she won't get out again until spring. She never has had any decent time off. There's no place to go, after all, and she's just spent a few hours once in a while in her room, resting and writing letters or something like that, poor dear. Yes, I think you should go, Tierney. I'll get along fine. There are no chickens to care for this time, and you'll only be gone for three days. One day going, a day there for business, and another day to return. You can stay with your friend, I'm sure."

"Buster?" Will asked. "Would you like him to go?"

"Not wise," Lavinia said. "It's too cold, for one thing, and you wouldn't know what to do with him the day you hope to transact your business. No; Buster will keep me company and be the man of the house. Right, Buster?"

Buster, thus appealed to, looked uncertain—whether to go, or stay.

"And of course," Lavinia said, "there'll be a present for such a fine young man. Right, Daddy?"

And so it was settled. Lavinia worked on her lists; Tierney worked on her clothes.

"You better take my heavy winter coat," Lavinia said. "It doesn't go around me very well now, anyway. I don't think I'd wear it even if I went some place, which I probably won't. I'll just wrap a horse blanket around me in such a case! I'm about as big as one," she said ruefully.

But it wasn't true. If her due date was the first part of December, as she thought, Lavinia was undersized, or so it seemed to Tierney, who had to admit she knew little or nothing about carrying and birthing babies.

And that worried her too. Who would "officiate" at the birth?

"We have a midwife in Fielding," Lavinia had assured her, "and if she can't make it, Will can take care of me. Can't you, dear?"

Will didn't look much more confident than did Tierney. "Between us," he said, "we'll do fine."

But Tierney wasn't so sure. Prairie blizzards were legendary. But babies were born all around the world and in some mighty out-of-the-way places without doctors or midwives, and had, ever since time began. They knew instinctively how to thrust their way into the world.

And so serious plans were laid for the trip to Saskatoon.

Early in the morning, before the sun was up—it was coming later and slower now—Tierney climbed into the wagon and onto the wagon seat, wearing Lavinia's coat and with a horse blanket wrapped around her dangling legs. Even so, it was nippy, and the tip of her nose was turning red before they were out of the yard.

Lavinia, waving good-bye, looked rather forlorn; but Buster would soon be up for the day and keeping things lively. Then too, their nearest neighbor, though he lived eight miles away, had promised to send his son to care for the milking of the cows and the watering and feeding of the animals. He would check on Lavinia; probably she would have cocoa ready for him and a snack of some kind before he started his trek back across the prairie.

"I hope the weather holds clear," Will said, scanning the wide blue sky rather anxiously. "For Lavinia's sake, even more than ours, I guess. It can change so quickly and with such drastic results. Fortunately we've never been caught out in a true blizzard. But

I've had to struggle back and forth to the barn through them, once for several days before it let up. It's no fun, I tell you for sure."

Colder than this? More wintry? It hardly seemed possible, thought Tierney, pulling a scarf up around her face, shielding herself from the winds that bent the brittle grass, heavily frosted though it was, to the ground. But as the sun came up the earth warmed a little, the wind abated, and she enjoyed the ride and the rest.

It had been a busy summer and fall. Will had brought wild plums from a nearby coulee, and these had been made into jam. There were beans and carrots and peas and tomatoes to can. Soon, she was told, Will would butcher one of the yearlings that had grown fat on the abundant grasses amid which it had been tethered, and she and Lavinia would put much of it up in jars for use next summer when it was impossible to keep meat from spoiling.

Tierney was tired of chickens! They were all tired of chickens! "Bring home a case of canned salmon, please!" Lavinia had implored as she prepared her massive list of needed supplies. With the long winter shutting them in, what they brought home now would probably have to do them until spring came, and the chinooks. This trip was imperative.

It was late afternoon when they reached Saskatoon; after all, they had bucked a considerable wind most of the way. Will deposited Tierney at the hostel and went on, promising to pick her up the day after the next one, early. Accustomed to buying the supplies and knowing how much he had to spend, Will would not need her help for that. Tierney's shopping, what she needed to do for herself, she would do tomorrow while Anne worked.

The clerk remembered her. "Same room," he directed and handed her a key.

Before taking off her coat, Tierney lit a fire in the small heater that had been brought in as soon as the weather turned cold. Annie, she knew, would appreciate the comfort and warmth when she came through the door.

It was almost ten o'clock before the door opened and Anne appeared, in a new coat and gloves and with a bright tam on her

head. Seeing Tierney, a glorious surprise, brightened her weary face dramatically, and before ever her wraps were loosened she flew into her friend's embrace. Soft coos and murmurs of happiness filled the sparsely furnished little room as Tierney and Anne wept a few tears together, laughed at their own silliness, and finally drew apart to wipe their eyes and study each other fixedly.

"You look so good to me!" Anne declared unsteadily.

"You look . . . oh, Annie, you look so tired! Good, of course, but tired."

"I *am* tired. I think I'm always tired. But oh, Tierney, guess what? I'm workin' in the dinin' room. Aye! I'm a waitress; can you believe that? I should have been off at nine, you know, having started at nine, but that's the way it goes—twelve hours we work; only twelve, if we're lucky. Mr. Whidby—"

"Of the rasping, rubbing hands?"

"The same Mr. Whidby. I'm grateful he has given me the chance in the dining room. I was sick and tired of peeling vegetables! And you know what, Tierney? I'm not nearly as afeart of men as I was. Mr. Whidby, laughable though he is and a pest in some ways, has taught me how to stand up to all these farmers and trappers and salesmen who coom through here."

"Oh, Annie, I'm so glad! I hated to see you so scared and intimidated!"

"Men!" Anne sniffed. "They're not as impossible as I thought. You know, Tierney, a lot of their ways are just put on." Anne was removing her wraps as she talked. "They are, mostly, far from home and wife or mither, and they love to tease. I'm learnin' to tease back, or ignore them, or, in some cases slap a hand. In fun, of course," she added quickly, seeing Tierney's shocked face, "and I get away with it!"

"Tha's . . . tha's good, Annie," Tierney said. Annie, slapping a man? If she'd only had some of that spunk where Lucian was concerned. But of course she had! She had fought tooth and nail, like a tiger, and she had kept her virginity no doubt because of it. Yes, Annie had been through the gamut of experiences. But it seemed she was coming out on top, her old self again. It was worth the trip just to find this out, Tierney thought, grateful she could relax her worries over her friend, in one way at least. Now, if she just didn't look so tired. . . .

In spite of her physical weariness, it seemed Anne was doing well. "Look here," she said, reaching a hand into her skirt pocket and producing a handful of change, walking to the dresser, and dropping it into a jar of coins.

"Are those . . ."

"Aye, tips. They call 'em tips, Tierney."

"And what do ye do to get 'em?" Tierney asked a trifle grimly.

Anne's laughter, tired though she was, trilled out blithely. "Naething, ye silly gowk! At least naething but give 'em good service. Oh, Tierney, ye should live in the city . . . weel, town, as I do."

Tierney glanced around the room, barren of anything homey—hosiery drying on a line across the corner; teacups stacked on the small table along with tea, bread, crackers, and a few other items of food; two straight-backed chairs.

"We're goin' to get a couple o' rocking chairs," Anne defended, rightly interpreting her friend's glance. "Wi' the fire lit, and the lamp, and a good book from the library—you would really love the library, Tierney—we are verra comfortable."

But Tierney thought of the Ketchum home, the love and accord there, her own room clean and attractive, the abundant food, the warm fireside, and wouldn't have changed places with Annie for anything.

"Weel, we're each contented then," she said. "An' so, it seems, is our Pearly. An' have ye heard anything from home?"

Anne had not. But there was much to talk about, so much in fact that they forgot about Tierney's supper until Fria came in, bearing a pail of hot soup. Greetings over, "There's plenty of soup for you, too," she said to Tierney.

There was a warm camaraderie around the small heater, Tierney and Fria eating soup and crackers at the table, Anne sitting on the bed nearby, all chattering a mile a minute.

Once again, at bedtime, it was three to a bed. But with the room cooling quickly as the fire was damped and the night wind

howled around, they were grateful for the extra body warmth and soon drifted off to sleep.

The next day, with directions from Anne, Tierney located a shoe store and purchased the overshoes she needed. In fact, she put them on and wore them. The wind was fierce, and her feet were freezing. After that she located a general store where she picked up a few personal items, found a top for Buster, and a book—*Medical Companion and Household Physician*—for Will and Lavinia, who had bemoaned their need of such a treatise several times. It pledged a concise presentation of "The Causes, the Symptoms and Treatment, demonstrating the cure of the various ills humanity is subject to." Following that, Tierney spent a good hour searching for and selecting something for each member of the family for Christmas; she'd not get back to town before then.

Following the "shopping spree," Tierney stopped by the Madeleine and the dining room, as Anne had suggested. At Anne's recommendation she did it in the middle of the afternoon, when business in the dining room was slowest. Anne, having obtained Mr. Whidby's graciously granted permission, took Tierney back to the kitchen and introduced her to the crew there, particularly Mrs. Corcoran and Spalpeen, whose shenanigans filled parts of every letter Anne wrote and kept Tierney amused as well as the hotel staff.

Nothing would do but Mrs. Corcoran, also ready for a break, would serve up—not only a glorious pot of tea, but, when she realized Tierney was staying at the hostel—a great platter of food, roast beef, pickles, cheese, boiled egg, and urged Tierney to "tuck in." And when Tierney left, it was with a package of dessert, doughnuts, tarts, fruit cake, plenty for treats that evening and to take back home to the farm with her.

"What a dear she is," Tierney said to Anne as she slipped on her coat again and prepared to go back to the room.

"I couldna have made it without her, the darlin'," Anne acknowledged. "Now, when ye get there, build up the fire and sit doon and read one o' the books. That'll keep ye goin' until I get back."

Another evening, a few more good laughs, much sharing, a few tears, and it was bedtime and sleep. The following morning, before eyes were hardly open and clothes donned, Will was there, knocking on the door.

"Five minutes," he said cheerily.

The short deadline was a good thing. It allowed for no weeping and few words. With one last hug Tierney was on her way, insisting Annie stay in by the fire, and bustling off with her packages, her overshoes on her feet and a new tight-fitting knitted cap on her head.

If she had thought the wind bitter when they came in, if she had thought the frozen roads rough, if she had supposed things couldn't get any worse, she had a lesson in store for her.

"I don't like this," Will declared, pulling an extra blanket up around his own legs, having first tucked Tierney in. "We better make tracks. Trouble is, the team can only go so fast, given the distance and the weather."

Perched on the wagon seat, the wind whipping around, snatching at the blankets, tossing the team's manes and tails, frosting Will's eyebrows, and in spite of hat and gloves and Lavinia's heavy coat sending shivers up and down her body, Tierney thought of Pearly and her prayers. What a shame that she, Tierney, hadn't been in a position to pray a few words of comfort over Anne when they parted; what a pity that she couldn't whisper a request for mercy as they tussled their way through the wind and the cold.

Perhaps she was too intent on the fact that God wouldn't hear if her heart wasn't right, and not bold enough when it came to her needs in the face of what seemed to be a near state of emergency. Certainly her heart was filled with uneasiness; certainly it was a time to pray, from desperation if not from faith.

She'd give it a try; it couldn't hurt, it might help. Squeezing her eyes shut against the storm, Tierney whispered a prayer that seemed, to her doubting heart, to be caught away in a whisk of wind, never to be heard by man, but perhaps by God, if He were being magnanimous.

24

When they reached the coulee, it promised to be a heart-clutching and body-wrenching experience to descend to the refuge below. But the team needed a rest, and so did the driver, of this Tierney was certain. Will was rigid and frigid, especially his hands, which had been holding the reins all the way and must be numb and stiff.

He drew the team to a halt momentarily and studied the trail down. The ground was frozen solid, lumpy and icy.

"I think," he said to Tierney, "I'll unhitch and lead the horses down. To try and wrestle the wagon down would be disastrous, I'm afraid, and I wonder if we'd ever get back up. Yet the team needs a drink and a rest."

Tierney nodded, peering out of the blanket she had finally pulled up around her, squawlike, for protection.

"I'd suggest you come on down, too," Will said, speaking into the wind. "It won't be easy, but you need the exercise—it'll get the blood flowing good again, and bring more feeling into your arms and, er, lower limbs."

As Will was unhitching the horses, Tierney unwrapped herself and clumsily climbed out of the wagon, realizing it was the height of foolishness to expect Will to be a gentleman under such circumstances and help her down. Just before clambering over the wheel, she thought of food and knew it wasn't likely Will would come back and rummage around for cheese and crackers or whatever.

Remembering the items Mrs. Corcoran had sent along, Tierney located the bag under the seat of the wagon where she had dropped it. She picked it up clumsily, tucked it under her arm, and prepared to climb over the wheel. One leg over the edge of the wagon, the wind found an entrance, and she caught her breath in a gasp as it swept up and under her full skirts, billowing them like a tent and chilling her in an instant. Startled, her gloved hand slipped from its grip, her foot slid off the hub, and she crashed to the ground. But she was down and apparently intact. And that included her dignity, for Will had not seen.

And she had the sack with her. Unfortunately it had opened in the fall and the tarts and doughnuts had scattered out like small wheels rolling across the prairie. And no wonder—they were frozen solid. She gathered them up and thrust them back in the bag, wondering if they could possibly be eaten. Of course she hadn't thought to get a cup or any means by which to get a drink. *Fine pioneer! My first emergency, and I lose my wits! And my balance!*

Stumbling over the broken clods of frozen ground that Will and the team had left behind as they half slid their way down the embankment, Tierney arrived at the bottom, more quickly than she had planned, but again, she was down, and again she was safe.

Sheltered as it was from the wind, still the coulee was cold, and the stream no longer ran, unless it did so under the ice.

Slipping and sliding down the side of the coulee, Will had followed the horses, to indeed find the stream frozen, but not solidly. Stamping and kicking, he broke the crust, and the horses lowered their frosty muzzles into the icy water. When they were finished drinking, he pulled them over to where dried grasses offered some sort of fodder, and they fell to nuzzling and eating.

Huddled under the bare branches of a bush of one sort or another, Tierney opened the sack, removed a doughnut, and passed the sack to Will. His expression as his teeth skidded off his first bite was enough to make her laugh, in spite of wind and weather and miserable circumstances.

Will, too, managed a grin. "I'll just chaw away at it," he decided and suited action to words. Gnawing and chewing, they managed some small sustenance. Will, never mentioning the missing cup, knelt on the frosted ground at the stream's edge, cupped his hand, and drank. Thirsty and having no other choice, Tierney did the same. Her hand tingled with cold and, before she put her glove back on, she slipped her hand inside her coat and into her armpit and shuddered again as another frisson of shivers ran over her.

Not caring to wait too long, the weather being what it was, Will led the horses above as soon as he could, Tierney following, the sack of goodies in one hand as, with the other, she clutched weeds and bushes along the trail to help herself up the bank. Will was, by then, hitching up the team, and Tierney climbed back into the wagon.

"Why don't you sit on the bottom," Will suggested, "instead of the seat? I would do it myself if I could trust the horses to make it home." But the trail over the prairie was indistinct, and there was too much at stake to delay even for a few minutes.

Tierney found a place among the horse blankets and quilts in the bottom of the wagon and hunkered down out of the worst of the wind. But she felt great sympathy for Will as he took his place again, to be battered by the fierce wind, and she watched him bow his head as though struggling through the gale. Ahead of him the horses bent their heads into the harness in much the same fashion and pulled doggedly onward.

It was the middle of the afternoon that the first flakes fell, softly at first, too light and dainty to be dangerous. Or so one would think, catching a single flake on the palm of a dark glove and examining it. But the glove, unwarmed by the hand within, was too cold to melt the unique thing, and one realized its potential for danger. Tierney blew the snowflake away, shivered again, and tucked herself more securely under the blanket. She tried leaning back against the side of the wagon, but the jouncing was terrific as the wagon made its way over a road turned solid, with no give to it whatsoever.

Frightening in their silent purpose the flakes fell. They swirled around the faces of Will and Tierney, they piled on the seat beside Will, on the wagon floor beside Tierney. Soon the road became obliterated and there were no landmarks, insofar as Tierney could see when she peeped over the edge of the wagon, looking with awe at the scene—white as far as the eye could see, and all within an hour of the first flake.

As though reading her thoughts, Will turned his head, and shouted, "Good thing we're as near home as we are. I know right where we are. The nearer we get to Fielding and home the more worn the road is, the deeper the ruts, and the better the horses can see it."

Tierney closed her eyes and thought of Pearly. What would Pearly do in such a circumstance? Pray, of course. Tierney had tried it earlier, but not in such a state of anxiety as now. Perhaps she hadn't been earnest enough before. Most desperately now she attempted it again: *O God of Abraham, Isaac, Jacob, and Pearly, please hear this plea for help and get us home safely!*

After that, jolted continually though she was, she must have dozed, although, to her panic-stricken thinking when she awoke, she feared she might have slipped into the sleep of death that fell on freezing people. But realizing that all her limbs felt the cold and that they moved satisfactorily at her command, she sighed with relief and felt a little foolish. Tierney knew, from conversations with Pearly, that she wasn't ready to meet God.

What would it be like, to face the living God and not have made your peace with Him? It was an uncomfortable thought, prompted by the desperate situation and her realization that it could happen, without warning and without preparation. Her earlier prayer, as with this one, had been one of desperation and not contrition. Did God get impatient with people who cried out to

Him in emergencies and forgot all about Him in better times? These uneasy speculations were interrupted by welcome news:

"Not far now!" Will sang out through frozen lips, and Tierney's thoughts turned with relief to happier things—a fire, a hot cup of tea, a good warm supper.

This time Will helped her down, having clambered out and made his way to the back of the wagon where he removed the tailgate. He began pulling boxes and crates and bags from under the great heap of blankets he had carefully spread over them to keep cans and jars from splitting and cracking. The food items had been warmer than she had, Tierney realized, wishing belatedly that she had crawled under the waterproof tarpaulin that sheltered the entire store of goods.

It was two snow-covered figures who trundled their way, arms laden, across the few feet of ground from the wagon to the porch.

There was no reason to find it ominous when Lavinia didn't come outside to welcome them. Perhaps she hadn't even heard them; the snowfall muffled most sounds. It was a white, silent world. And dark; even the moon and the stars hid themselves on this most stormy of nights. Tierney blessed the team that had, unerringly, trudged them homeward to their warm stalls, good grain, and satisfying currying, when Will would take a gunny sack and sweep them free of the last vestiges of snow still clinging to their broad, steamy backs, and rub and brush them dry.

There was no reason to feel alarm when there were no footsteps across the snow on the porch; it was too newly fallen, too recently come.

But when they stepped inside, to stand momentarily on the mat at the door, it was both ominous and alarming when Lavinia was nowhere to be seen, the house was colder than it ought to have been, and no tea kettle simmered on the stove and no supper.

"What the—?" Will muttered. "Vinnie! Lavinia—!"

It was a sleepy-eyed Buster who greeted them from the doorway to the front room, his hair touseled, clutching his "bankie" to him.

"Mama's sick," he said.

"O God!" Will exclaimed, and it was a prayer. Hastily setting down the box he carried, stamping his feet heavily on the mat, he began unwinding the scarf that obliterated most of his face and pulling off the flap-eared cap from his head. Sitting down, while Tierney stood dumbly by, beginning her own unwrapping, Will pulled off his galoshes, removed his coat on which the snow was quickly turning to water, dropped everything on the linoleum, and fled toward the front room and through it to the bedroom beyond.

Her own things removed at last, Tierney took a moment to hang up the coats and scarves and hats, set the overshoes aside, and then gathered up the bemused Buster in her arms.

"Mama's sick," he repeated. "Did you bring me something?"

What a long and lonely time it must have been for the child, his mother ill, perhaps in bed for goodness knew how long, and the time stretching interminably until his father should come home.

"Of course," Tierney reassured him. "Now first, let's go see if we can be of any help."

Tierney, with Buster by the hand, made her way to the bedroom. How cold it was! Obviously Lavinia hadn't been able to tend the fire. The little hand Tierney clasped was warm, however, as though the child had been cuddled warm and secure under blankets.

Standing in the bedroom door, she could see Will leaning over the bed. Lavinia, white-faced and obviously frightened, was stumblingly explaining.

"It's the baby, Will. Something's wrong. It's far, far too early, and yet . . . and yet I know it's trying to come. Ohhhh, *Will!*" Her explanation turned into a cry as, apparently, another pain struck. Even from the doorway, even through the covers, Tierney could see the turgid belly stiffen and distend.

Will looked around wildly. "My Lord," he said, just as wildly as before, though just as prayerfully, "what'll we do?"

Hesitantly Tierney stepped forward, leaned over, and brushed the damp hair back from Lavinia's forehead. With her eyes fixed on Will she said, just as tensely as he had spoken, "There's no question about going for . . . whoever it is . . . that midwife, I suppose?"

Knowing it was indeed out of the question, she added, hopefully, "Or your neighbor. But," she answered her own question, "she'd be only two miles closer than the woman in Fielding, right?"

Will, swallowing convulsively, nodded dumbly. "I could try—"

Not knowing much about blizzards, still Tierney had experienced enough in the last few hours to say, "It probably isn't a good thing. We—you and I—will have to manage alone—"

It was enough to startle Will into action. "I've got to try," he said, the muscles of his jaw working. "Listen, Lavinia—" he bent toward his panting, sweating wife, "I'm going for help. If I can get to Fielding, I will. Otherwise I'll stop at the Brokaws' and bring Lilyan. Hold on, Sweetheart. Be brave just a little longer."

He might just as well have said "a lot longer," for that's what it proved to be.

A lot longer, and still, when he and Lilyan Brokaw arrived, Lavinia struggled helplessly against the contractions, though weaker and weaker.

Frightened almost out of her wits, Tierney found herself actually wringing her hands as she waited. Her gripping fear was that the child would come with only herself to deliver it. And yet the fact that it didn't seem to budge was just as agonizing.

"Dear God," she whispered, "I can see how selfish and stupid our prayers can be, always telling You what to do, trying to decide for ourselves what's right. It's up to You to sort them out and do what's best for us. But please, please, don't let Lavinia die!"

It was a much-needed prayer, for by the time Will and Lilyan Brokaw arrived, dawn was coloring the sky with pale light and Lavinia was almost past help, having sunk into a state of half-awareness, rousing only to struggle and groan. Even that was becoming less with each futile effort to expel the burden from her body.

"How is she?" Will asked when his wraps had been laid aside and he had approached the bed. Lilyan Brokaw had preceded him, having been busy in the sickroom while Will was unhitching and caring—once again—for the weary team of horses.

Lilyan Brokaw, a hefty woman in her early fifties and the mother of eight, turned from the bed, and said in an aside, "Not good, Mr. Ketchum. Though it's early and the child is small, still there's something wrong. Very wrong."

Lilyan tried, with whatever skills she had, to advance the babe in the womb; Tierney, worn and trembling, turned to the kitchen to build up the fire, boil water, and make tea. Good reviving tea; even it failed in its restorative powers this time. Tierney was terribly afraid.

Creeping back, finally, with a cup of tea for Mrs. Brokaw, it was to hear the neighbor woman say, somberly, "It's never going to come on its own."

Will looked ghastly—worn with his two long trips, his lack of rest, his hunger, and his terror.

"Do *something!*" he pleaded.

Still Lilyan Brokaw hesitated.

But looking at that desperate face, perhaps thinking of the living child asleep now in his own bed upstairs, perhaps moved by the eloquence in Will's eyes, Lilyan Brokaw was moved to try that something, desperate measures indeed for an unskilled person.

"We have to get the child out," she said flatly, "though I've never done it. I had it done to me once, and it . . . well, it worked."

Her voice faded, and it was, in its way, as eloquent as the silent but speaking eyes of the husband on the other side of the bed.

"Bring a pan of hot, soapy water," Lilyan Brokaw said with a sigh, and Tierney did so, along with numerous clean towels.

And then she fled the scene, not needed, and totally unable to bear the screams that ripped through the house from the hoarse throat of the tortured woman as Lilyan Brokaw, stolidly and with dogged resolution, thrust her hand into the birth canal and, by force alone, withdrew the scrap of humanity that was the cause of it all.

Wet, bloody, and motionless it lay, at the last, on the towel Will held out, tremblingly, for the deposit of his second son.

When, ashamed, Tierney crept back, it was to see Will standing alone, his second-born in his arms, his wife unconscious, and Lilyan Brokaw, almost as pale as the patient, going about the job of cleanup. Here Tierney tried to help, bringing fresh water, finding an old sheet to be torn into padding, taking the bloody linen and putting it to soak.

Finally Will handed the dead babe to the reaching arms of Lilyan Brokaw, who took it to the kitchen area to be bathed and dressed in the clothing Tierney located, having helped sew on it across the past months. Finally, Lilyan wrapped the tiny mite in a small blanket, as Tierney stood by, feeling helpless in the face of so great a tragedy.

"Here," she said, feeling that, finally, there was something she could do. "I'll put it in the little crib in their bedroom. I'm sure, once she's . . . alert again, she'll want to see her baby."

But Will was waiting. As soon as he saw Tierney, he rose from his knees at the side of the bed, reaching one last time for his son. How pathetic the sight; how final the good-bye.

Lilyan, who was checking on the swooning Lavinia, said abruptly, "Miss Caulder, take the baby. Will, you need to be here by your wife."

It was difficult to say who was the most startled, Tierney or Will. He handed her the dead child and turned immediately to the bedside.

"What is it?" he asked.

"She hasn't stopped bleeding. It's . . . it's just *flooding* from her. Oh, Will, I'm not capable of the care she needs!" Lilyan, good, helpful neighbor, was in despair.

"Miss Caulder . . . Tierney," she called, "quickly, bring more towels! Lay the baby down and bring more towels!"

There were no more towels. Frightened and trembling, Tierney located what she could—extra sheeting, dish towels, even a thick, woolly blanket. Hurrying back with these it was to find Lilyan and Will lifting the supine Lavinia and shoving the rubberized sheet from the baby's crib under her body. Lilyan took the items Tierney offered and began stacking them also beneath Lavinia and packing them into place on her torn body.

Mesmerized, eyes staring, Tierney could see that it wasn't enough. Before their very eyes, Lavinia Ketchum was bleeding to death.

Will dropped to his knees beside his wife, murmuring her name brokenly, pleading for her to hold on, to stay with him, and, finally, to know that he loved her . . . loved her . . . loved her.

As the packing grew more and more brilliant, Lavinia's face grew more and more colorless. Her very life, it seemed, was flowing from her, collecting in a few towels while her husband pled his case and Tierney and Lilyan stood helplessly by.

Finally, feeling that she was listening in on things too private and personal to be shared, Tierney slipped out of the room. She stood in the kitchen, hands to her temples, weeping uncontrollably. How quickly autumn's glory had fallen prey to winter's invasion; how quickly health and vigor had surrendered to death's cold beckon.

It wasn't long until Lilyan Brokaw followed Tierney to the kitchen, her hands full of towels bearing her neighbor's life's blood, and feeling herself to be the cause of it all.

Lilyan all but collapsed onto a kitchen chair, staring blankly at the fire flickering around the range door. "I did it," she whispered.

"Of course you dinna do it!" Tierney answered, falling to her knees beside the suffering woman. "Someone had to do something. Will begged it of you. There was no doctor available . . . no doctor anywhere—"

"I shouldn't have done what I did . . ."

"You had to do it, Mrs. Brokaw! You had to! There was no other option; there was no one else."

Lilyan's gaze shifted to Tierney's face. As a thirsty person yearns toward a spring, so she looked for reassurance from Tierney.

It was a burden not to be borne for the rest of her life! It was a guilt that should not eat her heart out forever—so Tierney concluded. "Listen to me. Mrs. Brokaw, listen to me. Mr. Ketchum went for you. You had no choice but to come. Think—if you had turned him doon, which you had every right to do, being so stormy and all, how you'd feel now. In the midst of a blizzard you left your fireside and your children and came. The baby wouldna be born; it simply wouldna coom! I had watched by her side for hours and did nothing . . . could do nothing. You did what you could. It had to be done."

Anguish filled the fading eyes of the middle-aged woman.

"Listen," Tierney urged, feeling she had not yet banished the question of guilt, "the alternative was to leave her alone, let her struggle herself to death. *Isna that so?*"

Lilyan, finally, recognized and accepted the truth, releasing her own self from the blame that had fastened on her. With a sob she fell on Tierney's shoulder, her own thick shoulders heaving with the release of tears that came.

It was thus Will found them. Coming across the room he put his hand on Lilyan Brokaw's shoulder and said the words that would set her free for the remainder of her life, her working, serving, giving, helping life.

"You did what you could. Now, dear friend, will you help me one more time?"

The reservoir on the range yielded enough hot water for the final cleansing. Before they were through, Tierney and Lilyan—while Will sat in the kitchen with his head in his hands—dressed the cooling body of Lavinia Ketchum in her wedding dress, wrapped her in a quilt, and went, quietly, to inform Will that all was ready.

Tierney stood in the background, fighting horror; Lilyan Brokaw opened the outside door. The wind blasted in, hurling snow before it, almost snuffing out the lamp on the table. Will, in his heaviest coat, an ear-flapped hat tied under his chin and gloved hands gripping his burden, carried the mortal remains of his beloved wife out into the winter's bitterness, to lay her to rest, for the time being, on boards placed on sawhorses in a nearby shed. Then to return for the small bundle that was his son and struggle through the storm one more time, placing the babe—before her arms stiffened—on the breast of the one who had borne and given her life for him.

There, in the shadows and ice, they waited the far-distant spring and the thawing of the land, land which had called like a siren, and which, in the end, had demanded the ultimate payment.

Dearest Annie,

I should be in bed, but the days are so full that I hardly have time to write except now when things are quiet. Of course you understand, for you have had more than one letter from me before this, telling you of the horrible, awful thing that happened two months ago—the death of dear Lavinia. Being left here with Mr. Ketchum, without his wife, is strictly against the Society's policies, I know, but I feel that in some circumstances it is an unreasonable rule.

For, Annie, what am I to do? For one thing, how would I get away from here? We are snowed in. Mr. Ketchum makes a trip to Fielding whenever weather permits, which isn't often, but I'm here with Buster, poor boy, who can't understand it all.

I haven't had word from you, nor from Pearly, since before Christmas, which, of course, was a dreary affair. Mr. Ketchum tried to make it cheerful for Buster's sake, but it turned out being more sad than anything else. Of course we have no trees here, but Buster hung up his stocking, and we gave him the things we bought when we were last in Saskatoon. He can't really remember other Christmases much anyway, so he was satisfied. And we hung up some bells and other decorations that were in the attic. Mr. Ketchum brought in a frozen turkey that he had been saving, and I did the rest toward preparing a special dinner. I must say it was a dreary, dreadful day.

If the food wasn't satisfactory, he didn't say anything, but ate it as he has all else that I've fixed since Mrs. Ketchum died. What a chill it gives me, Annie, when I think of her and the babe, lying out there just a few yards away in the shed. I peeped in once when I was on my way to the toilet . . . I won't say anything more about the frost in there, on everything. They'll be buried when the ground melts. It is too awful for words.

The other reason I can't leave, of course, is Mr. Ketchum and Buster. How can I go off and leave them alone? Maybe with spring, and the thaw, they can find someone else to take my place. I know I really shouldn't be here. But Mr. Ketchum is so nice, Annie, you can't imagine what a gentleman he is, at all times. I don't feel a bit uneasy.

Mr. Ketchum says he has written to Mrs. Ketchum's family, who live north of here in the bush, in a place called, of all things, Bliss. How I wish that were a guarantee! I would go in a minute. Well, maybe not a minute. I don't seem to be going anywhere at all at the moment. He thought someone from Bliss might be able to come help him, for I've talked to him about how I should be moving on, going someplace else, or the Society will not like it and he may get in trouble. He's had no answer from Bliss . . . maybe they never got his letter. Mail delivery is uncertain at this time of year, with terrible blizzards from time to time, even worse than the one when we came home from Saskatoon. I wrote you all about that!

Word from James tells me that they are all well. The wedding has taken place, and Phrenia and he seem very happy. In spite of all that's happened here, Annie, I cannot wish myself back in Binkiebrae. With no Robbie there, it isna . . . isn't the same place at all. I know he is over here, <u>*someplace.*</u> *I feel a certain nearness to him just being on the same continent. Now isn't that silly!*

Mr. Ketchum and Buster are asleep. Perhaps I told you that he couldn't bear to sleep in this downstairs room after his wife died. So we spent one afternoon switching things around—I'm downstairs and he is with Buster upstairs.

I admired him before, Annie, and my appreciation for him has grown during these hard days and months. I declare I don't know how he'll carry on without Lavinia. When the chickens arrive in the spring and the workload increases . . . well, he'll need more help than I can give him, and he certainly needs more loving attention. Poor man. It is nearly midnight and I'm not sleepy, can't seem to sleep tonight, missing you . . . missing Pearly . . . missing Robbie, wondering what the future holds.

Love, Tierney.

The din of dishes clattering, people talking, and wind sweeping around the hotel, all served to create a turmoil that had Anne's head in a spin. It was almost time for her to go home, however, and so she straightened her aching back and smiled faintly at Mrs. Corcoran as she asked for a fresh supply of coffee in the dining room.

"Coming right up," that efficient lady said, brushing a wisp of graying hair out of her eyes. "Spalpeen—where's that kid when he's needed? *Spalpeen!*"

The boy, growing into a gangling youth, came galloping from the pantry, his mouth obviously stuffed with food. But did he have the grace to look abashed? Not at all. He knew who his friends were, and Mrs. Corcoran, lovely Irish colleen that she was—or so he was always telling her—was at the top of his list, and wouldn't begrudge him a treat or two.

Next on his list was Anne Fraser. And now here, truly, was a lovely—not colleen, but, being Scottish—lassie.

"Ah, Mrs. Corcoran, darlin'," he lilted now in her Irish brogue, "and what can I do for ye?"

"Fill the coffeepot, you rogue!" Mrs. Corcoran directed, and with a grin Spalpeen went to do as bidden. One thing about Spalpeen, he served—not only faithfully but cheerfully.

Spalpeen, everyone had to admit, was certain to make his mark in the hotel; already he'd risen from general flunkie to Mrs. Corcoran's right-hand helper. He would not be called a man for some time yet, but he was growing and filling out under the good and plentiful food and the tender consideration he received, in spite of the slapping and chaffing and haranguing that were signs, actually, of the cook's affection for him.

"How are you makin' it, lassie?" that good lady asked Anne. "You look weary tonight."

"I'm glad it's the end of the day for me," Anne admitted, preparing to go back for another half-hour's work in the dining room.

Anne was making a fine waitress. Her naturally sweet nature and desire to please stood her in good stead, and she found satisfaction in filling the needs of the people who passed through the Madeleine's dining room. Some were regulars, living in the hotel and working in the town, but most of her customers were transient, going or coming from their homesteads, dealing with the sale of land, working for the railroad or the fur trade, going to the gold strikes, lighting out for the Yukon, all traveling across the continent now that the railway had connected coast to coast.

It was a country filled with raw vigor, a new nation made up of many nationalities, and a wide smattering of them came through the Madeleine's big dining room.

Passing from table to table with her coffeepot, filling cups, Mr. Whidby approached her.

"That table by the window?" Mr. Whidby said, flicking a speck from the shoulder of her spotless waist, then resuming the rubbing of his hands together in his usual manner (Anne thought, at times, he'd wear them out, so religiously did he perform the rite of rubbing). "That's a bunch of remittance men. They need special attention, and I want you to take time, before you leave, to see that they get it."

Mr. Whidby knew money when he saw it; that table would be worth a nice bounty for the coffers of the Madeleine, and wouldn't hurt his own record and reputation, if handled correctly. No one would do it more satisfactorily than the beauteous Anne. These diners, being young men and full of "ginger," might be induced to indulge in dessert after a generous dinner as well as numerous cups of coffee. Moreover, proper service would encourage them to come back. No one knew just how long remittance men would stay in one place, but, being winter and with travel difficult, they might be around for a while. The Madeleine was as good a place as any to spend the money that flowed so freely, and which they had done nothing to deserve.

Remittance men—a term used only here, perhaps, although Australia also had its share of scapegraces, or ticket-of-leave men, called delinquents in another age. Rascals mostly, ne'er-do-wells, slothful or careless sons of the wealthy and titled. An embarrassment at home, in trouble with the law, hunted by some outraged father of a used and abused female, they were shipped off to another continent, there to play, laugh at their own stupidity as though it were a great lark, and, in general, lead useless lives, of interest only to each other and of importance to no one.

Anne sighed; Mr. Whidby's word was law. Worn out as she was, she was in no mood to deal with the shenanigans of foppish and foolish young males, with whose mischief, and worse, she was

already well acquainted. Having too much money, they lived from month to month for the check, or remittance, from home, and most of them felt the rubes in Canada were below their consideration, except as objects of fun.

Patting her hair, tucking into place a few recalcitrant curls, smoothing her apron and clutching her pad and pencil, Anne approached a table of six of these young men. Already they were laughing and shoving each other, too loudly and too pointlessly—no doubt they had visited a saloon before entering the Madeleine—their faces flushed, their eyes bright, their color high.

"Yes, sirs," Anne began. "What can I do for you gentlemen?"

"What we want isn't on the menu," one dandy said with a snicker, and the entire table laughed uproariously.

With her new fearlessness in the face of such waggishness, Anne bit her lip and hoped her cheeks would refrain from flushing—it would only add to their amusement—and prepared to speak cool words of dignity, somehow getting through this day's last assignment. Drawing in her breath, she opened her lips to speak.

Her mouth fell open, but no words came. She felt her eyes staring . . . staring . . .

Across from her, his mouth as wide as hers and slowly widening even further, a look of surprise on his face and a dawning of comprehension in his eyes, sat Lucian MacDermott.

"Well, what have we here?" he drawled, and the table fell silent, all eyes turning from him to the girl at whom he looked, standing before them with her lovely face as white as her apron, her eyes sick, her comely form frozen in time and place.

"Well, if it isn't Fanny."

26

Do you know this fair maiden?" someone asked mockingly, as all stared admiringly at Anne.

"Do I know her! Not as well as I will, given the chance!" came the drawling answer, Lucian licking his lips suggestively.

"And," he continued firmly, smirking horridly, "I plan to get the chance. You," he turned to Anne, "remember where we left off in our little, er, encounter, I'm sure. You see, men, Fanny and I have some unfinished business to take care of."

Anne's heart was racing, her mind whirling. And yet part of her was icily cold. Here, there would be no tussle and display of physical force. No, here she was safe. For the moment, she was safe.

While her heart pounded, her voice responded coolly. Habit and practice took over. "Sirs," she continued, as though she had not been interrupted, "may I take your orders, please?"

"Oh, she's a cool one, all right, Lucian. She'll be more than a match for you!"

"Lucian, I think you've met your match!"

"What do you have in mind, Lucian?"

These and other remarks swirled around as Anne stood, pencil poised, chin lifted, prepared to take their order. Finally, one after another, they decided what they'd eat. Anne wrote, tucked her pencil behind her ear, turned on her heel, and managed, in spite of shaking legs and weak knees, to walk to the kitchen.

Here she changed into another person entirely. White of face, trembling of limb, she flew to Mrs. Corcoran.

"He's here! He's found me! That man out there . . . Lucian—"

"Hush lassie," crooned Mrs. Corcoran, recognizing instantly that something serious had happened. She put her big arms around the quivering girl and patted her back soothingly. "Now," she continued, "tell me what this is all about. And who is this Lucian fellow?"

"From Sco'land, he's from Sco'land. An' he's the reason I got awae from there! Oh, Mrs. Corcoran, I dinna know wha' to do! He came near tae killin' me, he did; oh wha' shall I do?"

"Sit down, my dear. Now," she raised her voice to the kitchen crew standing around, transfixed, "get yourselves back to your work! None of your business, here!"

"He'll find oot whaur I live, I know he will; I'm no' safe from him anywhaur, it seems!" Anne, seated on a straight-backed chair, buried her face against Mrs. Corcoran's comfortable middle and shivered uncontrollably.

"Now, my dear, let's think—"

"I'm gettin' oot o' here, Mrs. Corcoran! Oot o' toon!"

"Think sensibly, Anne. Where on this earth could you go, out of town? And in this weather!"

"Tae Pearly; tae Tierney. Aye, tae Tierney; tha's whaur I'll go—"

Anne sprang to her feet, wringing her hands, eyes wild. "I've got to go, I've got to get home and get things packed and get oot o' here!"

"Annie, Annie," soothed the cook, but to no avail.

"Dinna tell anyone . . . dinna tell Mr. Whidby; he might tell Lucian. Jist say I'm sick or summat as that. Gi' me a chance to get awa'!"

Anne pressed through the encircling arms, brushed past the clinging hands of her concerned friend, ran to the wall where coats and hats were hung and beneath which overshoes were placed.

"Send someone else to wait on those daft loons," Anne directed, donning her wraps feverishly. "An' tell her to be slow aboot it. I've got to hae time to get awa'!"

Without her week's pay, without a formal termination of her job, Anne fled the premises of the Madeleine, unsure of where she would go or how she would get there. But her heart turned toward Tierney. Tierney, to whom she had fled when Lucian MacDermott had attacked her before. Tierney, who would understand, help her, hide her.

At the hostel she dragged her bags from under the bed and stuffed and rammed her belongings into them, lamp turned low all the while, blinds pulled and door locked. Every step in the hall caused her to stiffen, listening in agony until it faded away. Finally, she wrote a note to Fria (Fria knew all about Lucian MacDermott), but not revealing what she was going to do.

For in her mind a plan was shaping up: She would indeed go to Tierney. But first of all she would go to Pearly, because Pearly lived in or near a town that was on the railway—Hanover. With such a devious circuit, surely Lucian would be stymied, unable to follow, should he care to. And he would care to. His anger was too hot, his shame at her treatment of him too great, to be taken without retaliation.

Then out into the night she went, slipping past the desk when the clerk was absent from it. She was not far from the station; she remembered the way well and trudged toward it through the falling snow and the sweeping wind. Here she bought a ticket for Hanover, set her bags at her feet, and slumped on a bench in a corner of the waiting room among others who came and went.

Hours later, on the train, she relaxed a bit, though she studied everyone who entered the car, before settling back. It wasn't a great distance to the first stop, which was Hanover—towns were few and far apart on the prairie, but important, and rarely passed without a stop—to let someone off, let someone on, unload supplies, or take on cans of cream.

It was mid-morning; the storm was over, and the day was crisply cold and brilliantly beautiful, with a myriad scintillating diamonds displayed everywhere one looked. The town seemed snowed in and was quiet and peaceful in the storm's aftermath.

No one else got off the train, and Anne breathed a great sigh of relief. Carrying her bags, she went into the station house, up to the window, and spoke to the man there who was openly watching her. Anne, lovely Anne, drew attention wherever she went. For once she regretted it, knowing that, if he were to be quizzed, he would remember her, perhaps vividly.

She spoke quietly, respectfully . . . still, he'd remember. "Can you tell me where the Schmidts live? The Franz Schmidts?"

"Sure," the man said promptly, eyebrows raised—after all, the Schmidts already had one domestic. "Out thata way," and he pointed, "about three or four miles."

"The road—would it be open?" Anne was prepared to walk a dozen miles, if necessary.

"Not yet. Someone is sure to come in from that way sooner or later. Sit down and keep warm, Miss, if you wish, and we'll see what develops."

Again Anne sat and waited, her baggage at her feet. Fortunately she had eaten her supper last night at the Madeleine before Lucian had made his appearance, but she longed for a good cuppa.

Finally, "Miss, Miss," the same man called, and beckoned. "There's a team coming now from that direction. Seems to be—yes, it is—Schmidt's neighbor."

Anne rose indecisively to her feet, looking out the window at the rig slowly plowing its way toward the nearby general store.

"Want I should talk to him for you?" the man asked kindly, and Anne nodded her grateful appreciation.

Coming back in, stamping the snow from his feet, the stationmaster said, "Duncan—that's his name—has agreed to let you ride out with him. He'll be leaving in a half hour or so, probably less. Just needs to get the mail, drop off a cream can, do a little shopping. He'll give a wave when he's ready. Keep your eyes peeled. . . ."

Pearly was putting the last touches on a dried apple strudel; Gussie Schmidt sat nearby, comfortably rocking, having taught Pearly the rudiments of rich dough and confident it would turn out well, as did most everything under the quick fingers and alert mind of Pearly Chapel. The little London starveling had learned a lot from the elderly German woman. She had learned a lot from Frankie, the grandson. Learned a lot without many words being said; Frankie was not a garrulous man. But he was expressive in stolid, persistent ways, and Pearly was not slow in reading his eyes, his mind, his heart.

"There," she said, popping the strudel into the oven, "it'll be ready for dinner," and turned with interest toward a window, having heard the sound of sleigh bells.

"It's Mr. Duncan," she informed Gussie, who had paused in her sock knitting to raise curious eyes; visitors were rare in winter. "Frankie's comin' from the barn to meet him."

Gussie rose from her chair at the side of the stove, standing with Pearly at the window. So intense was the cold that only a small spot in the center of the pane was clear of the thick riming of frost that made it difficult to peer through, except for one person at a time.

"Look," Pearly said, relinquishing the viewing angle.

"Dat's Duncan," Gussie said. "And zomebody's mit him—a voman, seems." She gave the spot to the more bright-eyed Pearly and resumed her place at the side of the kitchen range. Oh, it was good, all right, to have the quick legs and strong arms of a domestic. And not just any domestic—Pearly Chapel of the happy heart, the willing spirit, and the vibrant Christian witness.

"Yes, and she's gettin' down and comin' in."

Pearly let the curtain fall back into place and hurried to the door, opening it to the bundled female form that turned out to be—Anne Fraser.

"Annie! *Annie!* I can't believe it! Come in, come in."

Pearly pulled Anne into the house, and in spite of her bulky clothing, wrapped her in loving arms, laying her warm cheek alongside the icy one, blending tear with tear until, at last, they stepped back from each other, laughing and weeping at the same time.

"It's Annie, Oma! Annie, who came across the ocean with me. Annie, this is Gussie, Frankie's grandmother—Oma."

Noting the surprised look on Anne's face, Pearly laughed and explained, "I call her Oma, same as Frankie does . . . she asked me to. Oh, Annie, it's good to have a grandmother. You know—I told you all about it. And here comes Frankie—"

Pearly began the task of unwinding Anne from the scarf around her face and neck and removing her heavy coat and snowy galoshes.

Frankie had bidden the neighbor good-bye and followed the figure of Anne into the house. Anne! Anne, who had refused to come with him to Hanover. Anne, who had sniveled at the very idea of riding across the prairie with him. Anne!

Frank Schmidt stepped into the warm, cozy kitchen of his grandparents' home, with its gay curtains at the windows, its coffeepot bubbling on the range, the aroma of apple strudel sweet in the air, and with the precious form of Pearly Chapel in the midst of it all, and could only thank God that Anne Fraser had crept her way out of his life and future.

And so he too was able to greet the newcomer with a welcoming, if cold, hand, and a tentative smile. Anne, shamefaced only for a moment, recalled all the good things Pearly had said in her letters, and immediately was released to feel at home, accepted, even loved, perhaps for Pearly's sake.

Nothing would do but that Anne should sit up near the stove alongside the grandmother's rocking chair and accept a good cup of hot tea, Pearly knowing it alone would warm the depths of her friend's being, seeping into her very heart, if such were possible.

"Soon," Pearly promised proudly to her friend's blissful face, "there'll be fresh strudel. It's Oma's recipe, but I made it."

Following the noon dinner hour and the doing up of the dishes, in which both girls shared, talking lightly the while, Gussie kindly encouraged Pearly to take her friend to her room, to do the serious talking that was necessary to get to the root of this business! For it was most unusual for anyone to brave the winter weather for a social visit alone; there had to be something serious behind it all. Gussie dozed beside the fire, content with her life and the wonderful turn of events a good God had brought her way in the thin figure and winsome face of Pearly Chapel.

At the table that night, as soon as supper was over, and with cups of coffee and tea in their hands, Pearly, with Anne's permission, made the necessary explanation to the family. She had already told—long ago, in the quiet, comfortable moments when she and the family sat of an evening around the stove, eyelids heavy, shoulders drooping, bodies wonderfully relaxed following a hard day's work—all she knew about her friends.

Now she had but to take up the tale: "That man that treated her so bad? That Lucian? He's showed up again! In Saskatoon! Right in the hotel dinin' room! An' in front of everybody, he threatened her. Yes, he's after her again! Of course she had to git away! I told you how he nearly kilt her before, and that was why she decided to come to Canada. Oh, he's evil, that 'un. Looks like a civil gentleman, acts like the worst of blackguards. He's a scurvy scoundrel—"

Poor Pearly; her vocabulary simply wasn't enough to express her feelings. Collecting herself with some effort, she remembered—a little belatedly, it's true—her teaching on compassion, and added, rather lamely, "I just hate the sin, you understand, but I . . . I—" Pearly paused a moment, and plunged on virtuously with what she thought to be right and proper, "but I love the sinner."

Pearly looked quickly around the table, fearful that her tirade of condemnation had exceeded her attempt at justification. As indeed it had.

"Well," she said, drawing a deep breath and being honest at last, "I'm *trying* to love the sinner."

Gussie, "Oma," patted the heaving shoulder. Frankie reached a sympathetic hand toward her. Franz, "Opa," smiled tenderly. Only Anne was left with flaring nostrils and heightened color as she contemplated the knavery of the absent Lucian.

"Aye, it's true," she finally added in a strangled voice, "he came nigh to killin' me. And the fear he has put in me is even worse. It's a cruel thing, is fear. I dinna know why I'm here, except that I had to get awa', and my first thought was to go to Tierney, who helped me before, in Binkiebrae. Weel, I hae nae family here, ye ken. An' e'en if I did," she added bitterly, "they're afeard o' the MacDermotts."

Many clucks of sympathy, several clearings of throats, a surreptitious wiping of Oma Gussie's eyes.

"You're velcome to stay here, liebchen," Frank Schmidt, the patriarch of the family said and meant it. "You'll be safe here."

"Thank you! Oh, thank you! But I feel like I want to be wi' Tierney. She's havin' a hard time herself. Perhaps Pearly has told you that the lady where she works—Mrs. Ketchum—died several months ago, and Tierney isna supposed to be there withoot another woman. And yet she feels such sympathy for Mr. Ketchum, and willna leave until someone cooms along to take her place, maybe a relative from Bliss. You know Bliss?"

Anne meant the town and district of Bliss, of course, but, looking around the loving circle, felt that this family, in the truer sense of the word, did indeed know the meaning of bliss.

Being assured that they all knew Bliss, a town north of here, in the bush, Anne continued.

"It'll ease the situation there, for Tierney, if I can be wi' her now. An' surely Lucian won't go way oot there. Think?"

"Surely not," Pearly "thought."

"But," Pearly continued, "how is she to get there?" Pearly, wise Pearly, did nothing but look around the room, and at Frankie in particular, with her pansy/purple eyes and, as ever, the heart of young Frankie turned over.

"I'll take her! Whattya say, Opa?" Frankie looked expectantly toward his grandfather.

"Shall I take her? There's not that much work to do here, being winter and all, and Pearly will be here to help. Right, Pearly?" Frankie, wise Frankie, looked at Pearly trustingly, and her heart turned over.

"Right. I can help outside, as well as in," she said eagerly. "I can help with the chickens—I feed 'em anyway—and I can even help with the milkin'." Pearly had learned much more than baking since she had been on the homestead.

Mr. Schmidt looked properly persuaded. "Da veather iss goot now," he said sagely, "and I tink iss gonna be fine for a few days, dough ve neffer can tell . . ."

"It'll just take two days, Opa. A day over and a day back. Whattya say?"

Frankie's strong, square face was confident. His broad shoulders straightened; he loved a challenge in his own quiet way. His heart, once testy with this Anne Fraser, had, in the space of a few minutes, come full circle, and he was ready to defend her with his dying breath.

Would he be called upon to give it?

27

The wind was muted, but still loose snow skirmished over hard-packed drifts, curiously resembling the breath that curled from the mouths of the team as Anne and young Frank left the homestead and headed out across the prairie.

As the cutter passed through Hanover, they could see children on their way to school, romping and playing, running up the frozen banks and sliding down with great glee and much shrieking, breath also curling in white mists around their tightly and brightly capped heads.

"It's a glorious day," the usually taciturn Frankie commented, having learned a new appreciation for his wintry surroundings from an ever-awed Pearly. Pearly thought Hanover, in winter, was almost as fine as in autumn, when the grain covered the fields in countless stalks of bound sheaves soon to become wagonloads of golden grain. Such bounty! Forgotten the long days of summer and the burning of a sun that came early, stayed late, and poured out its heat tirelessly, only occasionally routed by dark skies and enough rain to ensure a good crop for the hardworking people of the prairie lands. It had been a good year. Thank God! And thank Him they did, being, for the most part, God-fearing people, well aware of their puny ability and their heavy dependence on divine providence.

The parting from Pearly had been brief. Wrapped in their heavy outside garments, Anne and Frankie were too warm to linger in the house and too cold to linger on the step. Pearly had spent as much time fussing over Frankie's scarf as Anne's, and her farewell waves, if they but knew it—and perhaps they did—were as much for the man she saw every day as for the friend she hadn't seen for the best part of a year. Frankie drove away feeling like a king in his royal carriage and flourished the reins as happily. Anne departed feeling a warmth of family closeness she hadn't known . . . perhaps ever. That it was because of the Lord they loved and served, Anne recognized, and it made her own empty heart yearn for the same satisfaction and contentment.

"It worked out well, dinna it," Anne offered tentatively, finally. "For Pearly to coom work for ye instead o' me, I mean."

The younger Frank Schmidt, called Frankie to differentiate from his grandfather, looked down on the fair face of Anne Fraser and counted himself blessed that usually it was the thin little face of Pearly Chapel beside him. Consequently his answer was generous.

"Yah. Yah, it has. Pearly was God's choice for the Schmidt family. I—that is—everyone loves her."

"I ken that; I can tell," Anne said humbly, adding after a moment, "forgive me, Frankie, if ye will, for being such a . . . such a gowk. Please?"

Frankie slapped the broad backs of the team with the reins and his laugh soared out over the prairie, happy and content.

"It may just have been the best thing you could have done for me," he said, pale eyes alight, "and, I hope, for Pearly. Of course I forgive you. *I thank you!*"

Well! Anne thought to herself, slightly taken aback by his enthusiasm for her bad behavior, *he doesn't have to be that happy about it!*

The barriers between them, however, if they did indeed exist still, were broken, and the remainder of the day passed in harmony.

It was the northland at its best—shimmering in its beauty, snapping with cold at first, slowly growing milder as the day advanced, until Frankie was moved to say, "I feel the first hint of the coming spring in the air. Oh, it's not yet a chinook or anything like that, but it's definitely warming up. And it sure helps us get across this old prairie—not having to fight wind and weather, that is. We should be in Fielding by midafternoon. Then we'll ask where the Ketchum farm is and be there by supper time. Whattya think of that, Annie?"

His use of "Annie" set the seal on their new friendship, and Anne's heart, still feeling the faint touch of shame over her previous behavior, was finally absolved and cleared.

A sandwich at noon, as they drove, and a sip of milk from a bottle they had kept under wraps, and the miles slipped away almost happily. Anne was going to Tierney, and there she would be safe.

The proprietor of the general store in Fielding gave them clear directions to the Ketchum place. It wasn't difficult; there was only the single track to follow out across the vast expanse of white, turning right at the tenth meridian road. Ten meridian roads laid out precisely—ten miles.

"You'll pass the Brokaw place about two miles from here," he said, "then nothing, at least on this road, until you get to Will's. Say, you want land, young feller? I'm also a land agent, and there's still plenty abeggin' to be taken—"

Frankie proudly assured the man that he had a place of his own. "My Opa's," he said in an aside to Anne. "It's to be mine. That's why I stay and take care of the place, and of Opa and Oma."

"Strange, your asking about the Ketchum place," the man said thoughtfully to Frankie as Anne studied the candy counter and made a decision to take some licorice to small Buster. "Just finished directing another feller out there. But I guess he decided not to go. He went over to Swiger's Stopping Place; guess he got himself accommodations there."

"Come, Annie," Frankie called. "Best we get on our way if we want to pull in for supper. I could eat a horse and chase the rider, myself."

Annie laughed, admitted she would welcome a good meal, and followed Frankie back out to the cutter, where they crept back in among the cold quilts and blankets and shivered their way back onto the proper road out, once again, onto the broad prairie.

Jingling along through the otherwise silent landscape, they might as well have been on the moon, so remote were they, and so bleakly barren was the terrain. Thinking of the warm fire ahead and the warmer welcome, Frankie and Annie found their expectations rising, and their laughter rang out from time to time.

Eventually Anne took the opportunity to nap a little, her head bobbing in time with the horses' gait and the slipping and sliding of the cutter's runners on the road over which, it was apparent, only one or two other rigs had passed since the last snowstorm.

"That must be it," Frankie nudged Anne awake and pointed.

Smoke from a stovepipe drifted, white and pure, across the blue sky already dimming toward evening, as the house lifted over the curve of the horizon. Anne and Frankie watched as it seemed to move toward them, closer and closer until, with a flourish, Frankie urged the weary horses to a trot and curvetted between half-buried gate posts into the Ketchum yard.

It had been a long day. Tierney had spent several hours ironing, and her shoulders ached. Ironing was a wearying job, though the Ketchum equipment was the very latest and best. For one thing, there was a real ironing board, one that could be folded away when not in use and with a sadiron holder on one end. It was the first time in her life that Tierney had not ironed on a board set across two chair backs.

The irons themselves were at the root of her weariness. There were three of them, set to heat on the range top, each a different size: No. 1 weighed four pounds and had one end rounded "for polishing"; No. 2, 5 1/8 pounds; and No. 3, recommended for heavy overalls and the like, weighed 5 3/8 pounds. The detachable handle could be used on all three and, supposedly, "fit naturally to the hand without straining the arm or wrist."

Arm and wrist perhaps, nevertheless, as Tierney prepared a batch of macaroni and beef and tomatoes for their supper, she stopped from time to time to rub and manipulate her elbow and shoulder; it had indeed been a big ironing. Soiled clothes were left to accumulate through blizzards, and Tierney always hastened to get out a batch of laundry when a day dawned bright and clear and promised to be sunny long enough to dry clothes. Or stiffen them. It was a Herculean task to wrestle the garments, frozen into bizarre shapes, off the line, collapse them by main force into a basket, and take them into the house, there to warm, sag, and eventually finish drying. And of course such a hit-or-miss laundry schedule deviated sadly from the housewife's cardinal rule of washing on Monday and ironing on Tuesday and threw the entire week into housework chaos.

The macaroni dish, a sealer of green beans, and great slabs of bread—which Tierney had learned to make well under the direction of Lavinia—this would be their supper. Planning to serve a sauce dish of canned peaches for dessert, at the last moment Tierney had put together a cakelike topping called "Cobbler" in Lavinia's *White House Cook Book.* Written by Hugo Ziemann, chef of the United State's White House under President Harrison, it promised "1,600 tested cooking recipes, besides numerous hints and helps for the toilette and household" and was a great aid to proper cooking for Tierney.

She had barely taken the dessert from the oven when she had cause to rejoice in her decision—a rig was pulling into the yard. What a rare occurrence! And right at supper time. There was no thought of sending anyone on without food and drink and a good thawing out at the side of the heater. Tierney glanced at the cobbler, lifted the lid to the macaroni dish, sniffing appreciatively, stirred the beans, and felt herself prepared. Just pray it wasn't the preacher from Fielding with another stern rebuke for the arrangement at the Ketchum house!—a single female, *unchaperoned,* living with an eligible widower! Perhaps a good meal would soften his countenance and bend his rigid back. In his disapproval he made Tierney think of nothing so much as the misshapen, frozen balbriggans she wrestled from the line after washday.

"Who in the world—" Will had exclaimed, rising from his comfortable chair at the side of the front room heater, and stepping toward the door. "I can't imagine who this could be, this time of the day."

Peering from the window, Tierney muttered to herself, "If it's the preacher, he's brought his wife," and wondered if that meant more big guns trained her way, to get her to depart the premises. Tierney stiffened her back and her determination, and, standing by the kitchen range, waited for some word, some sign that would identify the guests.

"Tierney!" The word was a cry, a piercing cry.

Tierney started, as though struck a physical blow. Annie! Could it be—

Then Anne's woolly arms were around her, Anne's cold cheek was pressed to hers, Anne's voice was murmuring incoherently in her ear. It was indeed Annie Fraser.

Supper was late in being served. Even then, over what Anne pronounced a "masterpiece," the talk went on, explanations, newsy bits and, finally—over great cups of tea and sauce dishes of Chef Ziemann's peach cobbler—the account of the unexpected appearance of the dreaded and feared Lucian MacDermott, Anne's flight, her welcome into the Schmidt household, and Frankie's offer to drive her from Hanover to Fielding, and Tierney.

"Who would have thought," Anne concluded, shivering, "that the long arm of the MacDermott could reach e'en to the hinterlands o' the prairies."

"He won't get away with his shenanigans here," Will said stoutly. "Women are honored, almost revered, here on the prairies and in the backwoods. And we have law and order, whether he knows it or not. Our Mounties are able and capable, I can tell you that.

A better prepared force you won't find!" So spoke the son of immigrant parents, safe and secure in his chosen homeland.

"Lucian MacDermott ne'er cared for law and order; considered himself above it, I guess," Tierney said. "He was a law unto himself in Binkiebrae."

"Well, Anne," Will said, his gray eyes serious, "you are welcome here. In fact, your presence may be a blessing. We have," he said with a smile, "a watchdog of a preacher, and right after my wife's funeral he was out here, laying down the law of the church about our living arrangements. But I don't know how Buster and I would have made it without help. Tierney has been God's blessing to us. Right, son?"

Buster, in his high chair chewing with gusto on a piece of licorice, smiled a black and cherubic grin and took another bite.

While Anne and Tierney did the dishes and put Buster to bed, Will and Frankie got acquainted, pulled up to the fireside in the front room. The girls joined them, and the talk went on into the night. Finally—after the fires were stoked, the dampers set, and the lamps distributed—Anne and Tierney retired to her room, Will went to sleep with Buster, and Frankie took Will's bed. Peace settled on the Ketchum home—more than at any time since Lavinia's death, Will's great grief, and Tierney's several months of uneasy attendance on the man's and child's needs.

Tierney and Anne talked long into the night. "I'm so glad ye're here, Annie," Tierney said more than once, adding, "the Society would be verra vexed wi' me for bein' here, a lass alone. And yet I canna, in good conscience, look for another place—"

"Hae ye thought o' marryin' the man?" Anne asked thoughtfully. "He seems a fine sort, and o' course I know he is, from the letters ye've written. And what a wonderful place he has here! It's the best setup I've seen in all that trek across the plains. How about it, Tierney, hae ye considered marriage?"

"Why, Annie," Tierney said, surprised. "Ye know I'm pledged, in my heart, to Robbie Dunbar!"

Annie looked uncomfortable. "Aye, so ye've said. But coom now, is it sensible, lass, to consider such a thing when there's nae chance in a million ye'll e'er see Robbie Dunbar again?"

Tierney, plaiting her hair before the mirror, stared unbelievingly through it at her friend. "Annie Fraser, nev-er, ne-ver hint at such a thing," she said, low and fierce and enunciating every syllable clearly, "if you expect me to continue to call you my friend."

Anne had the grace to look shamefaced; such love was incomprehensible to one who'd never experienced it.

"I'm sorry!" she said, agitated, and Tierney immediately forgave her.

"Annie," Tierney said thoughtfully, laying aside her hairbrush and turning from the mirror, talking directly to Anne, "isna it time to do summat about . . . about God?"

Anne was immediately big-eyed. "Wha', wha', Tierney? Wha' shall we do?"

"Here we are, two lone lassies, far from home, at the mercy of anyone and everyone and needin' God's protection sae bad, and havin' nae right to coom to Him and ask fer it."

"We always went to kirk, Tierney."

"Aye, but was it enough? I think not. At least we dinna know God an' Jesus like Pearly does. And we dinna hae the peace and joy she has. I, for one, want . . . need that."

Tierney looked at Anne expectantly. Anne said, humbly, "Me too, Tierney. Me too. The last thing, almost, that Pearly said to me this mornin' is that she's still prayin' for us. So—what shall we do aboot it, Tierney?"

"I'm thinkin' lots aboot Pearly's verse, 'Coom unto me, all ye that labor and are heavy laden, and I will gi' ye rest.' The reason we don't hae that rest, Annie, is because we haven't coom. Reet?"

"Reet, I guess," Anne said uncertainly, but willing to be persuaded and led.

"Well, then, let's . . . coom."

"Aye."

Not knowing what else to do, the girls joined hands, closed their eyes, and Tierney prayed, Annie agreeing.

"Lord God o' Abraham, Isaac, Jacob, and Pearly, we coom to Ye jist now. We ken we need to be forgiven, and so we ask You to forgive our sins—do you mean that, too, Annie?" Tierney asked, digressing momentarily.

"Aye."

"An' make us clean an' pure in the blood o' Jesus, shed for us. An' . . ." Tierney proceeded more surely now, "an' we take Him as our Savior, right now, in this place, at this time—" her prayer grew in assurance and authority, until she ended on a high and happy note: "in Jesus' name, Ahhhh*men*." It may have been an ecclesiastical amen, but it was from the heart.

There was nothing left to do but fall into each other's arms and shed a few tears, tears of relief, tears of joy, tears of happy surprise that such a fine feeling should accompany such a simple transaction.

"Why are we cryin'?" Annie asked, eventually, "when we feel sae wonderful?"

"I dinna ken there'd be sich a . . . a feelin' in my heart," Tierney said, awed. "I remember Pearly said the Spirit bears witness wi' our spirit, that we are the children of God. That's it, Annie, it's the *witness*."

The girls, so new in the way and so wise already, rejoiced in the witness, finding it unexpectedly sweet and satisfying. Each attempted, in her own way, to express her thanks for the great gift of God's forgiving love and the accompanying gift of His joy.

"We better get some sleep," Tierney said, finally, their cold feet attesting to the lateness of the hour and the chilling of the house. With a hearty puff she extinguished the lamp and climbed into bed, there to hear her continued whispered prayers echoed from Annie's side of the bed.

"Won't Pearly be glad?" Annie murmured, just before they dropped off to sleep. "Frankie can tell her."

Sleep had almost overtaken both of them when Anne sat bolt upright. "Who do ye suppose that man was—that asked the store owner in Fielding how to get to this place?"

28

Next morning, Tierney came awake with another of Pearly's Scriptures running through her mind: *This is the day which the Lord hath made; we will rejoice and be glad in it.*

Or perhaps she had learned it at the kirk in Binkiebrae; suddenly her heart was opened and she realized how much the kirk, after all, had taught her. That it hadn't brought her to a personal relationship with Christ, she figured, was her own fault, and she would no longer belittle the blessings she had gleaned from her childhood spiritual upbringing. Certainly it had kept her from the sins of the world, had given her not only a biblical background but pious examples in the good people of Binkiebrae. And it had, in the end, pointed her toward the Christ she now knew in fulness.

"Wake up, Annie! This is the day the Lord hath made, and we are to rejoice and be glad!"

"This early?"

"Aye, this early. This early, and all the time. I hear Mr. Ketchum stirrin', fixin' the fires, and I like to get up and get coffee on for him."

"Are ye sure," Anne said, opening one eye, "ye dinna want to do it for him *permanently?*"

Then, catching sight of Tierney's frosty face, she added hastily, "But o' course not . . . I'm jist joshin'! I'm nae forgettin' aboot Robbie. Where, Tierney, do ye suppose he is, the dear man?"

"I dinna ken," Tierney said, slipping from the bed, shivering, reaching for a warm robe that had been Lavinia's, and shrugging it on. "But I'll tell ye this, Annie Fraser—this is the first day of praying that will not end until God brings us back together again. Oh," she carolled at the joyousness of the thought, *"hallelujah!"*

"Maircy! Ye're beginnin' to sound like Pearly hersel'!"

"Hallelujah!" Tierney said again, having already experienced the presence of the Lord close and available as soon as she had opened her eyes, and anticipating the day and the new blessings that would be hers.

"Ye're aboot to become a fanatic, just like Pearly," Anne said, with a sigh. "But I agree; 'tis sweet." After a moment she added a faint, "Hallelujah."

Tierney gave a peal of laughter that had Will, downstairs, picking up his ears. It had been a long time since laughter had played much of a part in his household's activities. It sounded good to his ears. It would be good to have Anne Fraser here—good for Tierney, good for Buster, who already loved her, good for . . . himself.

His opinion was only strengthened when Anne appeared, hastily dressed in the chilly room but lovely just the same. Her beauty was fresh and dewy, her spirit naturally light and happy, her smile ready and sweet. Yes, she would be a fine addition to the family.

"Good morning, Miss Fraser," he said, more cordially than one would have expected, new acquaintances that they were, and found her brown eyes turned on him with the full force of which they were capable. Will straightened from the heater, flushed, as though his heart was beating harder than was necessary.

"There's nae need tae call me Miss," Anne said with a dimpling smile. "Please make it Anne . . . Annie."

"Well, I will, if you'll drop the Mr. Ketchum and make it Will. I've never been able to get Tierney to break down and get that intimate." Will's fine face creased in a smile. "I don't know how we should ever have endured and survived without Tierney, Anne. We owe her a great debt, Buster and I. I live in fear of the day when she'll up and leave us, and yet I know she will. I'm well aware of the rules of the Society and that we are breaking them even now. I don't know how to solve it—our problem, that is. But come," Will gestured to a chair at the side of the heater, now glowing red, "sit by the fire and warm yourself."

"Well I will, for a few moments. I promised Tierney that I'd get Buster up when it's time and bring him doon and dress him by the fire. I can e'en feed him his breakfast—Scotch porridge, I would suppose. Reet?"

"Reet—that is, right." Will—staid, substantial, sensible Will—blushed.

Breakfast was a happy affair. Tierney and Anne, of course, had to share their "testimony," in fine Pearly fashion.

"An' you'll be sure and tell her, I know," the girls both urged Frankie. "An' we'll write her all aboot it verra soon."

Frank assured them that he'd tell her and assured them that he rejoiced now for her, as well as for himself, over their good news. His blessing over the porridge and toast, at Will's invitation, was fervent and covered much more territory than their appreciation for the food. Yes, it was a time of rejoicing for all concerned. Will's latent devotion was stirred until he, too, was caught up in the glory of the moment.

Tierney cleaned up the breakfast dishes while Anne dressed the pajama-clad Buster. With the day bright and beckoning, she said, "Buster, how would you like to take me on a tour of the place—show me the chicken runs and brooders, the barns and cows and barn cats. And do you know what? I've never been inside a soddy."

"We got one!" the child, big-eyed and important, told her.

"Really?" Anne feigned surprise and pleasure. "Then you'd be jist the one to show it to me."

So outside wraps were donned, and Buster and Anne, hand in mittened hand, squeaked in overshoes warmed at the fire out into the glories of the day and spent a happy half-hour playing with cats, squirting milk from cows' udders, and throwing snowballs at the side of the barn.

"An' now, the soddy," Buster said importantly. "Lemuel lived in it, Miss Annie, when he was here. But he's gone now. Daddy keeps things in there. Things like coal oil for the lamps. And he hangs meat in there when he butchers. We're going to butcher pretty soon. I don't like liver, Miss Annie."

"You know what, Buster—neither do I." And the two trudged their cheery way to the soddy, to Buster's pride and Anne's interest. Ever since her trek across the continent she had wanted to see inside one of the small, turf-topped sod buildings.

The door, frozen in its hinges, opened with effort. Once inside, it was hard to see, momentarily, having come from the outside glare to the dimness of the soddy. Though many soddies had no windows at all and were nothing but miserable burrows for humans, this one had two windows, one on each side of the door. But being set in walls two feet thick, the light was poor. Still Anne could see that the dirt walls had been hung with felt and that the ceiling, above poles, had been laid with tar paper, and the sod laid over that. Another innovation, perhaps.

Buster saw her looking up and said, "Daddy says the tar paper keeps the bugs and mice from falling through."

"That's . . . that's a good thing, I'm sure." Anne shivered—bugs and mice!

"I lived here," Buster said proudly, "when I was a baby."

"Well, you're a fine, big laddie now, and that's for sure," Anne said and Buster squirmed with pleasure.

The door squeaked open behind them and banged shut. Anne turned.

His back against the closed door, his arms crossed on his chest, his hat tipped rakishly back, and his lips curled in a smile that was colder than the day—Lucian MacDermott.

Anne staggered back a step, looked around wildly. There was nowhere to go, and the thick sod walls would effectively stifle all cries. Buster—could the child bring help, and in time?

"The brat can't get the door open by himself," Lucian said with a curl of the lip, as though reading her thoughts. "So he'll just have to be an onlooker; it will be his first lesson in intimate relations."

He stepped away from the door, his eyes narrowing. "Forget the brat. Get that heavy coat off, Miss *Fanny!* If you think you're getting away from me this time, you have another think coming. By the time your hoity-toity Mr. Ketchum goes through his buildings looking for the guest whose cutter sits in his yard, it'll be over and done. No need to dally, right, *Fanny?*"

Stepping forward, Lucian gave Buster, who had crowded close to Anne's side, a shove, toppling him onto the dirt floor.

Catatonic until that moment, a feeling as of fury itself arose in Anne's breast. She didn't have time to identify it as the rage that surfaces in the maternal breast when her young are threatened; she only knew it came naturally, like a flood. His treatment of Buster was not to be countenanced!

Automatically, without thinking, and hampered though she was with her heavy wraps, Anne flung herself at the weakly handsome face that was now filled with purpose and passion and intent on her and her alone. Surprised at the attack, Lucian spent a few moments defending himself from the spitting fury that was Anne Fraser. Hadn't he learned a thing? Almost . . . almost it was the Binkiebrae roadside affair all over again.

But this time Lucian had an advantage: Anne's fingernails, so effective last time, were inside her woolen gloves. Lucian's swift punch to her face sent her reeling, tripping over something behind her, falling . . .

With an oath and a snarl he was upon her, ripping at the opening to her coat, tearing off the buttons, struggling to tear the garment from her . . . rolling in the dirt, knocking items left and right, his hand going to her throat as she attempted to scream.

There was not a sound necessary, and none was made, when a hand that was calloused and square and strong grabbed Lucian's collar and an arm that was muscled and mighty yanked the fop from his prey. Through slitted and already-battered eyelids Anne looked up to see the flaring nostrils and clenched teeth of the man she had spurned to ride home with. The rock-solid, four-square, powerful Frank, the man to whom she had been reluctant to trust herself; Frank the quiet, the stolid, was going about the methodical business of thrashing her attacker.

Frankie, never out of control, knew when to quit. With a final smashing blow he straightened himself, dusted his hands on his pants, and leaned toward Anne. "Can you get up, Annie?" he said practically, his heavy breathing the only sign of his brief display of violence. And he helped her to her feet and moved her out of harm's way. Moved her into the sheltering arms of Will Ketchum.

For Will, having seen the strange cutter and horse, had made a survey of his outbuildings and found no one there, turned to the soddy and the tracks leading to it and had burst into a scene more terrible than he could have imagined.

While Frankie went about the business of trying to get the beaten Lucian to his feet, Will held a trembling Anne in his arms and felt a thrill all out of kilter with the horror of the moment. Looking over her and beyond to the tar paper roof, he mouthed a prayer more earnest than any uttered thus far this day: "Thank God! Oh, thank God!"

But just what Will was thankful for was not clear. Except, of course, to God, who has all things planned and must rejoice to see His children fulfilled and happy.

But the full understanding of all that was some way off—except to God with whom tomorrow is as today.

Buster came creeping out of the shadows, to be gathered into his father's arms and Anne's. For it seemed natural and good to her to slip one arm around Buster and another around Will, while both she and Buster leaned their heads on Will's shoulders.

Before they stepped out of the soddy—with its moments, its memories, and its madness—Frank had located a length of rope and was trussing the groaning form of Lucian MacDermott tightly, attempting again to yank him to his feet. When that didn't work

and Lucian collapsed, Frank heaved him over his broad shoulder, through the door, and to the great outside. Here he dumped him into his own cutter, tied him down, covered him up, and left him there, half conscious, and went inside to wash his bleeding knuckles, gather up his belongings, and say his good-byes.

Tierney, with Anne in her arms, her face shocked, was trying to grasp it all. Will set Buster down in a rocking chair and began to remove the child's overshoes and wraps, his gray eyes fixed on Anne, the light of discovery in them.

"I'll take this law-breaker to the proper authorities," Frank was saying. "We don't put up with things like this in the territories. I can guarantee," he said, looking at Anne, "that he'll never bother you again. You need to believe this, Annie. If I haven't put the fear of death into him, the Mounties will. After he sits in jail for a while—and they're not comfortable this time of year—he'll be glad to go back where he came from."

Anne—and who can blame her—turned from Tierney's arms and ran into Frank's. "Oh, Frankie . . . oh . . ." was all that she could say, but so much was said in that broken phrase. Frank patted her shoulder, shook hands with Tierney and Will, and turned to leave.

"I'll follow you," Will said. "I need to go to Fielding today anyway, and you may need a witness to corroborate your story. I have a certain standing in the community by now, and they'll believe me. Yes, Annie, I think you may rest secure from now on. And I trust *and pray,*" he said, looking directly at her, "you'll be doing that . . . from right here."

Anne's puffy eyes looked back, and even the swelling couldn't hide the answering glow in them. "Yes, Will," she breathed through equally puffy lips, "I'll . . . be . . . here."

Tierney, watching, amazed, believed she had seen and heard as definite a proposal of marriage as a girl might want. And had listened, amazed, to its response. Who'd have thought it! Anne and Will!

Now, what would she, Tierney, do; where would she go?

29

Will returned from Fielding brandishing a letter.

After putting the team away, bringing certain purchased items into the house, and removing his wraps, Will sat at the fireside, the girls gathered around him, and he spread the letter out before them.

"This is from Lavinia's parents, Herbert and Lydia Bloom, who live in the bush north of here, a place called Bliss."

To Tierney, it sounded like a state of being rather than a town or district.

"Of course I've already read it," Will said, "but some of it bears reading to you; at least it'll give you things to think about. It's written by Lavinia's father." Settling in the chair, he began to read:

We are slowly finding comfort for our broken hearts in regard to the loss of our Lavinia and quite understand your problem where the domestic help, Tierney Caulder, is concerned. How good of her to stay on in your time of need; we join you in gratitude. I should hate to think of you and Buster struggling on alone.

But of course, for her sake, you will be trying to make other arrangements, though what they might be we can't see from here. I know it is difficult in winter, and so far from the headquarters of the British Women's Emigration Society. But we are praying about it, and trust the best will be done.

Lydia is not doing well, and things here are too much for her. Maybe we are too old to take on homesteading at our age! We are making it through the winter, with its decline in our workload, but dread the spring with its garden work, broody hens to set, and baby chicks to care for, not to mention the new ducklings and goslings, and so on. Just the thought of the spring housecleaning is enough to almost make Mother swoon.

It's my suggestion, and Mother concurs, that when you find a substitute to take Miss Caulder's place, you send her on up to us. It would be a solution for her, I think, as well as for us. In the meantime you can prepare her for the idea, so that it won't be like going to strangers, exactly. Tell her how much we need her, and that we'll be willing to carry on with the terms of the Society's contract. I assure you we will be very good to her, for she will be doing us such a favor.

Will let his eyes roam down the pages.

Mother joins me in sending love to you and our dear Buster, whom we regret not having seen since you left here almost four years ago when he was just a baby. So near and yet so far! The workload, as you know, precludes any trips in the summer time, and the weather won't allow it in the winter, especially as the train doesn't come through either Bliss or Fielding.

Please let us know what Miss Caulder has to say about our proposal. Spring is almost upon us, and as soon as travel is open and you find a substitute, we hope she will agree to come to us.
Herbert S. Bloom.

"What do you say, Tierney?" Will said, looking up from the letter and studying Tierney's face. "Does it make sense to you? Do you think you could settle for life in the bush?"

Settle for life in the bush, when her heart rebelled daily against the bleakness and barrenness of the prairie? Settle for the bush, when her heart longed and cried out for something that grew higher than herself? Settle for the bush, when she thought of the shade, the beauty, the *greenery?*

"I believe," she said calmly enough, "that I could settle for the bush. I believe also," the newly praying Christian added, "that it's an answer to a prayer that I've barely put into thought, let alone words. I think it may be an example of 'before they call, I will answer; and while they are yet speaking, I will hear.'"

Tierney's eyes were starry. What a marvelous God! She wasn't afraid to trust herself and her future into His hands. "I'll go," she concluded, "jist as soon as you find someone to take my place."

All unplanned, the gray and gentle eyes of Will Ketchum sought the brown and gentle eyes of Anne Fraser, and what passed between them was enough for him to say, "I think you can begin to get your things in order, Tierney. Anne—unless I'm mistaken—will stay. Annie will stay with Buster and me. Am I right, Annie?"

Tierney may be excused if her mouth fell open. Anne may be excused if hers dimpled and smiled, both shyly and roguishly.

But Anne, being Anne, could only be simple and straightforward. "Ye're not mistaken, Mr. Ketchum—Will. I'll . . . stay. An'," she added, pinking beautifully, "happy to do so."

And so it was settled.

And so it was that, in the bright and blossoming month of May, Tierney found herself on a train, heading north.

At first the scenery was as she had known for the last three-quarters of a year, although the grasses were greener than she remembered. She had to admit that springtime on the prairie had its beautiful aspects. And though only a hint of it had been seen on the day when Lavinia and her baby had been taken from the small granary that had sheltered them and tenderly laid to rest in the bosom of the earth, it was enough to promise that there would be an awakening—on another day—and to dry the tears of those gathered at the graveside.

Spring had fully come when the preacher had been called to the homestead again, mollified that at last things would be done decently and in order. His wife and Tierney were witnesses to the simple but meaningful ceremony that united Will and Anne in marriage.

Anne was more beautiful than Tierney had ever seen her, with a new pale yellow waist and brown skirt that the girls had stitched as the winter went out on a whimper and a sigh and spring settled in with fresh breezes, birdsong, and prairie flowers. Anne had carried no bouquet, but her dark hair had been spangled with buttercups and one yellow dandelion, the offering of a capering and excited Buster. Will was the tower of strength Anne needed, and his supreme confidence in the rightness of what they were doing spread a peace and calmness over the day and the occasion.

Tierney had no qualms at all about leaving Anne in a household with two males—a son and a husband.

She was done with reminiscing when the bush began to appear; it was all she dreamed and more. Parkland, it was called. Seen at the springtime it was glorious—birds were returning by the thousands, with flashes of color and bursts of song; a million and more rivulets ran down every incline to form another slough, and they glittered in the sun and frisked in the gentle breezes; the fresh fragrances, the running sap, and a trillion and more buds breaking out everywhere—it was all too much for the senses to absorb at once. Tierney was heady with sight and sound and smell.

Looking out over the little farms coming awake with energy and new life, Tierney took her Bible—never far from her these days—from her bag, and turned to Psalm 65, a portion of Scripture that seemed to be written for this present place and this present time:

> Thou visitest the earth, and waterest it: thou greatly enrichest it with the river of God, which is full of water: thou preparest them corn, when thou hast so provided for it. Thou waterest the ridges thereof abundantly: thou settlest the furrows thereof: thou makest it soft with showers: thou blessest the springing thereof. Thou crownest the year with thy goodness; and thy paths drop fatness. They drop upon the pastures of the wilderness: and the little hills rejoice on every side. The pastures are clothed with flocks; the valleys also are covered over with corn; they shout for joy, they also sing.

Pondering on the pastoral picture the Scripture conjured up, Tierney was reminded, at last, of Pearly and her number one verse—Isaiah 40:11—*He shall feed his flock like a shepherd: he shall gather the lambs with his arm, and carry them in his bosom. . . .*

"Dear Pearly," she whispered to herself, "you were right. I know it now. Thank God! And thank you, Pearly Gates Chapel, for your faithful 'testimony'!"

For, noting the new-turned furrows, the springing growth everywhere, the words indeed seemed fitting, so right, that Tierney herself could have shouted for joy and sung, but, for the sake of her traveling companions, settled for a small hum instead.

That the bush seemed to wrap her in its very embrace was no problem for Tierney; she felt as though she were coming home, that every branch was a welcoming arm and that all roads, until now, had led directly to the Saskatchewan parkland.

And to Bliss in particular.

Mr. Bloom was at the station in Prince Albert to meet her. He was much as Tierney had pictured him—a man past middle age, of middle height, with nothing particularly outstanding to draw

the attention of anyone, but with the kindest eyes one could imagine, and a gentle, thoughtful way of speaking. Lavinia had chosen a husband much like her father. Herbert Bloom, like Will, would undoubtedly be the salt of the earth, of this Tierney felt quite sure. And then he spoke, and it was confirmed.

"Welcome to the bush, Miss Caulder! Mother, that is, Lydia, and I are so happy you've come. May we call you Tierney, even though the Society doesn't recommend it? We'd like it, you see, if you'd just consider yourself one of the family." Not only had the bush reached out to her but flesh and blood and bone!

Tierney felt a warm gush of tears behind her eyelids. It was all too much! God's loving kindness and constant presence, the loveliness of the bush, the Bloom welcome.

"I'd like it very much," she said unsteadily.

"I'm only sorry you couldn't bring our little Buster. But of course his place is with his father and his new mama. We're depending on you to tell us all about Anne and all about the wedding. We wish our dear ones much happiness and are glad their happiness resulted in your release to come be with us."

"They send their love, Mr. Bloom. And of course I'll tell you and Mrs. Bloom all about everything. You would love dear Annie. Will has made her one happy and contented woman."

The trip from Prince Albert to Bliss was heaven on earth to the beauty-starved girl. Mr. Bloom introduced her to the flora and fauna, pointed out features of the farms they passed, the acres and acres of virgin bush still unclaimed, the land still unworked, the new little homesteads taking shape, and the time flew by happily.

"Now this," he said eventually, "is the hamlet of Bliss. Named for the first settler, they say. And we've tried to live up to it," he grinned, "ever since. We'll stop for the mail and go on through. I've done what buying I needed to do in P.A. Choices are limited here. Will you get down and come in?"

"I'll wait in the buggy, I think," Tierney said, not yet ready to exchange the freshness and freedom for the lesser attractions of manmade structures.

Mr. Bloom climbed back into the buggy, and they were off again, passing through a leafy tunnel onto Bliss Road. "It's called that because the Bliss place is out this way," he explained.

But before they left Bliss he pointed out the small white building that was church and school. "It has great meaning for all of us," he said. "It's our spiritual home. You'll enjoy our pastor and our people, and soon they'll all feel like family to you." Blessing upon blessing!

The horse knew it was approaching home and stepped out. Tierney leaned back on the tufted seat, closed her eyes, breathed deeply of a fragrance that she was to come to know as the essence of the bush, and offered up a prayer—another one—of thanks for God's good provision and care.

"Now here," Herbert Bloom said, "is a comparatively new homestead just coming under cultivation. It's a good example of how we all begin. The owner got here last fall in time to put up his cabin for the winter, get up his wood, and lay in supplies. I believe he also got a cow and a horse or two. All winter, when weather allowed, we would see him out cutting bush, grub-hoeing, getting started on the clearing he has to do to prove up his land. That's him over there, getting ready, it looks like, to put the plow in the ground for the first time, turning over new soil, probably for a small garden. Yes, it's satisfying work, all right. Hardworking guy—he'll make it, I think."

It was a homey, nestling sort of place, set among poplars and bushes Tierney didn't recognize, some of them white with blossoms, with a small wisp of smoke coming from the stovepipe lifting above the rough, hand-made shingles on the cabin roof. It was new, and it was raw, but it looked as if it belonged and as if it would endure.

"I have some mail for him," Mr. Bloom said, sorting through the items he had picked up to be distributed along his route—the way of the bush. And with a flurry the buggy turned into the small clearing and pulled up and stopped beside the rough-hewn, woodsy cabin.

"I'll just run these letters over to him," Mr. Bloom said, preparing to hand the reins to Tierney, and get out of the buggy.

Tierney was studying the garden plot slowly appearing behind the moving plow, and, suddenly, longed for the feel of the earth between her toes. But that was foolish!

"Let me take it to him," she said impulsively. If not a barefoot run over the fresh-turned sod, then one with her shoes on—no matter, it would be an experience, a first-time experience, a strictly Bliss experience.

"Well, sure, if you want to. The exercise will seem good, I bet, after that long train ride and now this buggy ride—"

Tierney jumped from the rig, light as air, her serge skirt doing its best to swirl in the invigorating breeze. Holding one edge of it up to enable her to move freely, she stepped lightly and quickly toward the garden spot.

"Hey!" she hollered, waving the letter above her head.

The plow continued on its way, the man walking behind, the reins around his waist, his two hands firm on the plow handles. He was whistling, and the merry sound vied with the birdsong that never ceased from the surrounding bush.

The plow was heading away from her. Tierney stopped in frustration; it was either give chase or wait patiently until he made a turn this way. Tierney glanced back; Herbert Bloom waved her on, albeit with a grin.

Gathering up her skirt even more, Tierney ran after the plow. She had wanted the feel of the earth—well, it was getting into her slippers, ready enough! No problem! Bounding joyously, enjoying the freedom of movement and feeling younger and more alive than she had for a long time—particularly throughout the long, shut-in winter—Tierney quickly overtook the plodding horse and plowman.

"Hey!" she called again.

The man turned. The man turned, pushed his broad-brimmed hat to the back of his head. Turned, gaped, gave one shout, dropped the reins, and began to run toward her. Ran and leaped, even as Tierney had last seen him running and leaping, away from her, down the side of her hill in Binkiebrae. Running toward her, her name on his lips.

Her heart bursting with recognition and indescribable joy, her legs carrying her, like a thistle on the wind, to meet him.

Robbie Dunbar.

Ruth Glover was born and raised in the Saskatchewan bush country of Canada. As a writer, she has contributed to dozens of publications such as *Decision* and *Home Life.* Ruth and her husband, Hal, a pastor, now live in Oregon.